Riptide of Truth

ASHLEY RYNNE

RYNNE Publishing

RIPTIDE OF TRUTH

CONTENTS

~ *VII*

First published by RYNNE Publishing 2024
A catalogue record of this book is available at the Australian National Library and the Queensland State Library

Source ISBN: 978-1-7637837-0-6
eBook Edition © 2024 ISBN: 978-1-7637837-1-3
Version 1

~ One ~

Alison Carter stepped off the bus, her sandals kissing the warm pavement of Cairns while her heart raced with anticipation. The vast expanse of the Coral Sea stretched before her, a tapestry of shifting blues and greens that shimmered seductively under the sun. It was beautiful—a paradise that felt worlds away from the sterile confines of her apartment in Sydney, where shadows of her past echoed in the silence. Cairns was meant to be her blank canvas, a fresh start; yet, under the picturesque facade, she sensed turbulent waters beneath.

As she took in the sights, Alison felt a longing stir inside her—an overwhelming desire to breathe in the salty air and let the ocean wash away the burdens she carried. She had spent years in the unforgiving world of investigative journalism, exposing truths that often hid in the dark corners of society. But the resilience of the ocean called to her; it reminded her of her father, who had disappeared without a trace during one of his legendary marine excursions. His absence was a wound that had never fully healed, leaving behind a cocktail of unresolved grief and haunted memories.

Alison tried to shake off the unease that crept into her thoughts as she ambled along the waterfront. Locals bustled by, sharing easy laughter and warm greetings; it was the kind of tight-knit community she had always yearned for. The vibrant cafes and smile-filled marketplaces echoed with the spirit of the town, a stark contrast to the investigative grind that consumed her life. In time, she hoped to plant roots here, to find camaraderie among the people who shared her love for the reef—an activist's dream she had chased relentlessly.

Yet, even now, whispers of tension hung in the air like distant thunder. The recent discussions surrounding Coral Reef Enterprises, an organization that had supplanted its original noble intentions with questionable practices, stirred beneath the surface of casual conversations. Some locals expressed lament for the reef's declining health, while others clung tightly to the promises of financial gain from expanding tourism. Alison felt the weight of these opposing narratives—the delicate balance between preservation and profit echoed the internal conflict she had experienced since her father's disappearance.

Alison's thoughts turned to Mark Renshaw, her close friend and fellow marine conservationist. From the moment they met in college, their shared commitment to environmental justice had deepened into a profound friendship. They spent long nights poring over research papers, debating the ethics of marine science while their dreams danced on the horizon. With the thrill of possibility, Mark had poured himself into the work, tirelessly advocating for the reef. Having moved to Cairns ahead of her, he was the key she hoped would unlock her place amidst the community.

Remembering his easy smile brought both warmth and pangs of longing. Yet, in the shifting tides of their friendship loomed the tragedy of her father—a ghostly reminder that life was neither simple nor safe. If she truly wished to exert change, she must summon the courage to confront her fears.

As she strolled deeper into the heart of town, Alison noticed the art gallery showcasing local talent, the colors of each canvas pulsating with energy and life. One piece in particular caught her eye—a swirling depiction of the reef, vibrant and alive, yet shadowed by coal-gray strokes, hints of darkness lurking beneath the surface. It struck a chord within her, mirroring her own struggle—this idyllic facade, concealing layers of complexity begging to be unraveled.

Alison's heart swelled with a mix of hope and apprehension as she moved toward the gallery, a sudden gust of wind sending chills down her spine, cutting through her momentary reverie. The sun hung high in the sky, illuminating Cairns in a truth she yearned to believe—a truth of renewal, of promise. But she couldn't shake the feeling that the storm was brewing just out of sight, a tempest of emotions and revelations poised to shatter the calm facade of her new life.

Looking deeper into the gallery window, she thought of her purpose in Cairns—to experience the world she had dedicated her life to protecting, to heal from the sorrows that plagued her, and to explore the secrets waiting to be uncovered amid the paradox of beauty and peril.

As night fell, the vibrant community of Cairns began to glow with lights, amplifying the optimistic hum of life all around her. But Alison felt an unsettling cloud hover; the whispers of the reef and the shadows of loss intertwined in her mind. With her heart heavy yet hopeful, she took a step forward, unaware that the life she had imagined was about to be consuming—both in beauty and in chaos.

The calm before the storm wrapped around her like a gentle hug, as if the universe was granting her this fleeting moment of peace before plunging her into the depths of secrets, discoveries, and a fight for the truth. In that instant, she knew the storm would not just test her resilience—it would redefine her purpose.

The morning sun streamed through Alison's small kitchen window, illuminating the familiar clutter of boxes yet to be unpacked. She stood at her counter, holding a steaming mug of coffee, her eyes wandering to the wall that faced the ocean. A vivid mural created by the former tenant depicted the reef in all its glory—colorful corals and fish swirling in a vibrant dance. It reminded her of her college days, especially of Mark Renshaw.

The memories flooded back like waves crashing onto the shore. Their friendship had blossomed at university, forged through late-night study sessions and a shared passion for marine conservation that made them inseparable. Mark's infectious enthusiasm had drawn her in from the beginning. He was not just a brilliant marine biologist; he was a dreamer who maintained an unwavering belief in the possibility of change.

Alison set her mug down, determined to honor the memories that fueled her spirit. She rummaged through her unpacked boxes, searching for the photograph she kept tucked away. Finally, her fingers brushed against the thick, worn cardboard, revealing an image of them at a beach cleanup, grinning against the backdrop of the vibrant Sydney coastline. Mark's tousled hair danced in the wind, and Alison remembered how he had laughed as he attempted to pose with a giant piece of driftwood as if it were a trophy.

In that moment, she found clarity. Mark had dedicated his life to protecting the oceans, inspired by his mother's stories of overcoming hardships. She remembered how he often said that their fight for the marine world was not just about preserving beauty but about preserving life itself. They had shared a vision that stretched beyond their personal ambitions—a passion to illuminate the crucial connection between the ocean and communities. And now, with his recent death weighing heavily on her heart, that vision felt simultaneously more vital and more distant.

Alison needed to see Mark again, if only to carry his legacy forward. She picked up her phone, fingers hovering over the screen. She hadn't heard from him in weeks; he had mentioned organizing an event focused on sustainable practices in the community. But in the wake of tragedy, she found herself prioritizing a different kind of connection—the friendships that already existed, waiting patiently for her to tap into their strength.

That afternoon, she headed to the local café, the scent of freshly brewed coffee melding with salty sea air. As she entered, the melodic laughter of early patrons bubbled around, and Alison felt herself relax a little. The café walls were adorned with artwork showcasing the reef and all its splendor, a homage to the very landscape that had become her refuge and her passion.

"Alison! Over here!" a cheerful voice called out.

Alison turned to see Sarah Bennett waving from a table beside the window. Sarah was a familiar face, someone she had met through Mark during their college years. With her sun-kissed skin and easy smile, Sarah radiated an aura of genuine warmth. Alison approached her, taking in the lively discussion at the table—a mix of old friends who echoed their shared past with Mark.

"So good to see you! How's settling in?" Sarah asked, pulling Alison into a friendly embrace.

Alison felt a rush of affection as she settled into a chair, surrounded by the vibrant energy of laughter and chatter. "It's beautiful here. I think I'm really going to like it."

"But it's not the same without Mark," Sarah's expression faltered, her eyes glancing away momentarily. The shared grief hung heavily in the air, an unspoken acknowledgment of their collective loss.

"I still can't believe he's gone," Alison said quietly, her voice wavering. "He was so dedicated; it doesn't feel fair."

"Yeah," Sarah sighed, wiping a tear from her cheek. "We were working on some community initiatives together before..." She paused, a tremor of sorrow etched in her voice. "I thought we would do more together. He was so passionate about those campaigns."

Alison nodded, recalling how Mark had always recruited others to champion ocean rights—each meeting a rich dialogue of hopes and aspirations. They discussed the vision of a healthier ocean together, emphasizing their urgency to act. Learning that they couldn't add anything else to the locked chest of challenges felt impossible to bear.

As they talked, the group began exchanging stories of Mark, laughter occasionally punctuating their shared sorrow. Each memory became a thread, weaving together their bond, binding them in their quest for purpose. They shared tales about Mark encouraging them to participate in community beach cleanups, guiding discussions on ethical fishing, and painting murals meant to inspire change. With each story, the fabric of his life, stitched into their hearts, revealed itself anew.

"I want to continue his work," Alison declared as the discussions deepened, driven by conviction. "I want to bring attention to the reef, especially now with Coral Reef Enterprises moving forward with their projects. I can't just sit back and let it happen without us speaking out."

The group fell silent, taken aback by the force behind her words. Sarah broke the silence first. "That's what he would've wanted," she said, her voice soft yet resolute. "Mark believed in the power of community more than anything. If anyone can raise awareness, it's you, Alison."

Buoyed by Sarah's acceptance, the atmosphere shifted, gathering momentum. Support for Alison's intentions simmered, each person feeling empowered to contribute in their own way. It wasn't just a commitment to the oceans anymore; it was a pact between friends to carry the torch in Mark's honor.

As the afternoon sun dipped lower in the sky, casting a golden hue over Cairns, Alison felt the emergence of hope. The community slowly began to intertwine, building a network that embraced both their friendship and their shared mission for change. There, surrounded by friends in a café filled with laughter and stories, Alison recognized the first whispers of resilience—the foundation upon which they would bolster one another against the storms to come.

She took a breath, feeling the familiar stirrings of purpose ignite within her. The journey ahead wouldn't be easy, but Alison knew she wouldn't be alone. Together, they would navigate the tides of grief, uncertainty, and passion—all in the name of a cause that was larger than themselves. And through it all, Mark's memory would be the guiding force fueling their fight, ensuring that his legacy—and their friendship—remained forever anchored in their hearts.

~ Two ~

The sun rose early over Cairns, painting the landscape in bright hues of gold and emerald. Alison stepped onto the porch of her modest rental, her senses awakening to the vibrant energy of the coastal town. The lush foliage surrounding her home felt alive, and the continuous hum of cicadas added a lively soundtrack to her morning routine. Today, she had plans to dive deeper into the heart of Cairns, to meet the people who made this town as colorful as the reef itself.

As she wandered through the streets, Alison marveled at the charm of the vibrant architecture. Cafes spilled onto sidewalks adorned with blooming bougainvillea, while street vendors showcased handmade crafts and local produce that hinted at the rich culture embedded in every corner. The warmth of the sun felt like a friendly embrace, a reassuring reminder that she was exactly where she belonged.

Her first stop was Rusty's Market, renowned for its diverse offerings ranging from fresh tropical fruits to artisan products. The air buzzed with lively chatter and the scent of spices mingled with the sweetness of ripe mangoes. Alison couldn't resist the allure of the bustling atmosphere, and as she made her way through the market stalls, she felt a wave of excitement wash over her.

"Hey there! Looking for anything special?" a cheerful voice called out from a nearby stall, adorned with an array of colorful sarongs and handmade jewelry.

Alison turned to see a woman in her mid-thirties, her sun-kissed skin and warm smile radiating friendliness. "Just exploring," Alison replied, returning the smile. "Everything looks amazing! I'm new to Cairns."

"Welcome to our little slice of paradise! I'm Mia," the woman introduced herself and gestured toward her vibrant collection. "If you need any recommendations for the best places to eat or visit, I'm your girl."

As they chatted, Mia spoke passionately about local initiatives and community events supporting marine conservation—something Alison yearned to become part of. Both shared a moment of unspoken connection as they dove into discussions about the threats facing the reef, illuminating the importance of collective efforts.

"Mark Renshaw used to stop by here often," Mia shared as she pulled out a shell necklace from her display. "He was such a beacon for us, rallying community support for the reef. His passion really inspired everyone."

Alison's heart weighed heavy at the mention of Mark's name, a bittersweet reminder of the friend she had lost. "He meant a lot to me," she confessed, her voice softening. "I've come back to Cairns to honor his legacy."

Mia's eyes glimmered with understanding. "You're in the right place. This community rallies for what they believe in," she said, her voice filled with conviction. "Mark believed we could make a difference, and I think we still can, especially with fresh voices like yours to carry it forward."

Buoyed by Mia's encouraging words, Alison knew that the networks she sought were already here, intertwined within the vibrant pulse of the town. With a newfound sense of determination, she left the market with a few handmade treasures and a heart full of hope.

Following the market, Alison ventured toward the coastal path that wound along the shoreline, where the azure waves crashed against the rocks in rhythmic harmony. Here, children splashed in the shallow waters, while families gathered for picnics under the palm trees lining the beach. She felt an overwhelming sense of belonging in this quintessential coastal scene—a feeling that resonated intimately with her quest for renewal.

As she walked, she noticed a small art installation along the path—a whimsical series of sculptures made entirely from recycled materials, each depicting sea creatures that highlighted the fragility of marine life. Curious, she approached the vibrant display, where a group of artists was busy adding their final touches.

"Hello! This is incredible," Alison exclaimed, her eyes wide with admiration.

One of the artists, a tall woman with flowing hair and paint-splattered clothes, turned to her with a beaming smile. "Thanks! We're excited to bring awareness to marine conservation through art. I'm Gia," she introduced herself, extending her hand.

Alison shook her hand warmly. "I'm Alison. I just moved here, and I'm passionate about marine conservation as well."

Gia's expression brightened. "Perfect timing! We're gathering a team for an upcoming exhibit focused on the reef—local artists, activists, everyone's invited. We believe art can ignite conversations that lead to change."

A sense of exhilaration coursed through Alison. This was exactly the sort of collaborative spirit she had hoped to find. "I'd love to get involved," she replied earnestly. "Mark was a close friend, and I'm committed to continuing the work he started."

Gia's eyes softened. "Mark inspired us all. It feels only right that we keep his dream alive through this exhibition."

As they exchanged contact information, Alison could sense the seedlings of connections taking root. This was her entry point into the community—a thriving tapestry of creative minds intertwined with shared values and aspirations.

With a heart bursting with possibilities, Alison spent the rest of the day wandering through Cairns, introducing herself and connecting with the warm-hearted locals. She met café owners who shared their stories about the reef, passionate activists advocating for change, and artists whose works echoed the spirit of the ocean all around them. Each conversation deepened her understanding of the community's commitment to protecting the marine environment and her desire to be a part of it.

That evening, as the sun dipped below the horizon, casting a kaleidoscope of colors across the sky, Alison stood at the water's edge, enveloped by a sense of transformation. She let the gentle waves lap over her feet, grounding her in this new beginning.

With every handshake and heartfelt dialogue, Alison began to realize that her past did not need to haunt her—it could propel her forward in pursuit of a shared vision. The community of Cairns had welcomed her with open arms, setting the stage for her to forge new connections and rebuild her purpose in honor of Mark.

With renewed determination, she took a deep breath and whispered a silent promise to the ocean. She would give everything she had to protect its treasures and ensure that Mark's dream remained alive in the hearts of those who cherished the reef. The real journey of hope and resilience had just begun, and she was ready to navigate it alongside her new community, ignited by their collective passion for change.

As dawn broke over Cairns, the town was cloaked in a blanket of soft, golden light. But for Alison Carter, the new day felt heavy, shrouded in the lingering shadows of grief that had settled within her since Mark's unexpected death. Today was the day the community would gather to honor him, a celebration of his life intertwined with the cause they were all so passionate about. Yet, instead of excitement, Alison's heart was gripped by an overwhelming sorrow.

The remnants of her busy yesterday faded like the colors of a sunset, leaving nothing but the stark reality of loss. She moved through her small kitchen, preparing lukewarm coffee, her mind drifting to memories that played like an unending reel. Laughter and banter echoed in her thoughts—after all, how many times had she and Mark strategized over sustainable beach cleanups or brainstormed ideas to raise awareness about the reef? New plans. New beginnings. And now, all that remained was silence.

With a resigned sigh, Alison slipped into a simple black dress, a nod to both the occasion and the weight on her heart. She styled her hair and pressed a hand to her chest, willing herself to hold it together. Today was not about her; it was about Mark—about celebrating the light he had brought into their lives.

As she stepped outside, the brisk morning air slapped her face, momentarily distracting her from the clouds of sadness that loomed. She made her way toward the community center where the gathering would take place. The scent of the ocean mixed with the earthy aroma of early morning rain hung in the air—an olfactory reminder of the ocean she had come to love. Each step felt both heavy and necessary, a resolve forming within her to honor Mark's legacy with empathy and compassion.

The community center was lively, filled with friends, family, and fellow activists who had come to pay their respects. Colorful banners adorned the walls, each splashed with images of the coral reefs, while tables were laden with photographs of Mark's adventures—him laughing with local children, wading through shallow waters, and advocating passionately for marine protection. The visual tribute highlighted not just his dedication but also the impact he had left on everyone whose lives he touched.

Sarah was already there, her face painted with sorrow yet brimming with strength. The moment their eyes met, the two women shared an understanding glance, a silent acknowledgment of their shared grief. They met in a tight embrace, holding on for just a moment longer. Sarah's shoulder shook as she released a quiet sob, and Alison felt the same waves of heartache sweep over her—resonating with the lost potential of the future they had envisioned with Mark.

"Are you ready?" Sarah asked gently, pulling away, her voice steadier than before.

"Not sure I ever will be," Alison replied, wiping away unshed tears. "But I want to honor his memory today. We owe him that much."

The service began, with friends and family taking turns sharing stories and memories. The atmosphere was a poignant mix of laughter and tears, a celebration that echoed the essence of who Mark was—a passionate advocate, a loyal friend, and a soul who found beauty in every wave that crested against the shore.

"I met Mark during our first beach cleanup," a speaker said, her voice strong yet trembling. "I was skeptical at first. I thought, 'What difference could we make?' But Mark had this spark in his eye, a belief that change was possible if we all came together. He convinced me to keep going. And now, years later, I can't imagine my life without him."

With each heartfelt tribute, the collective grief swelled, weaving a tapestry of shared stories that captured Mark's spirit. Alison sat in the back, her heart both breaking and swelling with pride. Mark had touched lives far beyond her own, and the ripples of his dedication echoed in the hearts of those he had inspired.

But amid the stories of hope and resilience emerged an unsettling tension. As the celebration continued, whispers filled the room regarding Coral Reef Enterprises—rumors of misconduct and questionable dealings. Alison felt a pang of curiosity. Mark had never spoken about his concerns publicly, but there had always been an implicit urgency in his passion, and now that feeling lashed at her insides.

Towards the end of the ceremony, Sarah stood up, a resolve in her stance. "We all know that Mark believed in the strength of community. His fight does not end here. Together, we must continue the work he started. We can't let his vision of a thriving reef be silenced. We owe him that much."

The room erupted in applause, and an aching determination settled around them like a protective mantle. Alison felt her heartbeat faster, the grief mingling with a sense of purpose. She knew they had work to do, but beneath the surface, her mind wrestled with the shadows of doubt. How much of that work involved peeling back the layers around Coral Reef Enterprises?

Once the service began to wind down, Alison felt the weight of the day press upon her. She exchanged hugs with friends, sharing that bittersweet blend of comfort and sadness. Yet amid the heartache, the promise of continued advocacy washed over her—a tide rolling in to mirror the strength of their commitment to the ocean.

As the sun dipped lower in the sky, casting a warm glow over the horizon, Alison escaped to the quiet comfort of the beach. The waves lapped gently at her feet, and she closed her eyes, allowing the rhythmic sound to soothe her.

"Mark, I promise," she whispered into the wind, thinking of all he would have wanted for the community and the reef they cherished. "We'll fight for what you believed in. I won't let your memory fade."

The tide ebbed and flowed, and with every gentle caress of the water against her skin, she felt a connection to something greater—a bond between her and the ocean that would guide her every step in the days to come. Bursts of joy and grief swirled within her, each wave reinforcing the urgency of their cause and the necessity of digging deeper.

Today was just the beginning. As the sun set on this day of remembrance, Alison stood resolute, ready to navigate the storm that awaited her—both within herself and in the delicate waters of advocacy that lay ahead. Tidal waves of grief might threaten to engulf her, but she would rise, determined to honor Mark's legacy and protect the reef he fought so fervently for.

~ Three ~

The days following Mark's memorial blended together, a haze of muted colors wrapped in an undercurrent of grief that left Alison feeling both lost and strangely invigorated. The local community buzzed with whispers, each person grappling with their sorrow while simultaneously rallying to ensure that Mark's legacy continued. But as the days stretched on, Alison couldn't shake the unsettling feeling that shrouded the memory of her friend.

She found herself drawn to the Coral Reef Enterprises headquarters more than she intended. What started as a fleeting curiosity had transformed into an obsession, the weight of unanswered questions weighing heavily on her conscience. In the small, sunlit office of the Cairns branch, Alison navigated the crowded space filled with marine biologists collaborating over conservation projects and environmental policies—but what lay beneath their smiles? Rumors had danced through the air at the memorial, murmured conversations hinting at corruption and clandestine activities that had tarnished the organization's mission. And Mark had known something, had been worried, she realized.

Determined to get to the bottom of it, she decided to pay a visit to the local library that afternoon. The building was quaint, nestled between bright storefronts, its façade adorned with climbing ivy. As she entered, the familiar, earthy scent of old books enveloped her, offering a soothing balm against the turmoil brewing inside her. She made her way to the quiet research area, seeking to unearth any hidden truths regarding Coral Reef Enterprises and their impact on the reef.

Sifting through records and local archives, Alison pieced together the timeline of Coral Reef Enterprises. Initially founded as a bastion of marine conservation, it had progressively shifted toward profit-driven objectives—funding increasingly questioned. Environmental projects that had once promised to rejuvenate the reef now carried the weight of exploitation. Every press release she read echoed a troubling pattern.

"Alison?"

The soft voice jolted her out of her thoughts. She turned to find Eva Song standing nearby, a curious expression on her face. Eva had become a close friend over the past weeks, their shared loss knitting them together while their love for the reef fueled discussions both profound and lighthearted.

"What are you doing here?" Eva asked, sensing the intensity that underlay Alison's focused expression.

"Just digging into Coral Reef Enterprises," Alison replied, rubbing the back of her neck, a nervous habit she had developed. "I'm trying to find out what really happened with Mark. He was worried about them, and now I feel this pull to uncover the truth."

Eva approached, her brow furrowed with concern. "You know there've been whispers about shady practices, right? It's been a topic of heated discussion among activists lately."

"I picked that up at the memorial," Alison said, shifting her gaze back to the piles of papers. "I'm hoping to find something concrete here. I don't want to believe that Mark was entangled in anything corrupt, but something tells me he was onto something big."

Eva perched on the edge of the table, her fingers tracing the edges of a newspaper clipping. "What if you find something that could change everything? You'd need support—people who believe in the truth as much as you do."

Alison glanced up, her heart quickening. "Like starting a campaign to expose their actions? Mobilizing the community?"

"Exactly," Eva encouraged, her eyes sparkling with determination. "Mark believed in the power of community to facilitate change. You're already tied to his legacy. It's the next step."

Fueled by resolve, Alison and Eva dove deeper, poring over the archives, cross-referencing articles, and cataloging information about the organization's backers. Names began to surface—business leaders, politicians, and stakeholders who wielded power unfathomable to the everyday Cairns resident. The more they uncovered, the clearer it became that the threads of corruption had long entangled Coral Reef Enterprises within a web of deception.

After hours of sifting through documents, Alison's gaze fell upon a yellowed letter, its edges frayed from age. The letter contained concerns raised by scientists about lingering pollution from commercial operations, warnings that had been ignored or suppressed. Clinging tightly to her discovery, Alison's breath quickened. This letter could be a definitive expose, a voice that criminally echoed Mark's final thoughts.

"What is it?" Eva asked, her curiosity piqued.

"This—this letter suggests that the organization knew about the toxicity affecting the reefs and chose to bury it," Alison explained, her heart racing. "I think Mark may have stumbled onto something."

Eva's eyes widened as she processed the implications. "If they're actively hiding the damage they're causing, this could create a massive uproar. But this isn't just gossip—this is explosive."

"I need to confront them," Alison affirmed, the edges of her voice sharpening.

Eva's expression shifted to one of caution. "Are you sure? They may brush you off, or worse. It could put you in a precarious position, especially when people are still figuring out their loyalties after Mark's death."

The gravity of Eva's words settled like a weight on her chest. However, the fire inside Alison burned brightly, igniting a flicker of adventure as she wrestled with fear and determination. "If we don't stand up now, how can we ever hope to protect the reefs? Mark would've done it, and I won't let him down. I refuse to be complacent."

Eva held Alison's gaze, and for a moment, there was a shared understanding that transcended words. "Okay," she replied finally, her voice steady. "I'll help you, then. Mark wouldn't want you to fight this alone."

Grateful for her support, Alison felt a renewed surge of strength. Together, they could expose the darkness lurking beneath the surface. It would take courage to navigate through the secrecy, but as they gathered their notes and snapshots—evidence of hidden truths—the spark of rebellion ignited a path forward.

As they left the library, Alison's heart swelled with purpose. With one foot planted in the past and the other stepping boldly into the future, they forged a path meant to honor Mark's memory—a legacy redefined by a newfound quest for truth. The shadows of deception may loom large, but with friends like Eva at her side, she knew they would not falter. What began as a personal pursuit now transformed into a movement fueled by community—a tapestry woven by conviction and urgency, determined to reveal the secrets hidden in the shadows.

The following week unfolded with a renewed sense of purpose for Alison. Armed with evidence and buoyed by Eva's unwavering support, she began to prepare for an encounter with Dr. Samuel Grant, a key member of Coral Reef Enterprises. His reputation as a brilliant marine scientist preceded him, but there was an unsettling aura around the man that made Alison uneasy. The powerful man of influence, he had a knack for deflecting questions that could threaten his organization—a quality that lent him an air of enigma she could not ignore.

With a mixture of determination and nervous energy, Alison stood in front of the Coral Reef Enterprises office, mentally rehearsing what she planned to say. The building boasted an expansive glass façade that sparkled like the ocean on a clear day, but beneath that shiny exterior lay layer of complexity she was determined to uncover. The lobby was a blend of modern design and marine artistry—photos of vibrant reefs adorned the walls, while down the hall, an extensive library of marine studies loomed large.

"Alison! Glad you made it!" she heard a vibrant voice call out as Dr. Grant stepped into the lobby. His crisp white lab coat set him apart from the sleek professional attire worn by others around him. His striking blue eyes exuded intelligence, but there was an inscrutable quality to his demeanor, as if he held secrets that ran deeper than his academic accolades.

"Thank you for agreeing to meet with me," Alison said, forcing a smile while her heart raced. "I wanted to discuss some concerns I have about the organization—specifically regarding Mark and the impact of Coral Reef Enterprises on the reef."

Dr. Grant's brow furrowed, but he quickly reverted to a congenial façade. "Of course! Mark was a remarkable talent," he replied, his voice steady and composed. "I must say, it's unfortunate we lost him. He had such potential, and I wish he could have seen some of the projects we've been working on."

"Right, that's what I wanted to talk about," Alison pressed, trying to remain calm. "Mark was worried about the organization's practices. He expressed concern about pollution levels and the effects on coral health."

Dr. Grant paused, his expression cool and calculated. "It's a complex issue, Alison. Coral Reef Enterprises is dedicated to marine conservation, but with growth comes challenges. Unfortunately, it's often a balance. I can assure you, all proper protocols are followed in our projects."

"Are they?" She felt herself lean in, fueled by the urgency of her need for answers. "Some recent findings suggest otherwise. I found documents that indicate you were aware of the environmental impact and chose not to disclose it."

The atmosphere thickened between them, Dr. Grant's expression hardening ever so slightly. "Alison," he replied, his tone a mix of caution and authority, "the research and initiatives we implement aren't always black and white. You have to understand the nuances of science—advancing our mission means navigating complicated waters sometimes."

Alison felt her resolve waver momentarily. "But isn't that precisely where the problem lies?" she countered, her voice gaining strength. "If you're willing to turn a blind eye to the truth for the sake of progress, what was Mark fighting for? What are you really after?"

Dr. Grant regarded her with a penetrating gaze, as if assessing her courage. "What do you expect to accomplish, Alison? Mark was an idealist—a thinker who believed in changing the world through passion and hard work. But the real world demands compromise. You can't always stay on the shores of hope."

The pearls of doubt clutched at Alison's heart, yet she couldn't let hesitation dictate her path. "Maybe this world needs more people like Mark," she said, emboldened by the memory of her friend. "People willing to challenge the status quo. If I uncover the truth, I intend to honor the work he started."

Dr. Grant's expression shifted from intrigue to something akin to admonition. "Be mindful, Alison. The consequences of your pursuit may run deeper than you think. People notice when things aren't adding up, especially when it involves finances, politics, and relationships."

His warning plucked at her thoughts, threading fear into her resolve. "Are you suggesting that I back down?"

"I'm suggesting that you tread carefully," he replied enigmatically, his composure unwavering. "Investigating matters at Coral Reef Enterprises could lead to unexpected ramifications."

Alison found herself ensnared in his gaze, each word a delicate dance. Did he know more than he let on? Was he protecting secrets? A wave of determination surged within her, pushing her to probe deeper. "If I stumble upon evidence of wrongdoing, I won't ignore it. There are communities affected by your actions, and they deserve to know the truth."

Dr. Grant's eyes flickered with something between respect and caution. "Every choice has consequences, Alison. You might find that truth is more elusive than you expect," he said, his tone steely yet layered with intention.

With that, Alison understood their conversation had reached its conclusion. She forced herself to return his steady gaze, refusing to back down. "I'll pursue the truth, Samuel. Whether you like it or not, this story is going to surface," she declared.

"Very well," Dr. Grant replied, his voice smooth but edged like a double-edged sword. "You have the passion, and perhaps that's what the world needs more of. But remember, the ocean can be tempestuous. Choose wisely how you navigate it."

As Alison departed, the weight of their conversation pressed on her shoulders. She felt unsettled, as though she had ventured into murky waters, collecting debris that obscured the shimmering truths she sought. Dr. Grant was not merely a gatekeeper of information; he was a figure wrapped in riddles, each layer hinting at complexities beyond her comprehension.

The air outside was suffused with the scent of saltwater and the warm sun on her skin, but even the vibrant beauty of Cairns didn't quell the turmoil within her. She didn't just want to understand Coral Reef Enterprises; she needed to unravel the threads of influence and corruption that bound the organization to the fate of the reef.

As she walked away, the conversation with Dr. Grant lingered in her mind, causing her resolve to harden. If they really did have something worth hiding, it was only a matter of time before she unearthed the truth buried beneath the surface. Mark's fight belonged to her now, and with every step she took, she felt the ocean swell around her—an echo of hope, resilience, and the collective spirit of those who had gone before.

Alison knew the journey ahead would be fraught with obstacles, yet she stood undeterred, determined to dive deeper into the marine enigma that was Coral Reef Enterprises while shining a light on the shadows that had flickered around them for far too long.

~ Four ~

It had been a tumultuous few days since Alison's meeting with Dr. Samuel Grant, and the shadows of uncertainty loomed over her like a slow-rolling fog. The weight of the conversation nagged at her, breathy echoes of warning ricocheting in her mind as she tried to encapsulate the layers of secrets surrounding Coral Reef Enterprises. But unbeknownst to her, fate had a way of presenting unexpected artifacts from the depths—answers that might illuminate her path.

On a Friday afternoon, Alison and Eva decided to take advantage of the warm weather and visit a secluded beach that Mark had often spoken of fondly. The magical panorama of turquoise waters and powdery white sands had always served as an oasis for reflection and rejuvenation. With the weight of grief still palpable, the serene environment beckoned like a balm for their troubled hearts.

As they walked along the beach, the rhythmic clapping of the waves eased Alison's restless thoughts. The sight of the ocean sparkled with a beauty that felt both familiar and alien, a potent reminder of the dual nature of the world—one that could be breathtakingly beautiful while hiding peril beneath the surface. Eva moved with the fluidity of the water, her presence an anchor that kept Alison steady in her pursuit of purpose.

"This place is incredible," Eva exclaimed, her gaze captivated by the horizon. "I can see why Mark loved it here. It feels unspoiled, alive... an untouchable part of nature."

"It is," Alison agreed, a pang of nostalgia gripping her heart. "We spent countless hours here just talking about the future and all the things we wanted to achieve. I suppose I've taken a slice of that future with me, carrying it as a reminder."

As they continued to wander, Alison noticed something washed up on the shore—a bottle, half-buried in the sand, glimmering in the sunlight. Curiosity piqued; she hurried over to retrieve it, the wave of adrenaline rushing through her. It was a glass bottle, slightly worn, and inside, she could just make out the edges of what looked like a piece of paper.

"Look at this! I found a message in a bottle!" she called out, excitement underlying her voice as she held it high for Eva to see.

Eva approached, her eyes widening. "You've got to open it!" she urged, her enthusiasm mirrored in Alison's own.

With gentle care, Alison extracted the bottle from the sand and uncorked it, a faint pop echoing against the ambient sounds of the crashing waves. Rolling up her sleeves, she reached inside with trembling fingers, pulling out the parchment delicately. As she unrolled it, her heart raced with anticipation.

"What does it say?" Eva leaned closer, captivated.

The ink was slightly smudged, but the words were still legible, etched with the familiarity of Mark's handwriting.

"To the one who finds this, I hope my words reach someone who understands. There are truths buried beneath our feet, shadows lurking in both the depths of the ocean and the foundations of those we trust. Speak up for what you believe, seek the truth, and remember that the tides will always change. Protect the reef—it is not just about the coral; it's about our lives. I have faith in you. Remember me, and don't lose hope. - M."

Alison's breath caught in her throat as she processed the message—each stroke of Mark's pen resonating in her heart. "Wow," she whispered, the gravity of his words washing over her like a wave crashing down. "He knew something. He sensed the forces at play."

Tears pricked at the corners of her eyes as she absorbed the weight of his message. "This is not just a note; it's a call to action. He wanted me to keep fighting, even if he couldn't."

Eva looked intensely at Alison, her brow creased with both excitement and determination. "This is a huge sign, Alison. It confirms everything we've been discussing. Mark left this for you, knowing you would have the strength to carry his message forward."

Alison nodded, clutching the letter against her chest. "I need to protect his legacy, and that means not only advocating for the reef but also uncovering the truth behind Coral Reef Enterprises. They've hidden more than we can imagine."

As they stood together, the ocean wind blowing through their hair, Alison felt a swell of courage growing within her. What if Mark's message was more than just a reminder of his beliefs? What if it was a link to the very evidence, they needed to expose wrongdoing?

"Let's take this back," Alison declared, a spark of urgency igniting her voice. "We can analyze it further, look for clues that may connect it to Coral Reef Enterprises. There has to be more to this story."

Eva beamed, matching Alison's enthusiasm. "Yes, let's do it, together. We can start investigating tonight—gather all the intel we have. This is key to diving deeper."

Energized and determined, the two women headed back along the beach, the weight of grief lifting momentarily as they clung to the promise of mission that flowed from Mark's words.

Once back at Alison's apartment, they spread their notes out across the dining table, its surface cluttered with papers and empty coffee cups. Mark's letter lay like a glowing ember in the center—a beacon guiding their path.

"Based on what we've discovered about the organization, this message could be a turning point," Alison said, her voice steady as she squared her shoulders. "If we can link Mark's concerns to evidence of corruption, we're one step closer to bringing this to light."

As they worked late into the night, a sense of purpose enveloped Alison, igniting a fire within her that replaced the shadows of grief. Each word she read seemed to fuel her determination while the bond between her and Eva solidified, weaving together their thoughts like intricate threads.

They spent hours piecing together timelines, marking connections, and comparing their findings—all propelled by the raw energy of Mark's faith in them. His message had become more than just a letter; it was a rallying cry echoing in the depths of the ocean and within their hearts.

As dawn approached, the first rays of sunlight spilled through the window, illuminating their notes with golden light—a symbol of hope and the promise of a new beginning.

With the spirit of adventure and the echoes of Mark's legacy propelling them forward, Alison realized they were moving into uncharted waters, but they would never navigate alone. Together, they would face the tides of uncertainty, determined to uncover the truth hidden within the shadows and protect the world they cherished.

In that moment, with the ocean whispering beyond the horizon and Mark's words resonating within her, Alison understood that the journey ahead would be fraught with danger—but it was a risk she was willing to take.

The sun had barely kissed the horizon when Alison received a text from Eva, suggesting they meet at the café to strategize their next steps. A sense of urgency propelled her as she prepared for the day ahead. With Mark's recent message still fresh in her mind, she felt a mix of hope and determination—a powerful reminder that they were not just fighting for the reef but for the soul of their community.

Arriving at the café, the aroma of freshly brewed coffee enveloped her as she stepped inside. The morning light poured through the windows, illuminating the rustic decor that marked it as a beloved local haunt. She scanned the tables and spotted Eva seated in a corner, her head bent over a notebook, scratching furiously at the pages.

"Hey!" Alison greeted as she slid into the seat across from her. "You're up early."

Eva looked up, her eyes bright and excited. "I couldn't wait! I've been going through everything we discussed, and I think we can start laying out our plans today."

Alison smiled, grateful to have found such a steadfast ally in Eva. Their shared purpose had forged a bond stronger than she had anticipated, a friendship blossoming amid grief and determination. "What do you have so far?" she asked, leaning forward.

"I reached out to a few local environmental experts and activists," Eva replied, her excitement bubbling over. "They're all on board with coming together for a community meeting. If we can rally enough support and present our findings, it might push Coral Reef Enterprises to reconsider their practices."

Alison felt a rush of gratitude. "That's incredible! If we can gather their voices, the support could strengthen our case significantly. Mark always believed in the power of community advocacy."

Their conversation flowed organically, weaving between strategy and shared memories of Mark. Each recollection illuminated his impact, and the heavy burden of loss transformed momentarily into something almost comforting—a celebration of what they had lost, layered with their commitment to move forward.

"Do you remember that time at the beach cleanup?" Eva giggled, her eyes sparkling with nostalgia. "Mark made a speech, and we all stood there, captivated by his passion? There was a storm brewing, and you could feel the energy in the air as he declared 'We will not let this ocean suffer any longer!' He gave us all goosebumps!"

Alison laughed, her heartwarming at the memory. "Yes! And when the first raindrop fell, he lifted his arms as if to embrace the storm, calling it a sign of change. The passion he had was infectious. It's why we're all here—we're the ripple effect of his love for the environment."

As the sun climbed higher, the café bustled around them, creating a soundtrack of laughter and casual conversation. They continued to strategize, as building the foundation of the meeting became the focus of their morning together.

"Let's spread the word on social media too," Alison suggested. "We should create a hashtag to unify everyone's voices—something that captures both the urgency and hope of our mission."

Eva nodded, tapping her fingers against her notebook. "What about #SaveTheReefCairns? It's direct and impactful."

"I love it. It encapsulates everything we want to achieve," Alison agreed, her excitement rising.

With the ideas flowing, Alison's mind began to weave new visions of hope. It felt liberating to be actively participating in something so powerful, to speak up for what was right, to honor Mark's legacy not only with words but through action.

"Okay, so we'll gather our findings and share testimonials at the community meeting," Eva outlined, her energy palpable. "Then we can mobilize our supporters, drawing attention to the need for change at Coral Reef Enterprises."

Alison's heart swelled as they began drafting a plan. It was more than just a project; it was a way to channel their grief into something meaningful. The threads of their friendship wrapped around them—solidifying through collaboration and a shared mission.

Just as they were finalizing their strategy, a familiar face appeared at the counter. Tommy Ellis, Mark's long-time friend and fellow marine enthusiast, approached with a hesitant smile. "Hey, is this seat taken?" he asked, nodding toward the empty chair.

"Tommy! Not at all!" Alison replied, grateful for the distraction. "Join us!"

As he sat down, the initial awkwardness melted away. Tommy had been quiet since Mark's passing, burdened by the collective grief they all felt. But in this moment, among friends united in purpose, he began to open up.

"Hey, I've been hearing whispers around town about the community meetings," he said, his voice steady yet tinged with lingering sadness. "I think it's great you two are taking the lead. Mark would be so proud."

"Thank you, Tommy," Eva said warmly. "We're energized to keep his legacy alive, and we need as many voices as possible joining us."

"Count me in," he responded without hesitation. "If we can bring Coral Reef Enterprises to the table, I'll do whatever it takes to help. Mark was passionate about getting the community involved. Let's show them what we're made of."

Tommy's support brought another layer of strength to their plans. As they shared ideas and brainstormed, Alison felt the heaviness of sorrow lift, replaced by camaraderie. They had each lost something irreplaceable, yet together, they were building something beautiful.

"That's the spirit!" Alison exclaimed, leaning forward. "We'll all work as a unified voice—no more shadows, no more silence. We owe it to Mark and the reef."

The trio shared genuine laughter, forging a bond that not only honored Mark's memory but also inspired the strength they needed to confront the challenges ahead. In that small café, surrounded by the bustling life of Cairns, Alison felt her resolve solidify. They were not just carrying the burden of loss; they were creating a movement.

As the café filled with the vibrant energy of the morning, Alison knew that together, they were forming a network of support that would propel them forward. With the sea whispering beyond the horizon and the spirit of Mark lighting their path, they were preparing to ignite the passion of a community.

The future felt bright, the bonds of friendship strengthening with each moment they shared, all leading to a singular purpose—to protect the reef and honor the legacy of a man who had inspired them all. The tides may rise, but they would rise together, ready to navigate whatever storm lay ahead.

~ Five ~

The morning of the community meeting dawned bright and clear, the sun filtering through the seams of Alison's curtains as she paced around her apartment, the adrenaline of anticipation coursing through her veins. This was the culmination of everything they had been working toward—the chance to rally the community and shed light on Coral Reef Enterprises' troubling practices. She could hardly contain her excitement, but anxiety tugged at her gut, a reminder of the weight behind their mission.

She quickly donned a crisp blouse and jeans, then applied minimal makeup before glancing at herself in the mirror. The reflection staring back felt more determined than she had ever seen. They were no longer just a group of friends dealing with grief; they were becoming a unified voice, driven by purpose.

After a quick breakfast, she grabbed her notebook filled with research, testimonials, and Mark's message—now a talisman of their shared resolve—and headed out, her heart thrumming with a mix of nerves and fierce energy.

The community center where the meeting was set to take place buzzed with excited conversation, the air thick with anticipation. Alison stepped inside, immediately spotting familiar faces among the crowd. Sarah and Eva were already there, chatting with Tommy as they set up a table with flyers promoting their cause and inviting attendees to sign up for further involvement.

"Alison!" Sarah called, her face breaking into a wide smile. "You made it! We were just about to set up the projector for the presentation."

"Looks great!" Alison replied, her spirits lifting at the sight of hopeful faces in the crowd. "Is everyone ready?"

"Absolutely! The turnout is surprisingly good," Eva chimed in, her enthusiasm infectious. "I think people are just as passionate about preserving the reef as we are. We even have a few local journalists showing up!"

They gathered around the table, consolidating their materials and discussing how they would steer the presentation. The room was filled with the rustic charm of reclaimed wood and the scent of ocean air wafting in through the open windows, perfectly encapsulating their mission.

As the clock inched closer to the start time, Alison's nervous energy shifted into a quiet resolve. She spoke confidently to the assembled group, incorporating stories of how the community had come together for the reef in times past.

Then the moment came. The meeting kicked off, and together they took the stage, their hearts beating as one. Alison began by recounting the purpose of their gathering, sharing memories of Mark and the passion he exuded for conservation. Her words resonated through the room, stirring cheers and nods from those gathered.

As she transitioned into the core of the discussion—Coral Reef Enterprises and the growing concerns surrounding their operations—a tension settled in the air. The atmosphere shifted from hopeful excitement to a weighty seriousness as they revealed their findings. Videos of coral bleaching, photographs of declining marine life, and testimonials from community advocates painted a compelling picture that no one could ignore.

Tommy spoke next, detailing his personal experiences and emphasizing the importance of transparency within the organization they were addressing. "We can no longer be silent as the guardians of this reef. It's our responsibility to protect it—if we don't stand up for our home, then who will?"

The crowd erupted into applause, encouragement echoing through the room, a reflection of the collective determination igniting within them.

But as Alison and her friends moved through the presentations, the air began to crackle with tension. She was nearing the most vital and damning point of their argument: the allegations against Coral Reef Enterprises regarding environmental misconduct. By unearthing Mark's hidden fears—which she'd documented alongside other data—they were about to deliver a message that most would find hard to swallow.

"...and ultimately, the evidence suggests that Coral Reef Enterprises has not only ignored warnings about pollution but actively sought to conceal them," Alison concluded, her voice unwavering despite the apprehension rising in her throat. "If we allow this to continue unaddressed, we jeopardize not only the reef but the future of our community. We owe it to ourselves—and to Mark—to pursue the truth."

As the crowd buzzed with murmurs of concern and outrage, a figure from the back of the room stood up—O'Reilly, the local representative for Coral Reef Enterprises. His presence, once a shadow on the peripheral of mainstream discussions, cut through the mounting tensions like a blade.

"Excuse me," he interjected, his confidence apparent. "I think it's important to clarify some misconceptions." His tone was smooth, but there was an undertone of irritation simmering beneath the surface. "Coral Reef Enterprises has been an undeniable force for good in this community. We've done excellent work to promote marine conservation and awareness."

Alison's heart raced. She could feel the room shift as conversations erupted among the attendees—some defending her, while others hesitated, caught in the rhetoric that had sustained the organization for so long.

O'Reilly continued, his voice steady. "While there have been challenges—as there are in any large organization—the data presented today does not account for the positive impact we've made for marine life restoration projects."

Alison took a deep breath, rallying her thoughts, a surge of defiance igniting inside her. "But the truth matters more than the narrative you wish to maintain. Ignoring the scientific evidence and the community's voice for the sake of image is not conservation; it is a betrayal of everything we stand for."

The room wavered, anticipating the clash of ideals. Their crowd—fueled by grief, anger, and hope—faced off against the solidified front of the organization.

"We need to press for more transparency and accountability," Tommy echoed, his voice rising. "We cannot let fear dictate our mission or allow Coral Reef Enterprises to sweep these issues under the rug."

The tension reached a boiling point, but so did the passion within the crowd. Murmurs of approval and shouts of agreement filled the room, and each voice resonated, growing louder.

Alison's heart soared as she witnessed camaraderie blossom. People from all walks of life—local fishermen, artists, activists, and families—were uniting in their shared devotion to the reef. They were no longer shackled by uncertainty; they were connected by a collective hope.

O'Reilly's face tightened, a flicker of frustration crossing his features as he realized the tide was turning. "I think you'll find that the community is better served by collaboration instead of conflict. Perhaps we can discuss more productive measures... but this grandstanding will not help anyone," he challenged.

But it was too late; they were ready to stand firm. "We don't want mere promises; we want action!" Alison shouted, rallying the crowd behind her. "It's time for Coral Reef Enterprises to listen to the voices of the community—the voices of those who care for this reef as deeply as Mark did. We need their support, not just their rhetoric."

The room erupted into applause, a chorus of unity amplifying their resolve. The silence of complacency had been shattered; they had become a force to be reckoned with.

As the meeting began to conclude, it was clear that momentum had shifted in their favor. They had cast the hook, reeling in a wave of support that sparked new life into their cause. Alison felt a mixture of exhilaration and relief washing over her, knowing that the tide was beginning to turn—not just for them, but for the future of the reef.

Standing on the precipice of a new journey, she looked at her friends, each face lit with promise and determination. They were united, ready to lead the charge, and together, they would push for change.

As she stepped outside into the warm air, Alison realized this fight for the reef was more than a mission; it was the birth of a movement—one that honored Mark's legacy and connected the lives and dreams of those in Cairns to the heartbeat of the ocean they all cherished.

With the wind rustling through the palm trees and the sun warming her skin, Alison smiled, ready to navigate the waters ahead. Together, they would cast their nets, hooks, and lines not only to expose the truth but to ensure that every voice counted in the fight to preserve a precious world beneath the waves.

In the days following the community meeting, excitement swirled through Cairns like the salty breeze off the ocean. The tide of change was palpable, and people were emboldened to take action, rallying around the cause that Alison and her friends were championing. Yet alongside the momentum, there was an undercurrent of urgency—an acknowledgment that they needed to act swiftly to leverage the community's newfound energy.

Alison, fueled by their victories, decided to visit a local art exhibition that evening at the harbor. The exhibition had gained a reputation for celebrating environmental artistry, particularly works inspired by the ocean and its fragility. It seemed the perfect place to connect with other creatives who might share their passion for the reef, and she hoped to find fresh ideas and collaborations.

As she arrived, the evening sky dazzled in a palette of pinks and oranges, casting a warm glow over the gallery. The space bustled with activity—artists mingled with guests, sharing stories about their creations while others admired the breathtaking pieces adorning the walls. With each step, Alison felt invigorated by the blending of art, community, and activism, a fusion she hoped to weave into their efforts to protect the reef.

As she wandered through the gallery, one piece caught her eye—an expansive canvas bursting with color. Vivid blues and greens swirled together gracefully, depicting a vibrant coral reef teeming with life. Yet amidst this beauty lay hints of decay—a deliberate infusion of dark strokes that portrayed the stark reality of environmental degradation. The piece seemed to pulse with the very emotions Alison had been grappling with.

"Isn't it stunning?" a voice broke through her contemplation.

Alison turned to find Gia Leclerc standing alongside her, her artist's apron still smudged with paint, a proud smile dancing on her lips. "I painted this piece after my trip to the reef last summer," she explained, genuine passion infusing her words. "It embodies both the beauty and fragility of our ecosystem—but sometimes it feels like no one wants to see the darkness lurking beneath the surface."

"I can relate," Alison replied, her voice tinged with emotion. "Mark believed in revealing the truths that often get ignored. It's not enough just to showcase how beautiful something is; we need to confront the harsh realities if we are to protect it."

Gia's eyes sparkled with understanding. "Exactly! That's what art can do. It provokes thought, stirs emotions, and hopefully, inspires action. I've been thinking about how our work can contribute to the movement for the reef."

Alison's spirits lifted at the shared vision. "That's why I'm here tonight! I'm hoping to find ways to collaborate and amalgamate our efforts. With the community rallying around protecting the reef, I think art can be a powerful tool to amplify our message."

The two women discussed their dreams over the gallery's ambient hum—how they could combine art and activism to draw attention to the ecological crisis they faced. Ideas began flowing freely between them, each concept building upon the last like the waves crashing against the shore.

"Imagine hosting an exhibition dedicated solely to the reef—a showcase that features art intertwined with stories of the community's connection to the ocean," Gia proposed, her enthusiasm infectious.

"That could be incredible," Alison replied, her mind racing. "It'd bridge the gap between environmental science and community narratives. We could invite locals to contribute their own reflections and experiences!"

As they continued brainstorming, anxiety and excitement fused into a powerful wave of motivation. They envisioned a series of events that could raise awareness, culminating in a gallery opening that would serve as a rallying cry for conservation.

"Let's call it 'Tides of Change'," Alison suggested, a smile spreading across her face. "It reflects the movement we're initiating as we fight to preserve our waters."

Gia beamed. "I love it! Every piece can represent an aspect of the reef—its beauty, challenges, and the hope we have in preserving it. We shouldn't just showcase art; we need to spark conversations that encourage community involvement and action."

Excitedly, they delved into plans of how to mobilize the local artists, activists, and citizens. Their collaborative energy felt electric, each idea igniting another, and they began setting a timeline for outreach, promotion, and ultimately, execution.

As glasses clinked and guests mingled throughout the gallery, the atmosphere was thick with inspiration. Alison felt an exhilarating sense of purpose igniting within her; they were on the cusp of something significant—a fusion of art and activism that could resonate beyond the walls of the gallery, spilling into the streets of Cairns and beyond.

Before long, they were joined by other artists and community members, eager to share in the vision of using their craft for change. Each voice added depth to the discussion, generating momentum as Alison and Gia shared their ideas.

"This is what we need, folks!" Alison spoke to the small crowd that had gathered. "Art can provoke thought, but together with action, we can create real change for the reef! We need your stories, your talents—everyone's voice matters!"

Through discussions and the vibrant exchange of ideas, the spirits in the room lifted, each conversation a thread weaving a tapestry of hope. The gathering took on an air of reliability—there was power in numbers, power in purpose—and they were united.

As the evening unfolded, Alison stepped out onto the patio to catch a breath of fresh air. The harbor glimmered with moonlight, casting a soft glow on the water. With each wave crashing against the shore, she felt the swell of possibility surrounding her, a current of hope and resilience molding into something beautiful.

Her heart swelled at the thought of what they were cultivating—an artistic movement bound to the fight for the reef. It would not only honor Mark's legacy but also breathe life into the dreams of their community.

As she stood overlooking the water, Alison made a silent promise to herself: she would fight for the reefs in every way she could, using every tool at her disposal—words, art, and collaboration. The road ahead may not be easy, but they were embarking on a journey of discovery, intertwined with the essence of the ocean they cherished.

With renewed determination, she returned to the gallery, knowing that together, they were creating waves of change that would ripple far beyond their coastal town, setting a course toward a brighter, more hopeful future.

~ Six ~

The night of the "Tides of Change" exhibition arrived, and the energy in Cairns was electric. Alison stood near the entrance of the gallery, her heart racing in anticipation as guests began to arrive. She had worked tirelessly alongside Gia and a dedicated team of local artists and activists to pull this event together—a celebration intertwined with powerful messages urging community action in protecting the reef.

As people filtered in, gazing at the vivid artwork that adorned the walls, Alison sensed a harmony in the air—a reflective stillness that contrasted with the chaos of the past few weeks. The colors of the paintings popped, each piece telling a story that echoed the vibrancy of the coral reefs, while at the same time confronting the dire challenges they faced. Guests moved about, chatting excitedly, and a palpable sense of purpose permeated the room.

Alison took a deep breath, trying to calm her nerves. She had invited a diverse group of individuals to ensure a rich exchange of ideas; artists, activists, environmentalists, and even local farmers. Each one brought with them a unique perspective—and she hoped many would emerge inspired to join the movement.

As she began to mingle, Alison caught sight of Sarah, who was deep in conversation with Finn. The flicker of chemistry between them was evident even from afar. They had both taken time to navigate their feelings after Mark's death; the connection felt tenuous but real.

"Hey, you two!" Alison couldn't help but interject, moving closer. "How's it going?"

"Great! Finn was just telling me about his family history with Coral Reef Enterprises," Sarah said, glancing between them.

"Yeah," Finn replied, his tone somewhat guarded. "My family has been involved in the organization for years. My dad always emphasized the importance of balancing industry and conservation, but it's tough to navigate those waters when you hear these accusations."

Alison's interest piqued. "What do you think about what we're trying to accomplish here tonight?"

"It's admirable," Finn said, his expression serious. "But as someone watching from the inside, I worry about how deep this goes. Mark mentioned things, but I think—"

"Everyone has a right to be informed," Alison interrupted gently. "If there's any way your connections could help rally support on the inside, it could strengthen our cause."

Finn met her gaze, seeming to gauge the weight of her words. "I'd be lying if I said it's a straightforward situation. The organization's operations have always existed in a nuanced environment. But hearing what you're doing...it brings a refreshing perspective. Mark would have wanted us to unite."

The conversation shifted back to planning as they tapped into ideas around garnering support. The feeling of camaraderie hummed through the air, offering Alison a rare moment of warmth amidst the uncertainty.

Meanwhile, as the exhibition continued to swell with attendees, Dr. Samuel Grant arrived, cutting a distinct figure with his commanding presence. Alison felt tension ripple through her, realizing that although they had shared a cordial meeting, his arrival hung like an uninvited shadow.

"Alison," Dr. Grant greeted, his voice rich with precision. "I see the event has drawn quite the crowd."

"Thank you for coming," she replied, keeping her demeanor steady. "I hope you find our efforts uplifting."

"I must admit, I had my doubts," he said, scanning the room with an analytical gaze. His expression masked any hint of emotions, but Alison sensed an underlying tension. "You're drawing quite a bit of attention."

"Only the kind of attention we require to drive our mission forward," she countered, maintaining her composure. "This exhibition is about raising awareness and inspiring action for the reef."

"Awareness is one thing," he said, lowering his voice as if sharing a secret. "But how you frame that narrative can have consequences. Highlighting where the organization has strayed might cause unnecessary friction."

"Maybe friction is what we need," Alison shot back, unable to contain her frustration. "Ignoring the truth won't save the reef, Dr. Grant. The community deserves transparency."

He tilted his head slightly, a smirk pulling at the corners of his mouth. "Just remember, perceptions can be more powerful than facts. A false front can shield many truths."

Alison bristled, frustrated by his calm deciphering of the situation. "We're not masking truths; we're exposing them. This isn't just about environmental science; it's about our community. You don't understand what it feels like to have your home threatened. Mark understood that—he was passionate about preservation because he believed it was fundamentally about people."

Dr. Grant studied her closely. "You're entering perilous waters, Alison. Just ensure you choose your battles wisely. The ripple effect of discontent can feed into the very challenges you wish to address."

Before she could respond, their attention was drawn to the gallery's center, where a large canvas draped with a textured cover was unveiled, revealing a striking piece that depicted the reef in all its glory—stunningly vibrant on one side and darkly shadowed on the other, representing the duality of beauty and destruction.

Chatter erupted as guests gathered to dissect the new artwork, but Alison could sense the underlying tension shifting—the unease igniting a quiet fire among the attendees. A sense of solidarity blossomed; they were here collectively facing the challenges posed by Coral Reef Enterprises and the malice it had cast over their home.

A moment later, Eva rallied for attention, calling everyone to come together. "As you admire this stunning piece, let's remember why we're here," she said passionately. "It's not enough to appreciate the beauty of the reef; we must reconcile its fragility. Together, we can amplify our voices and ensure that the truths revealed tonight have lasting impact."

The audience erupted into applause, the sounds of solidarity echoing through the hall. Alison felt a swell of hope rise within her. Perhaps the tension sparked with Dr. Grant could be channeled into something meaningful—a challenge to break free from the confines of complacency.

As the evening wore on, Alison moved through the gallery, engaging with guests eager to share their stories. She felt invigorated, buoyed by the passion she witnessed among her peers, convinced that each shared experience was a building block for the community's future.

Yet, in the back of her mind, Dr. Grant's warning lingered visions of an insidious web of influence kept her aware that there were underlying currents they had yet to uncover. It would require vigilance, resilience, and unity among the community.

As the night folded into a gentle calm, Alison stepped outside to catch her breath, the cool breeze brushing against her skin. She took a moment to reflect, the sounds of laughter and conversations fading into the background. She could have never known how one exhibition would unveil both the beauty of their cause and the shadows that surrounded their battle.

The stakes were higher than ever, but the passion burning in her chest proved that they were ready to confront whatever came their way. Igniting the fires of change required both courage and authenticity, and with the community united behind her, she felt empowered to continue the fight, no matter how daunting the journey ahead might be.

Alison returned to the gallery, holding onto the resolve that had brought them all together, ready to transform concern into action. The real work was just beginning, and she knew—together, they would confront the false fronts, exposing the truths that lay hidden in the depths, ready to protect both the reef and the community they cherished.

As the sun rose over Cairns the morning after the "Tides of Change" exhibition, the excitement from the night before hung in the air like the salty breeze off the ocean. Alison felt energized, the shared expressions of hope and determination resonating within her. The community had rallied, and now they pressed forward, ready to demand accountability from Coral Reef Enterprises.

But beneath the surface of enthusiasm, a darker current swirled. Alison had spent the night poring over notes and research, her mind racing with the potential gravity of their findings and the looming threats that still hung over them. The message Mark had left her, combined with the new connections forged through the exhibition, had emboldened her. But deep down, she sensed that the fight was going to require more than just passion. They needed concrete evidence to back their claims.

She gathered Eva and Tommy at her apartment that morning, ready to brainstorm their next steps. As they settled around the table, the atmosphere buzzed with anticipation, but undercurrents of worry flashed across their faces.

"Okay, everyone! We need to strategize," Alison began, her pen poised over a fresh notebook. "After the exhibition, I feel we have the community's support, but we need to get more serious about the evidence and connections between Coral Reef Enterprises and the environmental degradation we've been witnessing."

"I've been speaking to some contacts in town," Tommy said, leaning forward, the urgency evident in his voice. "There have been whispers about the financial dealings of Coral Reef Enterprises. If we can get our hands on some of that information, it could bolster our case against them."

"Let's dig deeper," Eva added, her expression focused. "We know Mark was worried about possible cover-ups. If we can connect the dots, we could unearth something substantial."

Determined, Alison opened her laptop and began researching local financial disclosures and any public records related to Coral Reef Enterprises. As she sifted through databases and reports, something strange began to surface—discrepancies in funding allocations that didn't quite add up. While the organization touted its commitment to conservation, the financial trails hinted at something more sinister.

"Look at this." Alison pointed to a transaction marked for a supposed restoration project that revealed funds redirected to offshore accounts. "It doesn't make sense. If they're claiming to spend money here on the reef, why funnel it elsewhere? This raises serious red flags."

Tommy's brows knitted together as he absorbed the implications. "This might be the smoking gun we need. We should get our findings documented and then confront them with solid evidence. That means no backing down."

"I agree," Alison affirmed, her heart pounding with a mix of fear and exhilaration. "But we must be smart about how we approach it. We can't expose ourselves to legal backlash. If we tiptoe into dangerous waters, we need to prepare for what's coming."

As they continued to dissect the information, the atmosphere shifted from one of hopeful determination to a heavy understanding of the risks they were taking. The stakes for their fight had climbed higher; they were now treading on treacherous waters that could bring unintended consequences.

"Maybe we should bring in some legal help," Eva suggested cautiously. "If we're really going to confront them, we need to be armed with a strong understanding of our rights. I know a few attorneys who work in environmental law."

"That sounds like a smart move," Alison agreed, the tension easing slightly with the prospect of additional support. "However, we need to keep this close to the chest for now. The less noise we make before we're ready to go public, the better."

With a solid plan forming, they spent the remainder of the day compiling their findings and reviewing each piece of evidence meticulously. It was painstaking work, but the weight of purpose pushed them onward, albeit with the underlying tension of what lay ahead. They were setting their course to confront an organization shrouded in manipulation, and the ship they were captaining felt fragile in the looming storm.

Later that week, they arranged to meet with the attorney Eva had recommended—a straightforward figure named Michael, whose reputation for tackling environmental cases preceded him. As they gathered in his modest office, tinged with the scent of old books, it dawned on Alison how real their fight had become.

"Let's dive right in," Michael said, pulling out a stack of documents. "What have you gathered, and how can we support you?"

The trio exchanged glances before Tommy spoke, outlining their concerns about Coral Reef Enterprises and their financial discrepancies. As he spoke, Alison felt a sense of urgency compound—the recognition that they were becoming part of something larger than themselves. Each word he spoke only solidified her resolve.

"Very well," Michael said, his voice steady but firm. "What you're describing points to potential mismanagement or worse. If they're diverting funds intended for conservation into offshore accounts, that warrants serious inquiry. But if you want to challenge an organization of this magnitude, you must be prepared for backlash."

Alison's heart sank, a wave of anxiety crashing over her. "What kind of backlash are we talking about?"

"Legal threats, defamation lawsuits... They'll aim to discredit you, and anyone connected to this movement. Expect pushback from their supporters. It may become a difficult public battle."

The reality of what they faced settled heavily within the room. But alongside that heaviness ignited a spark of resilience; this wasn't just about them. The reef, their community, and Mark's legacy were worth every risk.

As they strategized over the coming weeks, tensions mounted. Alison felt as if they were sailing into uncharted waters—exciting yet fraught with uncertainty. Every new piece of information fueled their fire, but with it came the undeniable recognition that they had entered a realm of danger.

The soon-approaching meeting with Coral Reef Enterprises loomed before Alison like a storm on the horizon; she sensed their position would not be without challenges. But as they gathered momentum, she held tightly to the idea that they could make waves strong enough to shift even the deepest currents.

On the night before their scheduled confrontation, Alison sat on her porch, enveloped in the ocean air, reflecting on everything that had transpired. The path they were carving felt treacherous, yet within that treachery lay the potential for transformation.

She closed her eyes, imagining the reef thriving, the waters clear, and the community united. This vision remained a glimmer of hope—a guiding star illuminating their way through the darkness. Together, they would confront the storm ahead and navigate the treacherous waters.

With determination coursing through her veins, she whispered a vow into the night air: they would fight for the reef, for the truth, and for the future—a future where every voice could rise above the waves, echoing the call for change that she promised Mark she would uphold.

~ Seven ~

The day of the confrontation with Coral Reef Enterprises had finally arrived, and a thick cloud of anticipation hung over Alison and her friends as they gathered at the community center. The atmosphere felt electric, charged with both excitement and anxiety. This was the moment they had been preparing for—a culmination of weeks spent gathering evidence, rallying support, and solidifying their stance.

As Alison arrived early, she took a moment to gather her thoughts. The sun was just beginning to rise, painting the sky with soft hues of orange and pink. She stood by the window, looking out at the harbor, where the soft lapping of waves onto the shore seemed to echo the rhythm of her racing heartbeat.

"Hey," Eva's voice broke through her reverie, her face brightening the dim room. "You ready for this? It's going to be overwhelming, but we've got this!"

"Yeah, I know," Alison said, forcing a smile. "It's just that I can't shake this feeling of dread. What if they come at us with everything they've got? We know they won't just roll over."

"It's normal to feel that way but remember—we've sunk our hearts and souls into this. We have the community behind us," Eva replied, squeezing Alison's shoulder for reassurance.

As the clock ticked closer to the meeting time, other supporters began to filter in, their faces filled with expressions of solidarity and determination. Each individual brought energy into the chamber, fueling the collective resolve to address the issues at hand.

Tommy arrived, looking composed despite the chaotic thoughts likely swirling in his mind. "Everyone's here," he announced, glancing around the room. "This is it."

Moments later, Dr. Samuel Grant entered with an air of confidence that filled the room. Behind him trailed O'Reilly, a smug smile plastered on his face. Their presence sent a ripple of tension through the crowd. As the representatives of Coral Reef Enterprises, they had arrived to stand against the tide of allegations being thrown their way.

"Thank you all for coming," Alison spoke, standing tall before the assembly. "Today, we gather to discuss the future of our reef and the accountability we seek from Coral Reef Enterprises. We stand united in our love for this community and the ocean that sustains it."

With that, she turned her attention to Dr. Grant. "Dr. Grant, thank you for joining us. We'd like to start with some concerns raised by community members regarding the impact your organization has on our local waters."

Dr. Grant cleared his throat, glancing around at the assembled crowd. "Thank you for the opportunity to address these issues," he began, his tone measured but laced with underlying arrogance. "Coral Reef Enterprises has always prioritized conservation efforts, and perceived shortcomings are often part of larger challenges in marine research and advocacy."

The crowd shifted restlessly, and Alison felt the tension thickening. She sensed that this was their moment to unveil their findings and confront the representations that had long allowed the organization to prosper without scrutiny.

Alison stepped forward, clutching her folder filled with notes and gathered evidence. "We have spent countless hours researching your organization," she stated firmly, "and we have uncovered alarming discrepancies in your funding and operations. The financial reports indicate that funds meant for conservation have been misallocated or even diverted to offshore entities."

Gasps trickled through the audience as murmurs of disbelief ricocheted off the walls. O'Reilly immediately fired back, his voice booming with indignation. "These allegations are completely baseless! Our finances are transparent, and we have been leading efforts in marine conservation for years. What you're doing is reckless, and frankly, damaging to our reputation."

Alison felt a surge of adrenaline pushing her forward. "It's not recklessness; it's a call for accountability. We have a right to know how funds designated for our reef are being used. Our community deserves transparency!"

"Let's not forget the good that Coral Reef Enterprises has done," Dr. Grant interjected smoothly, attempting to regain control of the narrative. "We've implemented educational programs, restoration efforts, and promoted sustainable practices that benefit both the marine and local communities."

"But at what cost?" Eva piped up, her voice ringing with conviction. "If you continue to skirt the truth, those promises mean nothing to the very people you're claiming to protect. We cannot allow you to manipulate the conversation while the ocean suffers."

The atmosphere crackled with tension as supporters began to murmur in agreement, emboldened by Eva's words. The dynamic in the room had shifted; with each exchange, the urgency of their cause became more palpable. It was no longer a mere confrontation about finances; it had evolved into a clash of ethical principles.

Just then, a familiar face entered the room, an unannounced surprise. It was Finn, his expression resolute as he scanned the crowd, finally locking eyes with Alison. She felt a rush of relief wash over her, buoyed by his presence and alignment with their mission.

"There's something deeper at play here," Finn said, raising his hand to speak. "I may have insights from the inside—my family has long been involved with Coral Reef Enterprises, and I've seen how the organization has shifted over the years. If they're hiding funds or mismanaging projects, it's essential we address it head-on."

Dr. Grant's face paled for a fleeting moment, eyes narrowing at Finn. "You're stepping into your own peril, Finn. Is this truly the stance you wish to take?"

Alison could feel the intensity rising; she knew this moment could slip through their fingers if they weren't careful. "Finn is right, Dr. Grant. Transparency means acknowledging uncomfortable truths. It's time for Coral Reef Enterprises to demonstrate genuine accountability rather than masking failures with a glossy façade."

The audience erupted into applause, fueling the tension between the two sides. Dr. Grant frowned, and she could see the strain beginning to crack his composed exterior.

"Enough with these theatrics!" O'Reilly's voice boomed. "You all speak with such conviction, but you are tarnishing the reputation of this organization based on speculations and unsubstantiated claims!"

Alison took a deep breath, grounding herself amid the storm brewing around them. "It's not just speculation when communities are reporting negative effects on the ecosystem or experiencing shifts in fish populations. We have the data, evidence, and stories from concerned residents. We need action, not deflection."

Just then, someone in the audience raised their hand. "Is your organization willing to open the books and allow for an independent audit of the financing? This isn't just about perception—it's about the truth."

Dr. Grant cast a sidelong glance at O'Reilly, and for a moment, Alison hoped they could sense the momentum building against them. If they could push for transparency, this battle could shift in their favor.

O'Reilly spoke up again, irritation evident in his tone. "There's no need for such drastic measures. I assure you, our records align with the guidelines," he countered, but the crack in his confidence began to show.

The murmurs intensified, and the sense of urgency in the room grew. Each question thrown their way chipped away at the veneer, and triumph surged in Alison's heart.

"Then why not prove it?" Alison pressed, her voice steady. "This is an opportunity for you to regain the community's trust. A display of transparency could be the turning point in this ongoing battle, rather than digging trenches."

As the meeting continued, discussions turned into an urgency that pressed against the representatives of Coral Reef Enterprises, their strongholds trembling while anger swelled within the community. Together, they pushed for answers, demanding clarity after years of complacency shrouded their concerns.

Later that evening, as the meeting came to a close, Alison stood by the door, mind racing with the conversations still echoing in her thoughts. The battle they had fought that day may have only been the beginning, but they had made significant strides.

And as she glanced out at the ocean, she felt a strong resolve settle around her, knowing they had carved space for not just their voices, but the voices of the community. The tides were turning, but the real fight was far from over.

Together, they would navigate these treacherous waters, rallying against the currents of deception, prepared to uncover every hidden truth. They would fight for the reef and all who called it home—champions of hope rising together to create a world where transparency produced foundational resilience.

The echoes of the community meeting lingered in Alison's mind as she returned home that evening. The intensity of the day's confrontations had ignited something fierce within her, but it also left behind a lingering uncertainty. The representatives from Coral Reef Enterprises had maintained their facade, but the cracks were beginning to show. She sensed a storm brewing, both in their community and beyond, and the stakes felt higher than ever.

The following day, Alison received an unexpected text from Tommy, urging her to meet at the local pub—a gathering spot where they could strategize further and digest the fallout from the meeting. "It's time to talk about next steps," it read, accompanied by a series of urgent emoji.

As she made her way through the bustling streets of Cairns, Alison's thoughts drifted to the upcoming days. Would they face retaliation for their boldness? Would their quest for transparency lead to backlash that could threaten their movement? She knew they would need to fortify their resolve and prepare for whatever would come next.

Inside the pub, the atmosphere was alive with energy. Laughter and chatter filled the air, a stark contrast to the tension of the previous night. Spotting Tommy at a booth in the corner, she made her way over, finding him animatedly discussing plans with Finn and Eva.

"Hey, you made it!" Tommy exclaimed, his expression brightening. "We need to figure out how to keep this momentum going."

"Definitely," Alison agreed, sliding into the booth. "It feels as if we've cracked open a door, but I'm concerned about how they might react."

"Yeah," Finn interjected, his expression thoughtful. "I spent some time thinking about how Coral Reef Enterprises might retaliate. My family has connections to them, and I know firsthand how they operate when challenged."

"What do you mean?" Eva asked, her brow furrowing.

Finn hesitated, glancing around as if to ensure no eavesdroppers were lurking nearby. "They don't take threats lightly. If this turns into a public battle, they may label you as adversaries and attempt to discredit everything you're doing. They'll push back hard."

Tommy leaned forward, a mix of determination and worry evident on his face. "We need to reinforce our support. If we can solidify the community's backing, their tactics will have less impact."

Alison nodded, feeling the weight of responsibility settle on her shoulders. "I think we should organize another community gathering—this time to discuss concrete actions we can take. Let's mobilize everyone in our corner."

With the seeds of a plan budding, the conversation flowed. They spent the next hour crafting ideas while enjoying casual banter, each of them contributing with renewed enthusiasm. But as they geared up for their next steps, something ominous lingered in the air—the tension that often accompanies impending confrontation.

Just as they began to outline the logistics of the community gathering, a familiar figure entered the pub. Dr. Samuel Grant strolled in, his demeanor just as poised and authoritative as before. The sight of him ignited a mix of apprehension and anger in Alison. Was he here to intimidate them further?

Before she could process her thoughts, he spotted their table and approached with that signature smirk. "Well, if it isn't the champions of the reef," he said, his voice dripping with condescension. "Meeting in secret, are we?"

"We're not hiding anything," Tommy snapped back, irritation flashing in his eyes. "We're working to protect our community. You should be more concerned about why we're here and less about how we're meeting."

Dr. Grant's expression turned from smirking amusement to cold appraisal. "You should think carefully about the game you're playing. Your little movement, as noble as it sounds, is treading dangerously close to slander. You don't know the forces you're provoking."

"Is that a threat?" Alison shot back, unable to keep the edge out of her voice. "We've done our research, Dr. Grant. We know what's happening beneath the surface, and we refuse to let you, and your organization play fast and loose with the facts. The community deserves better."

A feral glint sparked in Dr. Grant's eyes. "You're playing with fire, Alison. People like you think they can change the tide, but you might find that you're out of your depth. The repercussions of challenging us could be... significant."

Alison stood her ground, although her heart raced. "We're not afraid. We have right on our side and the support of the community. If you think you can intimidate us into silence, you're mistaken."

The atmosphere in the pub shifted; other patrons turned their heads, drawn in by the escalating tension at the table. Dr. Grant's composure faltered for a fraction of a second, but he quickly regained control. "I advise you to consider the consequences of your actions. The business of environmental conservation is convoluted, and misunderstandings can lead to dangerous situations."

Before Alison could respond, he turned, shooting them one last contemptuous glance as he left. The moment he stepped outside, the tension around their table mingled with relief, but undercurrents of worry remained palpable.

"What the hell was that?" Eva exclaimed, crossing her arms. "He thinks he can scare us into submission. We need to be smarter about how we approach this from now on."

"I didn't think he'd have the audacity to confront us here," Tommy added, running a hand through his hair. "We need to be cautious. They may try to undermine us with lies or create divisions amongst our allies. We can't afford to let them succeed."

Alison took a deep breath, the blend of adrenaline and determination surging within her. "We need to keep pushing. What Dr. Grant said doesn't scare me—it only strengthens my resolve. Those threats only solidify why we're here. We're not just fighting for ourselves; we're fighting for our community and the reef."

As their discussions resumed, they brainstormed strategies to counter any attacks, emphasizing the importance of transparency, community engagement, and so much more. But the shadow of Dr. Grant's warning lingered, reminding them of the complex web of power and influence they were challenging.

The next few days flew by as the group worked diligently to prepare for the upcoming community gathering, aware that the confrontation with Coral Reef Enterprises was just the beginning of their fight. The fire within them grew, fueled by the desire to protect their home, but as they navigated these treacherous waters, the realization hit that they could very well be swimming against the tide of a formidable opponent.

As they finalized their plans and reached out to local media, Alison found herself caught in a maelstrom of emotions. With every ounce of determination bolstering them, doubt still slithered in the corners of her mind. They were ready to confront the storm brewing around them, but the knowledge that Coral Reef Enterprises would retaliate loomed larger than the waves crashing against the shore.

It was evident they would need each other more than ever. Together, they would withstand the turmoil ahead. They would not simply survive; they would rise, stronger and more resolute, vowing to protect the ocean that bound them together. The fight for the reef—and their community—had only just begun.

~ Eight ~

The day of the community gathering arrived, carrying with it an electric air of anticipation. Alison arrived early to the community center, her heart racing with a mix of excitement and nerves. The stakes had never been higher. They had chosen this venue deliberately, aware that it would serve as a symbol of unity and resilience—a platform for the community's voice to rise against the threats posed by Coral Reef Enterprises.

As Alison stepped inside, she was met with a flurry of activity. Banners decorated with the title "Tides of Change" hung around the room, vibrant artworks adorned the walls, and tables were lined with pamphlets highlighting their cause. The canvases from the previous exhibition were strategically placed, their vivid imagery showcasing both the beauty of the reef and the stark realities of its decline.

"Alison!" Eva called out as she stepped through the door, a confident smile plastered across her face. "Look at this turnout! Can you believe how many people showed up?"

Alison's heart swelled at the sight of familiar faces filling the space—friends, advocates, and those who had quietly watched from the sidelines but were now stepping up to demand change. "This is incredible!" she replied. "We might just have enough momentum to make a real impact today."

Together, they worked to finalize their setup, ensuring that everything appeared cohesive while maintaining the artistic expression that had become synonymous with their mission. The evening's program would blend presentations with storytelling; community members could share their experiences with the reef, fostering a deeper emotional connection to their cause.

Around the room, sparks of conversation ignited the atmosphere, each participant engaging with their passions and hopes for their collective future. Alison moved from group to group, feeling energized by the camaraderie that enveloped them. Even the looming threat of Coral Reef Enterprises felt less overwhelming in the presence of so much shared resolve.

As they prepared to kick off the gathering, the air shifted, and Alison felt a pang of anxiety as she caught sight of a familiar figure lurking at the edges of the crowd—Dr. Grant. His intimidating presence was hard to ignore, but she maintained her composure, willing to push through whatever challenges awaited. It was time to confront the very truths they had worked so hard to uncover.

Finally, the gathering commenced. Alison took the stage, her heart pounding as she looked out at the sea of expectant faces. "Thank you all for coming today," she said, her voice steady even as adrenaline coursed through her veins. "We stand here together, not as individuals, but as a community united by our love and concern for the reef."

The crowd responded with an enthusiastic cheer, fueling her determination. "Today, we will listen to stories, share our findings, and elevate our voices to hold Coral Reef Enterprises accountable for their actions. This is a pivotal moment for ours and future generations, and we need every one of you as part of this movement."

She glanced at Eva and Tommy, who smiled encouragingly, and began to outline their findings regarding Coral Reef Enterprises—discrepancies in financial reports, testimonies from local fishermen who had witnessed declining fish populations, and firsthand accounts of the impact the organization's alleged practices had inflicted on the ecosystem.

Each revelation poured forth, stirring emotions within the crowd. Gasps of shock and murmurs of disbelief rippled through the audience, punctuated by expressions of solidarity.

Then, it was time for the heart of the gathering—the community storytellers. One by one, local residents took to the stage, sharing personal experiences that evoked both sadness and determination. Among them was an elderly fisherman named Hank, whose stories of vibrant waters had turned murky echoed the urgency of the cause.

"I've seen the waters change under my boat," Hank said, his voice rich with conviction as he gripped the podium. "Decades ago, the reef flourished. We fished sustainably. But now, it's becoming harder, and I fear what that means for my grandchildren. We need to fight for our home, and we can no longer remain silent."

The audience erupted into applause, the connection between Hank's story and their mission solidifying the bonds of community that had formed around their cause. Alison could feel the energy building—a collective commitment to protecting the reef they all cherished.

As the gathering continued, Dr. Grant remained on the fringes, a watchful sentry simmering with irritation. At times, he shifted in his seat or whispered to O'Reilly, only for angry expressions to contort his otherwise composed demeanor. Alison sensed that the more they revealed, the more uneasy he became, realizing their voices were gaining strength.

Just as they reached the climax of the gathering, with emotions running high, Alison decided to introduce a surprise element. "I'd like to invite a special guest to the stage," she announced, her heart racing with anticipation. "Someone who has seen the inner workings of Coral Reef Enterprises firsthand."

Finn stepped forward, and the room went quiet, his presence carrying both weight and nervous energy. The tension settled over them like a blanket, as Alison watched Finn take a deep breath before beginning his remarks.

"Some of you know me, and a lot of you know my family's long history with Coral Reef Enterprises," he began, his voice steady despite the intensity of the moment. "I grew up seeing the good the organization has done, but I also saw how things shifted—not just in their practices but in their treatment of the community."

He continued, recounting tales of previous initiatives that had sparked optimism, only for the organization to gradually claw back from commitments to the community. "I've heard whispers of the truth being hidden beneath layers of pretenses, and as I stand here today, I can no longer uphold that silence. We cannot let this system continue unchecked; we must hold them accountable."

With each word, the room vibrated with energy, the connection between Finn's insights and their campaign against Coral Reef Enterprises strengthening their resolve.

"Thank you, Finn," Alison called out as the crowd erupted into applause. "Your courage to step forward amplifies our movement."

But before they could bask in the waves of unity washing over them, Dr. Grant stood up, his posture rigid with indignation. "This is not only an inaccurate portrayal of reality, but it's also reckless. Accusing Coral Reef Enterprises of wrongdoing—based solely on hearsay and innuendo—is a dangerous game."

"Reckless?" Finn replied, stepping forward, the fire igniting in his eyes. "You think silence is more prudent than transparency? We have a right to know how our community is affected, and withholding information is a betrayal to everyone here."

Dr. Grant sneered, now visibly rattled. "You may not comprehend the implications of stirring the pot, young man. There are consequences for challenging institutions like ours."

Alison interjected, moving to stand beside Finn. "The only consequences here are for the environment. We're not afraid of your threats. Together, our community will hold you accountable."

With a final glare, Dr. Grant turned on his heel, storming out of the gathering, leaving behind an almost tangible tension in the air.

The room erupted in applause once more, and Alison felt the adrenaline course through her. They had successfully stood up to the organization's representatives, and in doing so, they had taken a giant step forward toward building the momentum they needed—and the realization of their community standing together rang loud and clear.

As the gathering began to wind down and attendees conversed animatedly, Alison turned to Finn and Tommy, meeting their eyes with a mix of gratitude and determination.

"We did it! We took a huge stand today," she exclaimed, her heart racing. "This was just the beginning. We have to keep this movement alive and strong."

Finn nodded, his expression softening with relief. "Together, we can weather any storm that heads our way."

The energy in the room was palpable as they exchanged hopeful glances, fueled by the bond that had forged between them through advocacy. They had confronted the darkness; now, they were ready to press forward, armed with the strength of their community and the truth on their side.

With renewed conviction, Alison took a moment to reflect on how far they had come, the connections they had built, and the fight that lay ahead. Nothing would deter them from championing the reef—their home. The storm they faced would test their resolve, but she had faith in the strength they shared. They would navigate these turbulent waters together, unyielding in their mission to protect what mattered most.

The days following the community gathering felt electrifying; momentum surged through Cairns like a swift current. Alison and her allies, bolstered by the unity displayed at the meeting, were determined to capitalize on the wave of support they had generated. The hours leading up to each subsequent community discussion felt laden with anticipation, as if every moment were laden with potential for both hope and challenge.

However, as they delved deeper into their investigations of Coral Reef Enterprises, a sense of unease began to creep into the atmosphere. Rumors swirled, whispers of retaliation and intimidation tactics began to emerge from various corners. Those who had been supportive now tread cautiously, unsure if aligning with Alison and her team would provoke reprisals from the organization.

Alison leaned back in her chair, staring at the stack of notes before her, her brow furrowed in thought. The evidence they had compiled growing by the day was starting to paint a picture of corruption rooted deep within the organization. As the details unfolded, one thing became clear: the net around Coral Reef Enterprises was tightening, but so too were the threats against their advocacy.

"I've been hearing things," Eva said, her voice low and tinged with concern as she joined Alison at their table in the café. "Some folks are starting to pull away. They're worried about repercussion if they continue to support us."

"Damn it," Alison muttered, running a hand through her hair in frustration. "I knew this would happen. They'll try to isolate us, hit us where it hurts, but we can't let their fear dictate our mission."

Finn joined them, his expression serious. "I've got some contacts from within the organization. If we can obtain anything concrete about upcoming changes or dealings, it might give us the ammunition we need."

"Good! We need to get a hold of anything that can corroborate what we already suspect," Alison replied, feeling a renewed sense of urgency. "Especially if we're going to confront them again. But we need to be careful now. They may get desperate and resort to tactics we wouldn't expect."

As the three continued dissecting their findings and next steps, Tommy entered the café, his expression anxious. "Guys, I just bumped into O'Reilly on my way over. He wasn't subtle at all; the threats have started."

"What do you mean?" Alison and Eva said in unison, their apprehension peaking.

"He hinted that they know who's been behind the campaign. He implied that anyone speaking against the organization better just 'mind their business' before they find out what happens to those who cross Coral Reef Enterprises." Tommy's voice trembled slightly at the weight of what he was sharing.

Alison felt a chill sweep over her. "They're escalating things. We should gather at my place tonight—bring everyone who's been involved, people need to be aware of the risks."

The remainder of the day passed in a blur of anxious energy, and that evening, Alison's apartment became a hub of fervent discussion. Activists, artists, and individuals who had stepped forward to support their fight clustered together, their faces reflecting concern.

"I hate that we're living in fear," Hank, the elderly fisherman, shared as he shuffled nervously in his seat. "I've been fishing these waters my whole life, and I've never seen anything like what it is now—what the reef is facing. We've got to come together."

As the group exchanged ideas and strategies, Alison noticed the apprehension growing among those gathered. In as much as they were united by purpose, the fear of retaliation instilled doubt.

"We can't let them divide us," Alison urged, pacing before her audience. "We've come too far to back down now. If they seek to intimidate us into silence, then that alone proves how right we are in our fight. This makes us stronger."

But just as she was about to outline a plan for their next public statement, a loud knock on the door jolted the room. The air turned heavy, tension coiling around them like a snake preparing to strike.

"Who's that?" Eva whispered, her voice tense.

"It's late; could just be a neighbor, maybe they need something," Finn replied, his brows furrowing as he approached the door cautiously.

Alison felt her heart race as Finn pulled the door open, revealing Dr. Grant and O'Reilly standing on the threshold, flanked by a few stern-looking individuals.

"I think we need to have a little chat," Dr. Grant said, his calm demeanor contrasting sharply with the underlying threat lingering in the air.

Alison felt a wave of heat wash over her; the confrontation had come to her doorstep. "What do you want?" she demanded, clenching her fists at her sides.

Dr. Grant stepped into the room, O'Reilly following closely behind. "We'd like to discuss your actions and the consequences they could yield—for both you and your newfound allies. This movement of yours is drawing attention in ways you do not comprehend."

Alison felt her friends stiffen beside her, their expressions a mix of defiance and concern. "We're not afraid of your veiled threats," she replied. "We're here to protect our home, and that means exposing the truth."

"Truth? It's a slippery concept," O'Reilly interjected, his voice smooth yet patronizing. "The truth you declare may have dire ramifications, not just for our organization but for all your friends gathered here. If you insist on pursuing this campaign recklessly, you might find your community turning against you instead."

"You think you can intimidate us?" Tommy shouted, stepping forward. "We have every right to seek the truth."

Dr. Grant glanced at O'Reilly, a hint of amusement in his eyes. "This isn't intimidation, but rather a reality check. We can ensure your campaign fizzles out before it gains momentum. The ramifications of this war are far-reaching, and should you choose to continue, you might find the waters becoming far more hostile than what you anticipated."

Alison's breath hitched in her throat, both scared and furious. "This movement isn't about just us; it encompasses everyone here, the future of the reef, and the community that relies on it. If you want to threaten us, you need to understand that it only strengthens our resolve to bring this to light."

Dr. Grant stepped back slightly, now observing her with a curious intensity. "You seem more passionate than the others. But passion alone won't shield you from the truth about Coral Reef Enterprises. If you're wise, you'll retreat."

As tensions simmered, Alison could feel a shift; the community was strong behind her, and these threats only solidified her purpose. "We're not turning back. If anything, we'll work harder, unite stronger, and hold you accountable," she said, her voice unwavering.

With that declaration, she felt the collective strength of her friends around her—encouragement radiating through each of them, standing firm against the heavy storm that had just pushed its way through their door.

Dr. Grant and O'Reilly shared a moment of silent understanding, a flicker of acknowledgment passing between them as they recognized the unyielding spirit within the room. "Very well," Dr. Grant said finally, his voice low and incisive. "We'll see how this plays out. But remember—it won't be easy."

With that, they turned and left, leaving a trail of unease in their wake. The door swung shut behind them, and for a moment, the room remaincd silent, everyone processing what had just transpired.

Full of emotion, Alison stood still as concern mingled with adrenaline. "We will rise to this challenge," she declared, her voice firm as steel. "We know our purpose, and we know it's worth."

As waves crashed outside, they recognized the storm was upon them—both literally and metaphorically. They would face threats, intimidation, and resistance, but they would stand together, bound by a shared mission to protect the reef and their community. The net may have tightened around them, but with each passing moment, their pursuit of truth became a beacon of strength—a light cutting through the darkness, guiding them toward unity, resilience, and a fight worth making.

~ Nine ~

The intensity of the past few weeks weighed heavily on Alison as she walked down the sun-soaked streets of Cairns. The work surrounding the "Tides of Change" movements had consumed her, but mingled with the urgency of the mission was something deeper—an undeniable connection to the people around her, especially Finn.

As she reached the harbor, memories of their recent meetings filled her mind, especially the moments when their conversations drifted from strategy to more personal territory. Whether punctuated by shared laughter or contemplative silences, each interaction revealed layers of emotion neither had fully acknowledged. Flashes of longing flickered behind their shared glances, but the weight of their collective activism always pushed those feelings back into the shadows.

Today, they were all set to regroup at the community center to outline their next steps following Dr. Grant and O'Reilly's visit. But before returning to the fervor of advocacy, Alison felt a need to talk to Finn—to confront the surge of emotions that arose each time their paths crossed.

As she arrived, she spotted Finn standing outside the community center, seemingly preoccupied as he gazed out at the harbor. The sunlight danced on the waves, casting glimmers that sparkled in the wind. He turned as she approached, the corners of his mouth lifting in a tentative smile that sent a thrill racing through her.

"Hey, Alison," he greeted, a hint of warmth in his voice. "You're just in time. We were about to go over the plans for the meeting."

"I know. I just thought I'd take a moment," she replied, her heart pounding. "It's beautiful today, isn't it?"

"It is," he said, his gaze steady and searching. "The colors of this place always amaze me. But there's something about them today." He paused, his expression carrying an intensity that both thrilled and unsettled her. "Like they're reflecting a lot of emotion."

Alison felt her pulse quicken. "Yeah, it's a reminder of everything we're fighting for," she agreed, wishing to convey her awareness of their shared connection. "Despite the challenges, there's so much beauty here."

"Exactly," Finn said softly, stepping closer. The space between them felt charged, each heartbeat echoing in the stillness that surrounded them. "Sometimes it's hard to focus on the beauty when there's so much at stake."

Their conversation drifted to a comfortable silence, tension spiraling between them. Alison's heart began to race as she realized how close they were, the distance vanishing as she lingered in his gaze.

"Finn," she started, drawing a breath to steady her thoughts. "I know we're focused on the reef and the fight ahead, but... there's something about this that I can't ignore. It's been hard for me to discern what I'm feeling, especially amidst all this chaos."

His eyes widened, and she could see the flicker of something in his expression—a mixture of surprise and vulnerability. "I feel it too, Alison," he confessed quietly, the tension palpable. "With everything that's happened, it's hard not to. I've enjoyed spending time with you, but I've been hesitant to say anything."

Emboldened, she pressed on, "If we're going to navigate this fight together, shouldn't we also be honest about what else is brewing?" The words escaped her lips with a softness that carried the uncertainty they both sensed.

Finn glanced away for a moment, the tension rising between them palpable. "Absolutely. If we're standing together for something this important, we shouldn't mask the personal connections we're building." He paused, searching her gaze. "I don't want to complicate things amid everything that's happening, but I can't help how I feel."

As their eyes met again, the vulnerability in Finn's expression ignited something in Alison. She reached out, brushing her fingers against his hand, an electric jolt pulsing between them. "You don't have to hold back. We're in this together, and that includes every shade of our lives—even the complicated parts."

Their silence gave way to unspoken understanding, a sense of freedom blooming amidst the uncertainty. The tragic beauty of their fight for the reef intertwined with the budding desire that lingered between them, a tapestry of emotions woven through their shared experiences.

"Then let's be honest," Finn said, his voice a gentle whisper, his heart racing in sync with hers. "It's hard not to feel a bond with you. Things changed when we stood together against the tide."

Alison's heart raced as she acknowledged the truth in his words. "I feel it too. This fight has created something deeper within us, hasn't it?"

"I want to explore this—what we have," he confessed, stepping even closer, inching toward the precipice of vulnerability. "But we also have to focus on what we stand for. It wouldn't be right to let distractions pull us apart."

"Of course," she replied softly, her pulse thrumming in her veins. "We can navigate this together. We'll make sure our mission always comes first. But in moments like this, I want to acknowledge the connection we share."

Finn smiled, warmth radiating through him. They lingered on the threshold of their unspoken feelings, aware of the complexities ahead, yet embracing the alliance forming between them.

There, amidst the natural beauty surrounding them, the chaotic seriousness of their fight felt simultaneously tangled and clear.

Just then, Eva emerged from the community center, bringing with her the seriousness of the moment. "Hey, you two! Are you ready to discuss our next steps?"

Breaking their gaze, Alison and Finn stepped back, a subtle shift in the atmosphere. "Absolutely," Alison responded, trying to conceal the undeniable chemistry that still lingered like an unmade promise.

As they walked into the center, the excitement surrounding the upcoming gathering once again awaited them. The discussions around plans and community outreach began to flow, the momentum driving them forward into the fray. But Alison couldn't shake the sensation that something deeper had ignited between her and Finn—a new layer to their alliance that blurred the lines between emotion and purpose.

Together, they were not just fighting for the future of the reef; they were also coming to terms with their own intentions and desires, wrapping their cause with threads of connection that fortified their resolve.

With their hearts now intertwined amidst the currents of activism, Alison felt invigorated. Whatever storms lay ahead—personal or otherwise—they would face them together. The collective strength of their newfound connections only solidified the spirit of the movement they had created, propelling them onward in the pursuit of their mission and towards the deeper complexities of what it meant to truly stand united.

The days that followed the "Tides of Change" exhibition were a whirlwind of energy and purpose. The excitement of the community gathering had fueled their momentum, and Alison felt an electric current coursing through Cairns as they pressed on with their mission to rally support against Coral Reef Enterprises. Yet, even within the thriving community, cracks began to form beneath the surface, filled with whispers that hinted at tensions rising among their ranks.

Alison had spent hours drafting press releases, organizing outreach efforts, and refining their narrative, but she couldn't shake the feeling that trust was beginning to wane. Restlessness lingered in the air—a tension she sensed during their meetings and discussions as groups formed around differing opinions.

On a particularly busy afternoon, she and Eva were at the local café, huddled over cups of coffee and notes, preparing for an upcoming meeting with local environmental groups. As the conversation flowed, Tommy entered, his expression betraying a mix of nerves and determination.

"Hey, can we talk?" he asked, glancing around as if ensuring no one was listening. The seriousness in his tone caused alarm bells to chime in Alison's head.

"Of course. What's going on?" she replied, motioning for him to join their table.

"I think we might have a problem," he said, lowering his voice as he joined them. "I've been hearing rumors that some people in the community aren't happy with how we're handling things. There are whispers of discontent with our tactics, especially after O'Reilly's other threats."

"What? Why would anyone want to turn against our cause?" Eva interjected, disbelief etched on her face.

"It seems there are factions forming," Tommy explained, scrubbing a hand over his face in frustration. "Some people feel we're drawing too much attention to ourselves, that we're rattling a cage we shouldn't be. They're worried about backlash from Coral Reef Enterprises and how it could harm local businesses."

Alison felt the tension clamp down over her heart. "This can't be happening. We're fighting for the reef, for everyone's future! If they're turning away from that, we need to know who we're working with."

"I overheard a few conversations where people expressed concern," Tommy continued. "Some are worried that if we keep pushing, it could lead to economic fallout for the town. They think our actions could risk jobs and livelihoods."

Alison's mind raced with frustration. "That's exactly what they want! To create doubts and fears that divide us. This isn't just about any single organization or business; it's about protecting our resource!"

Finishing her cup of coffee, she stood. "If this is happening, we need to address it directly. We can't let Coral Reef Enterprises use intimidation to fracture our solidarity."

Tommy glanced around nervously. "But how do we do that without appearing combative? We're already walking a tightrope as is."

"We'll hold another community gathering," Alison decided swiftly, her heart steeled by the challenge. "A space where anyone can share their concerns and fears. We need to address this head-on, transparently. If we don't, the divisiveness will fester."

"Agreed," Eva said, her voice resolute. "We'll provide a platform for people to express their worries openly. We can't allow misleading narratives to win out."

With a plan taking shape, they went to work, organizing the details of the upcoming gathering. Alison remained hopeful that by nurturing open dialogue, they could help temper the fears swirling around the community. It was essential for them to unify behind a shared commitment to the reef and the values that tied them together—a challenging task, but one they would face with courage and transparency.

As the date of the gathering approached, anticipation built in the community. Posters adorned storefronts, and the sentiment that had drawn people together previously had transformed into inquiry and speculation. Would they still support Alison and their movement against Coral Reef Enterprises, or would the divisions take root?

On the night of the meeting, the community center overflowed with attendees; Alison stood at the front, trying to keep her nerves steady. She had set the stage for an open forum—a safe space for concerns, questions, and feedback. Anxiety coursed through her as she felt all eyes resting on her.

"Thank you all for coming," she began. "As we adapt to the ongoing challenges we face, it's essential that we come together as a community. I understand that there are concerns about the direction we've taken, especially regarding our advocacy efforts against Coral Reef Enterprises, and I want to invite you to share your thoughts."

As she spoke, Alison noticed a group forming at the back of the room—faces she recognized, but with expressions that betrayed their apprehension. Among them was a group of local business owners who had never shied away from voicing concerns. They had enjoyed a tenuous rapport with Coral Reef Enterprises and worried about the fallout from confronting the organization.

One of the men, David, stepped forward, his apprehension obvious. "Can I say something?" He cleared his throat, voice shaky but determined. "I run a small dive shop in town, and I've been hearing what's being said about Coral Reef Enterprises. I understand their practices have flaws, but we also rely on them for our livelihoods. If we push too hard, it could jeopardize our businesses."

Murmurs of agreement rippled through the crowd. The divide began to reveal itself as voices emerged both in support of and against Alison's movement.

Alison felt her heart sink. "David, I understand your concerns, but what about the long-term health of the reef? If we don't address the issues, there may not be a reef left to dive into."

"I see your point," he replied warily. "But we're walking a fragile line. If Coral Reef Enterprises retaliates and jobs are lost, that's a reality we cannot ignore."

Another voice piped up from the crowd. "But isn't the future of the reef just as important? If their practices continue unchecked, it's us, the local community, who will suffer in the long run."

The room erupted into scattered discussions, fears intensifying as differing opinions clashed. Wild gestures and animated expressions filled the air like a tempest, emotions rising to a boiling point, and Alison felt the tension that had been brewing finally erupt.

As the dialogue escalated, Alison realized they were at a precipice—one that could fracture the very movement she had sought to strengthen. "Everyone here understands our shared passion for the reef. But we need to find common ground rather than allow divisions to cloud our purpose," she urged, raising her voice to regain control.

Yet it seemed the fractures had soon spread into the very hearts of her allies, and a sense of betrayal hung thick in the air. "What's the point in risking everything when the organization could retaliate?" Tommy said, frustration tinging his voice as dissent grew louder.

"Are you saying we should back down?" Eva challenged, eyes locked on Tommy. "This is our moment to stand up for the cause we all care about! We can't afford to shrink back in fear!"

Alison sensed the tension morphing into something harder and darker—an unclear path that threatened to transform allies into foes. "We cannot allow Coral Reef Enterprises to dictate our unity. If we tear apart our community now, we betray everything we've fought for," she pleaded, her voice shaking but earnest.

The room quieted slightly, but the thick air was still steeped in dissent. Fractures had appeared within their ranks, fueled by fear and uncertainty, and it seemed the storm was threatening to consume them whole.

Realizing the weight of the moment, Alison stood tall, determined not to let divisiveness take root. "If you feel afraid, share it. If you have doubts, voice them. But we must do so together. We can navigate these rocky waters without losing sight of our commitment to one another and to protect our reef."

The sincerity in her message appeared to resonate among the crowd, even as the unease lingered. Slowly but surely, people began to share their concerns, expressing their fears about backlash, the economic impact of their advocacy, and the future of their livelihoods.

But as some began to advocate for unity, others still felt hesitant, caught against the current of progress.

"Compromise creates opportunity," one of the business owners stated firmly, standing up in a show of conviction. "We can't disrupt the status quo without understanding the potential fallout. We need to keep the dialogue open with Coral Reef Enterprises to protect our interests!"

Someone else shot back, "Keeping the status quo means continuing to let them operate unchecked! We can't keep living under this shadow!"

The tension hung palpably as voices continued to clash. Alison felt the ground beneath her shaky as the line between allies and foes blurred. The gathering once intended to unify now reflected the storm inside as tempers flared—a portrait of a community divided.

John, an older gentleman and longtime advocate for the reef, finally raised his hand to quiet the room. "We've been here before. Fear of retaliation has kept us quiet, but we cannot let fear dictate our actions any longer. If we want a healthy reef, we need complete honesty within our ranks and willingness to confront those who threaten our future."

With that simple yet profound statement, a newfound air of solidarity emerged. Even as tensions flared, Alison recognized that the battle they faced was part of a larger journey—one of learning to balance strong emotions and different perspectives.

As conversations shifted and voices softened, Alison felt a sense of reassurance envelop the room. They were in the midst of a storm, one that could certainly tear them apart unless they addressed the fears lingering in the shadows. But she also knew that in forging their path forward, they would emerge stronger together.

While the waters ahead remained uncertain, Alison resolved not to back down. She felt an unwavering need to bridge the divides forming within their ranks. They would not only stand for the reef but also for each other—woven together in a tapestry of resilience, courage, and hope that could weather any tempest.

~ Ten ~

The days that followed the community gathering were a tempest of emotions—renewed enthusiasm mingled with the uncertainty that hung in the air like clouds before a downpour. Alison found herself questioning the very foundations of her movement amidst the swirling rumors and unrest in Cairns.

Dr. Samuel Grant's warning still echoed in her mind, a cold reminder of the intricate web they were all entangled in as they pressed on against Coral Reef Enterprises. With tensions rising within their ranks, Alison knew they needed not only the support of the community but also the confidence to confront the organization directly. It was time to gather their evidence, sharpen their strategy, and plan how to approach the impending confrontation with clarity and purpose.

That afternoon, Alison, Eva, and Tommy met at the community center to regroup and review the evidence they had collected. The room was filled with art pieces from the "Tides of Change" exhibition, each one serving as a vibrant reminder of what they were fighting for. But for Alison, the space also felt heavy with the whispers of dissent they had faced during the recent gathering.

"Okay, let's look at everything we've got," Alison said, spreading out the documents across the table. The pieces of evidence included financial reports, testimonies, and even social media comments echoed from their community discussions.

As they sorted through the paperwork, Alison felt her heart flutter with both hope and apprehension. "We need to ensure we present a solid case against Coral Reef Enterprises," she said, her fingers brushing over the papers. "Every piece here needs to connect clearly to show the bigger picture of negligence and deception."

"I agree," Eva chimed in, her brow creased in concentration. "It's critical that we guide this narrative, not just react to their pushback. We need to present ourselves as informed advocates for the reef—professionals who mean business."

Just then, the door swung open, and Finn stepped in, his expression a mix of determination and uncertainty. "Hey, I wanted to touch base with you all and share what I learned from my contacts," he said, clutching a folder close to his chest.

Alison felt a surge of hope. "Great, we could use any insider knowledge right now!"

Finn reached the table, and as he laid his folder down, a tense silence enveloped the room. "I finally got in touch with someone who has insights into Coral Reef Enterprises' internal dealings. They... shared some potentially explosive information."

Curiosity mingled with anxiety as the group leaned closer, eager to absorb every detail. "Go on," Alison encouraged as Finn opened the folder, revealing several documents and notes.

"There's been talk about ethical violations in their recent projects, especially those tied to the government contracts," Finn began. "Some projects weren't just mismanaged; they were underfunded and poorly executed. The funding was misrepresented in reports—what was labeled as ecological restoration was often channeled elsewhere without proper reporting."

The air felt electric as Alison processed the implications. "If this is true, it could expose their entire operation. We need to act on this quickly."

Just then, a text buzzed on Alison's phone, its unexpected presence pulling her attention. Glancing down, she saw a message from an unknown number. The text read, *"Meet me tonight at the docks—urgent information about Coral Reef Enterprises. Come alone."

Her heart raced, and a rush of adrenaline coursed through her. "I just got a text from someone claiming they have more information on Coral Reef Enterprises... but they want me to meet alone. What do you all think?"

"Be careful, Alison," Tommy cautioned, a shadow of concern crossing his face. "It could be a trap."

"Or an opportunity," she replied, determination igniting in her chest. "This could be the break we need—clear, concrete proof to back up everything we're gathering."

"I say we all go together," Eva interjected firmly. "If someone is reaching out with important information, we shouldn't let you face it alone. They may be trying to intimidate or manipulate you."

"No, I think it's best if I handle this myself," she insisted, a flurry of mixed emotions churning inside her. "If they're trying to lure me into a trap, it could be worse if you guys are involved. If we plan to confront them, I need to know what this person has to say first."

Finn, sensing the weight of her decision, leaned in closer. "Then let's at least ensure you have a plan. I can stay close by and watch from a distance—if things go south, I'll be ready to help."

The group felt the tension throbbing, each member processing the risks. Though they had all fought so hard and forged bonds in their cause, the stakes of this potential meeting felt palpable.

"Alright," Alison relented. "I'll go. But everyone else—stay alert and remain nearby. Don't let me out of your sight, and if anything feels off, don't hesitate to intervene."

As night began to settle in and shadows crept across the town, Alison prepared herself. She felt a blend of trepidation and resolve. If there was information out there—crucial insights that could tilt the balance in their favor—she needed to uncover it, no matter the personal risk.

Under the cover of twilight, she made her way to the docks, her heart pounding as she scanned her surroundings. The sound of water lapping against the hulls of boats was the only noise as she approached their meeting spot—an isolated dock lit by soft lanterns flickering nearby.

The figure standing at the end of the dock was silhouetted against the water's glow, a shadowy presence that felt both familiar and ominous. As she approached, she steeled herself for whatever truth awaited her.

"Are you Alison?" the figure called out, their voice echoing across the stillness.

"Yes," she replied cautiously, eyeing the figure as she stepped closer. "What information do you have about Coral Reef Enterprises?"

The stranger stepped into the light, revealing a woman with dark hair tied back in a ponytail. Her face bore the lines of experience—a mix of anxiety and determination. "I've worked behind the scenes for years. I can't stay silent about what I've seen."

Alison felt a flutter of anticipation spark within her. "Then tell me everything," she urged, her breath hitching with the weight of what might come. "The community needs to know the truth."

But just as the woman began to speak, a sudden shout broke through the night, echoing from behind Alison. "Alison, look out!"

Momentarily caught off guard, Alison turned, feeling panic rush through her veins as shadowy figures emerged from the darkness, advancing toward her with intent. Before she could react, she felt the air shift, and it became clear that the storm she had been warned of was upon her—both literally and metaphorically.

Fear washed over her as the realization hit. The unfolding fight for the reef had drawn them into treacherous territory, and as the figures loomed closer, she understood that the consequences of their activism were beginning to reveal themselves in stark, undeniable ways.

The battle was far from over; it was only just beginning.

Adrenaline surged through Alison as she turned to face the shadowy figures heading toward her from the darkness of the docks. The familiar feeling of dread wrapped around her like a cold blanket, intensifying with each passing second. The urgency of the moment crashed against her, and instinct kicked in—the gathering storm she had feared was now crashing against them.

"Alison, run!" the woman at the dock shouted before she was abruptly shoved to the side, silenced by the advancing figures.

Without hesitation, Alison bolted away from the approaching threat, feet pounding against the wooden planks of the dock as she sprinted toward safety. Her heart raced, drowning out the sounds of the night—a chaotic symphony of fear and adrenaline fueling her escape.

She heard footsteps chasing after her, their shouts echoing across the water. "Stop! We just want to talk!" one of the figures called out. But the urgency in their tone reeked of anything but friendly intent.

As she reached the edge of the dock, she took in her surroundings. The light from the nearby lanterns flickered, illuminating the dark water below. Despite the panic rising within her, a small voice in her mind urged her to focus. She glanced back—was there still time to escape?

Alison turned and focused ahead, running down the narrow path that led to the street. The figures were gaining on her, their taunts ringing out as they closed the distance. "You can't run from the truth!" one voice shouted, but she refused to yield.

Just as she reached the end of the docks, she spotted movement out of the corner of her eye—Finn was there, positioned strategically nearby, having kept his promise to watch her from a distance. He saw her expression of fear, instantaneously shifting into action.

"Alison!" he shouted, his voice cutting through the tension. "This way!"

She veered toward him, heart pounding with gratitude and fear. With Finn by her side, they raced across the street and ducked behind the nearest building as the group pursuing them drew closer.

"What happened?" Finn asked, his voice urgent, scanning the darkness for any signs of the figures. "Are you okay?"

"I don't know! They were just—" she gasped, breathless from her sprint, her mind racing as they crouched in the shadows. "They were going to confront me. I don't know what they wanted, but it didn't feel safe. We need to warn everyone!"

"Let's get back to the others first," he said, glancing around the corner to ensure the coastline was clear. "You go first. I'll follow."

Alison nodded, adrenaline still pumping as they moved swiftly back towards the community center, her thoughts buzzing with what just transpired. What were Dr. Grant and Coral Reef Enterprises doing lurking in the shadows? What do they hope to gain from intimidating the very community they claimed to protect?

As they entered the community center, they found a pulse of activity still buzzing within. Supporters milled about, discussing the day's events. But the atmosphere shifted when Alison and Finn burst through the door.

"Where's Tommy?" she asked, scanning the crowd.

"He's in the back with Eva," a voice called out—it was Sarah, concern etching her features. "What happened? You look shaken."

"Dr. Grant was there," Finn blurted out, still catching his breath. "Alison was approached by someone with information… but they were ambushed. We need to figure out our next steps immediately."

The room fell silent, all eyes on Alison as her heart raced. "They're watching us, and they won't hesitate to intimidate us into silence," she said, steeling her resolve. "But we have each other. We have evidence to support our case against Coral Reef Enterprises. We can't let fear win."

Tommy, who had been discussing details with Eva, joined their circle, his expression serious. "We need to prepare to confront them head-on. But now, we also have to make sure we keep everyone aware of the danger."

As they shared what had just occurred, the atmosphere grew tense again, uncertainty flickering among the supporters who had shown unwavering strength in previous gatherings. The palpable fear of retaliation began to wrap its tendrils around the discussions, causing doubt to seep into the collective mindset.

"We need to protect this movement," Eva spoke up, her voice steady despite their trepidation. "Let's organize within our ranks. Make sure everyone is aware of the risks and stay vigilant. We can't let their intimidation tactics divide us."

Alison took a deep breath, feeling the weight of leadership settle firmly on her shoulders once more. "Right. Our movement must remain united, strong, and aware. If we're informed, they can't shake us."

But as the hours wore on, deadlines loomed in both their activism and the impending backlash from Coral Reef Enterprises. They worked tirelessly, strategizing the best way to push forward with their evidence and rallying the community. Each piece of evidence stood as a sturdy pillar in their fight, and as they dove deeper into their strategy, Alison felt a gripping sense of fear and determination intertwine within her.

But in the back of her mind, hesitation rooted itself—a question lingering like a vine: what truly lay beneath the surface of the battle they were waging? The potential darkness within Coral Reef Enterprises loomed like a storm ready to break, and Alison wondered if the truth they sought would come alongside consequences they could not fathom.

That evening, as they prepared to send out invitations for their next gathering—one where they'd address the community's concerns and present the hard evidence—Alison looked around at her friends. They had bonded in this fight, but the stakes were higher than any of them had anticipated.

As she gazed out the windows, watching the sun setting over the horizon, a surge of determination enveloped her. "We'll face this all together," she whispered to herself, gripping the edge of the table with conviction.

With every challenge, storm, and shadow thrown their way, they were becoming stronger—not just for the reef but for each other. And as she took her seat among her friends, ready to dive further into the murky depths of the truth they sought, she felt hope rising like the tide—a promise to stand unwavering against the darkness that sought to engulf them. The hour was growing late, but their resolve was only just beginning to bloom. Together, they would shine light on the secrets buried beneath the pressures of power & corruption.

~ Eleven ~

As the days turned into weeks, the tension in Cairns continued to escalate. Alison and her team worked tirelessly, gathering evidence and rallying community support against Coral Reef Enterprises. The stakes were higher than ever, and with each passing moment, the riptide of pressure pulled harder at the fabric of their movement. But in the heat of their fight, unexpected strains began to surface within their ranks, revealing fissures that threatened to split them apart.

The community was abuzz with anticipation for the next gathering, where they would present their findings and call for accountability. The venue was packed with engaged residents, all eager to join the fight for the reef. But among the camaraderie, Alison sensed an undercurrent of doubt brewing beneath the surface, fueled by fear and insecurity as some within the community began to question the path they were taking.

"No one wants to be the target of Coral Reef's wrath," said one local business owner during a pre-meeting discussion, his voice thin with concern. "We're risking everything by standing against them, especially when they've already shown they're willing to stifle dissent."

Tommy interjected, trying to reassure the group. "But we have to fight for the future of the reef! If we don't stand together, we allow them to manipulate the narrative and silence us."

Alison felt the weight of the assembled voices pressing down on her, tension crackling in the air. She had been so focused on unit-

ing the community in their shared cause that she hadn't anticipated the fissures forming within them—dissent festering in the
shadows.

As the crowd dwindled and people trickled into the main meeting area, Alison took a deep breath, steeling her nerves. "Let's focus on our goal tonight. We need to emphasize that the fight is
about more than just us—it's about the future of our community
and its most precious resource."

Tommy nodded, his determination unwavering. "We're
stronger together. We can and will face whatever comes our way."

Just then, Sarah joined the group, her expression somber.
"Have you heard the latest? Some people are whispering about
backing down. They're scared of possible repercussions," she said
quietly, glancing around as if afraid someone might overhear.

Alison's heart sank. The shadows had taken on a life of their
own. "We can't let fear dictate our actions. I'll address these concerns head-on tonight," she resolved, ready to reaffirm frontlines
for their cause.

As the gathering commenced, Alison stood at the front, surveying the crowd that sat packed into the community center. She took
a deep breath before speaking. "Thank you all for coming tonight.
We're here to discuss the future of our reef—our shared responsibility. But we need to have an honest conversation about the fears
that have emerged as we've pushed forward."

Murmurs of concern spread through the crowd, and Alison felt
the weight of their uncertainty hanging in the air. "I understand
that there are real worries about speaking out against Coral Reef
Enterprises," she continued, her heart steady. "But we owe it to
ourselves and to future generations to confront this head-on."

Just as she prepared to continue, a voice cut through the
room—one she recognized but didn't expect to hear. It was Lucas,
the local gossip whose innocuous presence often masked shrewd

observation. "But what if this fight puts our businesses at risk? What if solidarity isn't enough?"

Several nods of agreement rippled through the audience, and Alison's heart raced. "If we allow fear to win, we may not have any businesses left to protect!" she countered, urgency creeping into her voice. "The reef is not just our environment; it's a part of our culture, our economy, and our lives!"

With the audience engaged, she began to present the evidence they had gathered, documenting the inconsistencies and injustices tied to Coral Reef Enterprises. Each fact seemed to resonate deeply, shifting the crowd's angst into a collective determination to demand change.

But as the meeting progressed, she noticed a shadow lingering at the back of the room—Dr. Grant, his demeanor unreadable as he studied their gathering. The tension coiled tighter around her, but she pressed on, not allowing himself to deter their mission.

After the presentations, she opened the floor for questions, eager to hear from the community. But as hands rose hesitantly, the atmosphere shifted, and the energy became electric with anxiety.

"I just want to know—what happens if Coral Reef puts up a fight?" one of the attendees asked, her voice trembling. "What if they turn against us? What if someone gets hurt?"

"I don't think we should take that risk!" another voice called out. "There's too much at stake here, and it feels like an uphill battle."

Alison felt the room tightening around her—a visceral reminder that while they fought for unity, fear was already beginning to splinter their foundations. She had prepared for pushback but never anticipated an escalation of doubt that could trigger fractures among allies.

Much to her dismay, Tommy piped up. "Standing up to an organization like Coral Reef Enterprises means we must face the consequences. I understand everyone's apprehension, but we can't allow fear to dictate our actions! We need to stick together!"

But the whispers among the crowd grew louder, and Alison heard the discontent beginning to fester like an untreated wound. A small faction from the back whispered about negotiating terms with Coral Reef Enterprises rather than confronting them directly.

She felt the walls closing in, realizing a rift was forming—a moment that could either galvanize their resolve or lead to disbandment.

As tempers flared and anxiety grew, another person raised their hand, and Alison's heart sank further. It was one of the key locals invested in Coral Reef Enterprises, a known supporter of theirs. "Look, we need to consider the long-term implications. If we approach them too aggressively, we jeopardize future partnerships that could actually help the reef," he argued, drawing a few nods from his supporters.

In that instant, Alison felt the fragile alliances begin to splinter, allies turning against one another. "No, what we jeopardize is our integrity and the state of the environment!" she shot back, her voice steady but tinged with frustration. "If we can't be honest about the corrupt practices harming our ocean, then we aren't being good stewards of our community."

But doubt had taken root, sowing discord as various factions began to form—some advocating for negotiation, while others insisted on outright confrontation. The very unity they had forged began to crumble under the weight of uncertainty and fear.

"Alison, you can't ignore the fears people have!" Sarah pleaded, but even her usually supportive tone turned wary. "Not everyone will feel safe standing against Coral Reef without a solid foundation."

The clash intensified, voices overlapping, creating an almost chaotic symphony of divergence. Fear, doubt, and anger began to take on lives of their own, swirling around the room and threatening to pull them under.

Realizing the fracture before her was threatening to spread chaos, Alison took a deep breath, steeling herself to reclaim the narrative. "This isn't just about us; it's about who we are as a community. At this moment, we face a choice between integrity and complacency. We must remember why we came together in the first place."

Determined, she locked eyes with Finn, who stood steadfastly beside her. "And remember that we have to face this storm together. We can find common ground and grow our movement from the roots up. If we don't address the issues head-on, we'll all sink."

Gradually, the din of dissent faded as Alison's words settled over the crowd, grounding them. "Let's redirect our energy toward forming a cohesive strategy that addresses everyone's fears. Together, we are stronger—no matter where we stand on confrontational tactics. But we must not let fear divide us."

As the gathering continued, Alison sensed a shift in energy; though the divisions had surfaced, they had also opened the door to dialogues that could mend rifts if conducted with care. They would have to bridge the chasms of doubt that had begun to fracture their unity to forge ahead and ensure their movement remained resolute.

Changes loomed ahead, but this was not the beginning of the end. It was merely a storm to navigate—one that could lead to renewed unity and shared purpose if they stood firm against the tides that threatened to tear them apart.

With each voice, they had a story to share, and each story threaded them together, reminding them of why they were united in the first place. Faced against a formidable adversary, they could either disband into fears or intertwine their purposes, standing stronger against the turbulent sea. Together, they would weather the storm. Together, they could uncover the truths left submerged in shadows.

The chaos from the previous community gathering echoed in Alison's mind as she stepped into the community center for the follow-up meeting. The atmosphere was thick with tension and uncertainty; their unified front had shown signs of cracking, and whispers of dissent had circulated among attendees like confusing ripples across the calm waters.

Even as she arrived, Alison felt the buzz of anxiety swirling through the crowd. More faces had surfaced, but so had new divides—factions forming around differing opinions on how to confront Coral Reef Enterprises. The once-shared mission now faced the threat of fragmentation.

"Alison!" Eva called out, her expression a mix of apprehension and resolve. "I'm glad you're here. The discussions are starting, but people seem on edge."

"I know," Alison replied, her heart quickening. "We need to regain focus and remind everyone what brought us together. If we don't, fear could derail our movement."

Throughout the hall, attendees gathered in small clusters, murmuring amongst themselves. Some exchanged hushed words of doubt about the movement's tactics; others clung to the desire for a unified front. It was clear that anxiety was infectious, and time was running short to redirect those emotions into collective action.

"Gather 'round, everyone!" Eva called, clapping her hands to draw attention to their small group. "Let's come together and find a way to collectively address our next steps."

As people settled into their seats, some looked cautiously at one another, tension still palpable in the air. The room buzzed with a mix of nervous energy and unease, as if everyone was tiptoeing around invisible landmines of confrontation.

Once the crowd quieted, Alison stood to address them. Her heart raced—not with fear, but with a determination to unify them in their cause. "Thank you all for coming again. I understand that the discussions from the last gathering have stirred up worries. I want us to have an open conversation about how we can continue moving forward while addressing whatever concerns you may have."

"Do we really have the right plan?" said one local fisherman named Carl, raising his hand. "Coral Reef has connections that could hit us where it hurts if we push too hard. What if we lose our businesses or worse? I've heard they're already looking for ways to discredit us. They'll fight back."

"Sticking our heads in the sand won't help us either!" came a voice from the back of the room. It was a young environmental activist who had been vocal during previous gatherings. "We can't let them silence us. Yes, we risk backlash, but we must stand firm."

Alison felt her heart surge with gratitude for emerging voices willing to speak out. "Exactly! If we let fear dictate our path, the fight becomes futile. Our focus must remain on action, but we need to make sure every voice feels heard and valued."

The room began to stir, but it was undeniable that the fissures still lingered beneath the surface, each one threatening to deepen. Alison searched for a way to break through the discontent, but before she could redirect their focus, another voice cut through the air.

"I think it's all too risky," a member of the local business association chimed in. "The negative press has already started. We can't afford to alienate ourselves from Coral Reef. They provide vital support to our economy."

Angry murmurs ripple through the crowd, frustration boiling beneath the surface.

"Yes, but that support comes at the cost of the environment! We're not speaking for just ourselves; we're speaking for our home," Eva countered. "We need to become the voice for the reef before it's too late. If we turn our backs on this movement, we risk losing even more."

But as quickly as she spoke, the divisions grew clearer, each side building tension as arguments flared. The cacophony of voices grew louder as individuals leaned into their own perspectives, feelings juxtaposing against one another in a tumultuous display of dissent.

"Calm down! Calm down!" Alison shouted, attempting to regain control. "We can't afford to turn on one another! We're all here because we care about the same thing. We're fighting for the future!"

Yet, as the spirited discussion continued, the emotions swelled and turned, and what began as an earnest dialogue morphed into arguments, accusations, and rising tempers. The overwhelming sense of unity became a chaotic and stormy sea of diverging opinions.

From the corner of the room, Lucas, the local gossip, interjected. "If you're all so worried about how the fight affects you, have you thought about how Coral Reef Enterprises can manipulate what's being said? They'll use any crack they can find to undermine our movement."

Alison felt the unsettling tension thicken as Lucas's words reverberated through the crowd. Uncertainty and fear danced in the faces surrounding her, echoing the vulnerability that threatened to split them apart.

"I hate to say it," Finn spoke up, his voice steady yet weighed down by the truth. "But this conflict won't just touch us; it will reach into the very essence of this community. If we don't stand resolutely against exploitation, we risk losing more than just businesses—we risk losing our sense of identity."

The silence that followed his words broke through the frenzy, as every person present began to acknowledge the truth in his statement. The collective realization of what was at stake floated over them—or maybe it was the weight of doubt that enveloped their unity. Either way, Alison could see that every face in the room was grappling with their own fears while desperately trying to find common ground.

Alison pressed on, her voice trembling yet resolute. "This is our moment to address our concerns, our fears, and any doubts head-on. We need to pull together instead of letting fear divide us. Our strength lies in standing united for something bigger than ourselves."

Gradually, the fervor quelled, and Alison could see a flicker of understanding start to spread. Voices softened as members slowly shifted their perspectives, recognizing that they were on the precipice of a critical moment in their fight—not just for the reef, but to safeguard their community.

As the gathering continued, they openly nurtured each other's expressions, drawing in their shared fears while reinforcing the unyielding desire to confront the truths surrounding Coral Reef Enterprises. Emotions, once volatile, began to blend, recognizing that they could form a tapestry of unity from the colorful pieces of their thoughts and experiences.

Though fear and uncertainty still hung in the air, they had ensured that the community stood together, fortified from shared purpose and resolve. Alison held steadfast, knowing they could navigate these waves together and emerged as a voice that would call to the cracks that had begun to show.

As the sun dipped low on the horizon, casting a soft golden glow over the room, Alison felt her heart swell with the hope that they could weave their diverse voices into a powerful force for change. The battle was at a crossroads, but the fight for the reef had only just begun to settle in the hearts of an unwilling yet resolute community. Together, they would surf the tides of uncertainty—not just as allies, but as a collective force ready to confront whatever storm lay ahead.

~ Twelve ~

The tension in Cairns had reached a fever pitch, and the impact of the community's recent discussions about Coral Reef Enterprises hung over everyone like a dark cloud. Rumors and whispers ricocheted through the streets, and as Alison navigated her way through the bustling markets filled with tourists, she felt a sense of unease settling within her.

It was an odd juxtaposition to witness the vibrant tourism sector thriving under the warm sun while the looming threat of their ongoing battle loomed ever larger. Brightly colored stalls showcased local crafts and produce, and the laughter of children echoed through the air, an innocent contrast to the storm of turmoil brewing behind the scenes.

Alison glanced back toward one of the café patios, where she spotted Finn speaking to a group of tourists, his demeanor friendly and engaging. It struck her how seamlessly he shifted roles—sharing the beauty of the reef's ecosystem while also encapsulating the urgency of its preservation. But beneath the charm, she perceived his conflicts surfacing; she knew he too was grappling with divided loyalties between his family's ties to Coral Reef Enterprises and his burgeoning commitment to their cause.

Steeling herself, Alison made her way over to him, a sense of apprehension tinged with affection bubbling beneath the surface. It would be hard for them to sustain the momentum of their mission with distractions forming all around them, yet she longed to support him in this intersection of their lives.

"Hey!" Finn turned as she approached, a warm smile brightening his features. "I was just telling these folks about the reef and its impact on the local community."

"Hi there!" Alison greeted the tourists, her mood lifting slightly despite the underlying tension. "It's wonderful to hear people appreciate the reef. Are you enjoying your time in Cairns?"

As they exchanged pleasantries, she caught snippets of Finn's conversation, where he effortlessly highlighted the significance of marine life and local culture. But she also detected an undercurrent of discomfort within him, as if navigating the complexities of their fight made his heart heavy.

Once the tourists moved on, Finn turned to Alison, his expression shifting to one of concern. "I hate this duality. It's hard to balance sharing how beautiful this place is while fighting for its future. Sometimes I feel like I'm shutting off one part of who I am for another."

"I get that," Alison replied gently, her fingers brushing against his arm before pulling away. "But you're doing the right thing, Finn. This is as much about protecting our home as it is about preserving the community's future. It's a balancing act—and it takes time for all of us."

Finn nodded, a mixture of appreciation and trepidation in his eyes. "But it's exhausting. The more I dig into Coral Reef Enterprises, the more I learn about what's happening behind closed doors. It's shaping me in ways I hadn't prepared for."

Alison's heart twisted slightly. "It must be tough to reconcile those feelings, especially considering your family ties," she urged. "But I see the passion you have for our cause. We can navigate these waters together, you and I."

Before they could delve any deeper, a figure stepped into view from the bustling crowd—a familiar face. It was Lucas, the local gossip who often provided insight into the dynamics of Cairns.

"Hey, you two!" Lucas called out, a buoyant energy radiating from him. "Just thought I'd pop by. Have you heard about the latest developments in the Coral Reef controversy? It's creating quite the stir around town."

"What's happening?" Finn asked, his focus sharpening.

"Seems like the company is rallying its supporters big time," Lucas replied, a knowing smile on his face. "Some of the business owners are starting to backtrack on their support of you all. They're worried about the collateral damage from going head-to-head with a corporation this large."

"Great," Alison quipped, frustration simmering beneath her words. "They're letting fear dictate their decisions."

"It gets more interesting," Lucas continued, unfurling a piece of paper from his pocket that was filled with hastily scrawled notes. "I caught wind that Coral Reef Enterprises is also planning a PR campaign. They're going to try and divert attention, painting themselves as heroes in the fight for coral conservation. They could twist the narrative to discredit you, claiming you've acted irresponsibly."

Alison felt a wave of anger wash over her. "They're going to manipulate the truth to save face. That's outrageous! The community deserves to know what's really at stake!"

"Yes, but remember," Finn warned, his voice serious. "If they succeed in sowing doubt, we could lose any traction we've gained. This is a dangerous game."

"What do we do?" Alison asked, the tension knotting in her stomach as she sensed the threat looming closer. "We can't let them drown out our message."

"We need to fight back," Lucas said, a fire igniting in his eyes. "If they're preparing to go public, we can use our platform and get ahead of their narrative. Let's strategize and be proactive. Use social media to highlight our evidence, rallying the community before they have a chance to spin the truth."

"Agreed," Finn said, nodding. "If we unify the voice amongst our supporters and spotlight the true impact of Coral Reef Enterprises, we can shift the momentum. We need to create our own campaign—even if it means getting a little louder ourselves."

With determination building, Alison could feel the adrenaline coursing through her veins. "Let's organize a press conference or another community event. We'll showcase the truth we've gathered and stand together, reminding everyone why this fight matters. We need to be ready to defend against their narrative."

As the trio brainstormed ideas, determination surged through them, fueled by their commitment to the reef and the community they cherished. Together, they were ready to rise against whatever storm Coral Reef Enterprises threw at them.

Yet, one question lingered in Alison's mind—how well would they navigate these waters when faced with the powerful currents of manipulation? The realization struck her that their mission would require more than passion and resolve; it would demand strategy, transparency, and the strength of unity.

As they put their plan into action, the sun began to set, casting a warm glow over the bustling market. Alison felt a surge of hope and purpose under the fading light—the fight for the reef had forged something much greater than herself. Yet, she could sense the oncoming storm as shadows of doubt and fear began to drift around them.

But that night, as they solidified their plans and prepared for the confrontation looming just ahead, Alison knew that no matter what challenges lay before them, they would face them together ready to unveil the hidden truths that Coral Reef Enterprises wished would remain buried and prepared to withstand the growing tide of their fight for change.

The air outside felt thick with tension as Alison and her team prepared for the press conference, a mounting sense of urgency enveloping them. The sun had risen early over Cairns, but the warmth did little to ease Alison's nerves. Today was the day they would unveil their evidence against Coral Reef Enterprises, laying bare the discrepancies that had festered beneath the surface for too long.

Alison arrived at the community center early, her mind racing with all the details she had to remember. Tomorrow, their community would be watching, and if they wanted to protect their reef and their livelihoods, they needed to be ready.

As she stepped inside, she was greeted by the sight of familiar faces. Finn was adjusting the projector while Eva made sure the banners were properly hung—everything aligned and ready to showcase their mission. Tommy was poring over notes, reviewing their evidence one last time.

"Hey!" Alison called out, feeling a tight knot of excitement combined with anxiety. "How's it going?"

"Almost ready," Finn replied, glancing up with a reassuring smile. "Just double-checking the slides to ensure everything's set for the presentation. We'll get through this."

Eva joined them, her organizing skills on full display. "We need to remember our focus," she reminded them. "This is about bringing the community together empowering them with the truth. Remember why we're here."

The trio spent the next few hours finalizing their preparations, but as the time drew nearer, Alison felt the weight of responsibility settle on her shoulders. They were prepared to face Coral Reef Enterprises, ready to challenge the narrative both sides had crafted in this heated battle. But what caught her attention was the feel of someone watching—the sensation of eyes trailing her every move.

After grabbing a moment to compose herself outside, Alison turned to find Lucas waiting nearby, his demeanor earnest but crestfallen. "We need to talk," he said quietly, his brows drawn together in concern.

"About what?" Alison asked, wary of the unease in his tone.

"I've been hearing rumors—people are saying this is all going to end badly. The business owners are concerned, and some are thinking of siding with Coral Reef Enterprises to distance themselves from what we're trying to do. They want to play it safe."

Alison felt her stomach drop, frustration and disappointment swelling within her. "So, some think they can save their businesses by turning their backs on our fight? After everything we've endured, after finally finding our voice?"

Lucas shook his head, exasperation coloring his voice. "It's not just about cowardice; people are scared. They see the power that organization has, the influence they wield. They're afraid of the potential fallout."

"I understand that fear, but if we don't stand firm now, we will lose everything—our connection to the reef, our community, and the very core of who we are!" she expressed vehemently, feeling the urgency building within her.

"Yes, but if we push too hard, we won't just lose support—we'll create enemies," he replied, his voice cautious. "We need to keep an eye out, as Dr. Grant suggested. They're watching us closely, and if we make them the enemy, it won't end well."

Sighing, Alison realized they would have to tread carefully. "How do we make sure that we're still fighting for a cause without alienating those who just want to survive?"

"Small steps," Lucas suggested, his demeanor shifting. "Empower them. Show a united front that reassures them we're all in this together."

As they spoke, a small crowd gathered, preparing for the press conference to begin. Alison felt a mixture of hope and anxiety sack her heart as she noticed some familiar figures standing apart—Tommy and Eva picked up on her concerns, struggling to catch her eye while a cloud of uncertainty loomed.

They would need to rally as one solid front, but the fissures were starting to become evident. "Let's convene the crowd and start discussing the upcoming plans," Alison urged Lucas, before motioning toward the main area where people were gathering.

The press conference commenced in the central meeting room, filled with locals eager to witness the promised evidence against Coral Reef Enterprises. One by one, community members shared their thoughts, expressing solidarity while voicing concern about their livelihoods. The combination of heart-wrenching stories and yearning voices ignited the room with an urgency to confront the entity threatening their lives.

As Alison stepped up to the podium, she searched the crowd, allowing her personal connection to guide her. "Thank you all for being here today. We gather not just for ourselves, but in unity to protect our reef and our community."

The applause that erupted from those gathered set her heart alight, but as she looked at the crowd, some faces remained hesitant—a mixture of support and retreat drawn upon them like oil slicks in water.

She launched into the presentation, outlining their findings with clarity, displaying each piece of evidence they had collected. Images of the reef's deterioration flashed on the screen—the stark contrast between vibrant ecosystems and the creeping shadows of neglect. Concern rippled through the audience, and the air grew thick with their acknowledgement of the truths being unveiled.

But just as she was about to dive deeper into their findings, an unexpected voice rang out from the back—a voice Alison recognized all too well.

"Your facts are misleading!" It was O'Reilly, rising from the audience, steadfast in his defiance. "Coral Reef Enterprises has always operated above board! You're attempting to paint them as villains with no basis in reality!"

The crowd shifted nervously at the sudden confrontation, tension crackling across the room. Alison's heart pounded, remembering Dr. Grant's earlier threats—as well as the unease that had settled among their supporters.

"Your organization stands on shaky ground when dealing with a community who cares," Alison asserted, fighting to maintain control. "If you care for this place, prove it! Show that your commitments align with what you claim while we work together towards a brighter future!"

"We don't need a corrupted narrative to justify our business practices!" O'Reilly shouted back. "You're coercing the community to turn against us without reason. You've manipulated facts to serve your own agenda!"

The audience began to stir, their anxiety palpable as they watched the confrontation unfold. Some seemed swayed by O'Reilly's claims, while others grew restless at his aggression.

Alison felt frustration simmering beneath the surface. "We can't allow intimidation to dictate our actions! We represent the voice of those who are suffering, who can no longer ignore the damage being done to our home. I won't let you discredit our shared fight!"

Yet the tumultuous exchange had begun to fracture the unity present in the room, revealing the delicate balance between fear and solidarity.

"People might question everything we're claiming!" Eva murmured, concerned. "We can't afford to lose the trust of the individuals we've brought together tonight."

"I know," Alison replied quietly, minute yet fierce desperation threading through her voice. "But we must remain steadfast. We fight for the truth, and truth alone must be our compass."

As the crowd responded with electrifying energy, the gathering took on a life of its own, spirits rising as calls for action spread throughout the room. Yet O'Reilly's targeted remarks continued to loom over them, casting uncertainty into the corners of their collective resolve.

With each clash of words, the invisible lines separating allies began to blur once more, revealing how easily fear could turn friends into foes—both within themselves and their burgeoning movement.

Still, amidst the chaos, Alison felt compelled to drive home the message that Coral Reef Enterprises was evoking fear for a reason. If they sought to fracture the very community that relied upon one another, they faced a formidable challenge that could easily slip from their fingers.

As the confrontation raged on, Alison heard echoes of hope amidst the discord, reminding her that they were stronger together. They stood at a pivotal crossroads, empowered by truth, but wary of the tenuous alliances that splayed before them.

"Together, we will not be swept away by torrents of deceit or fear. Our commitment to one another, as a community, is our greatest strength!" she declared, feeling the warmth of unity rising beneath her words.

And deep down, she knew that the truth they uncovered would shatter the nets woven by Coral Reef Enterprises for too long—it was time to emerge stronger and more resolute than ever, ready to confront whatever storms lay ahead.

~ Thirteen ~

The tension that hung in the air after the confrontational press conference lingered long after attendees had departed. As Alison and her allies gathered to regroup, each face reflected a mixture of determination and uncertainty. Their movement had solidified feelings of unity and purpose, but the echoes of dissent that had surfaced during the meeting cast shadows over their progress.

"Did you see the way O'Reilly reacted during the conference?" Finn said, his voice heavy with concern. "It felt so aggressive. They're becoming desperate."

Alison leaned against the table, her mind racing. "They know we're getting close to exposing the truth. It's clear they'll do anything to maintain their facade, including threatening our community."

"Speaking of threats," Eva interjected, her voice steady yet urgent. "I think we need to address the possibility of retaliation—both for us as individuals and for anyone who has spoken out in our favor. People are scared."

"I hate to admit it," Tommy added quietly, "but I've overheard conversations at the local pub—business owners considering backing down. They're worried about Coral Reef Enterprises' influence in our community."

Feeling frustration bubble, Alison met Tommy's gaze. "Fear should not dictate our actions. Our fight is about bringing the truth to light. If we lose this momentum, it's as if we're handing the victory to the very organization that has harmed our waters."

"And we can't let one group intimidate the entire community," Finn said resolutely. "There's too much at stake for everyone involved."

Alison steadied herself, feeling the weight of responsibility settle over her. "We need to meet with community leaders, the ones who have shown support thus far. If we can solidify our alliances, we can discourage any wavering. But first, we should gather more concrete evidence—find connections that expose the heart of the corruption at Coral Reef Enterprises."

With a renewed sense of purpose, they huddled together, brainstorming ideas on how to pry deeper into the organization's hidden workings. Alison recalled the recent interactions she had with Finn's family, as well as conversations through local networks. Secrets burrowed within the organization could prove to be pivotal, and she wanted to ensure she wasn't missing a single piece of evidence.

That night, Alison climbed into bed with thoughts racing, her brain buzzing with possibilities. Just as sleep began to descend, a new text from an anonymous number cut through the night's stillness: *"Meet me at the old pier tomorrow night. I have critical information about Coral Reef Enterprises. Come alone."

Her heart pounding, she stared at the screen. Should she trust this unknown source? And what kind of information could this person possess that would add to their fight? Uneasy but intrigued, she decided she needed to hear more, determined that understanding these connections could fortify their strategy.

The next day was a flurry of activity. She and her team went over their plans as they awaited the evening's meeting. As dusk began to fall, Alison made her way to the old pier, anxiety riding her every step. The area was known for its deserted atmosphere; it could easily become an echo of silence, amplifying her unease.

As she reached the pier, she felt the ocean breeze brush against her skin, chilling her despite the summer warmth. She scanned the area, lit only by the faint glow of the moon and the remnants of fading sunlight. It looked ominous, shadowy curves obscured by darkness.

Minutes ticked by like hours as she waited, emotions ebbing and flowing as she thought carefully about the potential information to come. Suddenly, a figure stepped from the shadows—a woman with striking features and a determined look.

"You must be Alison," she said, her voice steady but urgent.

"Yes, I am," Alison replied, instinctively cautious as she approached. "What information do you have?"

The woman took a moment to steady her breath, her eyes darting around the pier nervously. "I've been working closely with Coral Reef Enterprises for years. I've seen things that I shouldn't have, things that would shock the community if they knew."

Alison felt her heart race—this was the clarity she had been seeking. "What kinds of things?"

"The mishandling of funds, misrepresentation of projects, and outright deception regarding the ecological projects they claim to support. They've been covering their tracks with false reports," the woman explained. "But it runs deeper than that. They're connected to certain local politicians who benefit from their operations. If they can keep the reef suffering, they can continue to siphon off funding for projects while reporting false outcomes."

Alison could barely believe the weight of the information being laid before her. "This could change everything. We need proof—records, documents that substantiate your claims."

"I have copies, but I need assurance of anonymity. They've already been watching me," she said, fear pooling in her eyes. "If they find out I'm leaking this information..." she trailed off, the implications clearly weighing on her.

"Of course, you have my word. Your safety is our priority," Alison promised, feeling the gravity of the situation tighten around her.

Seconds turned into minutes as the woman shifted uncomfortably, and Alison's mind raced with the possibilities. This could be the evidence that would expose Coral Reef Enterprises. This could empower them all to rise against the organization's relentless grasp.

Before long, the woman reached into her bag and pulled out a folder stuffed with documents, handing it over with trembling hands. "Here. Just be careful. They have their eyes everywhere, and I fear for what will happen if they discover this leak."

Alison nodded, gratitude blending with determination. "Thank you so much for your courage. We'll make sure your involvement stays confidential."

As she returned to the street, the weight of the folder felt like a lifeline—a tool that could potentially turn the tide in their fight. But something tugged at her heart, and trepidation bloomed within her. Would the truth wield the power she sought, or would it lead her into deeper waters of betrayal?

Once back at the community center, she shared her discoveries with Eva and Tommy, their reactions a whirlwind of excitement and caution. They delved into the folders, poring over the evidence, each piece carefully dissected.

"This is it," Eva said, her excitement contagious. "This solidifies everything we've accused Coral Reef Enterprises of. They can't run from this."

"But we need to be strategic about how we release this information," Tommy cautioned. "They'll come out swinging, trying to discredit us. We have to ensure we handle this carefully to avoid backlash."

The group worked tirelessly through the night, strategizing their next steps while pouring over the extensive evidence. It was exhilarating, yet Alison felt a growing sense of unease. The darkness tied to the information they had just received lingered, threatening to consume them if they weren't careful.

As dawn broke on a new day, a fierce storm rolled in, black clouds swirling, revealing the tumult within. Just like the weather, Alison could feel the shifting tides of their fight against Coral Reef Enterprises—how easily alliances could be broken and how fragile trust had become.

Together, they would unveil the truth stowed away in the shadows, but they would do so with caution. As they navigated through the storm ahead, Alison resolved to keep her friends close and maintain a vigilant watch for the dangers that circled them like sharks in murky water. In their quest for the truth, they would have to weather not just external conflicts but also the treacherous currents that threatened to pull them apart.

The storm that had rolled into Cairns left a trail of dark clouds heavy in the sky, but that gloom was nothing compared to the tension roiling within the community. The days following the unveiling of evidence against Coral Reef Enterprises had become a frenzy of activity and anxiety. While the buzz around Alison and her team's revelations initially stirred enthusiasm in the community, it also catalyzed desperation from their adversaries, sparking fear of retaliation among their supporters.

Alison stood at the community center, surrounded by flyers and notes for the next gathering, her heart racing as she absorbed the electric atmosphere. Anxiety pulsated in her veins, knowing that the upcoming meeting would serve as a crucial pivot point, determining whether their efforts would unify the community or further fracture it under external pressure.

"Alison," Eva called, approaching her with a worried look. "Have you seen the latest news? Coral Reef Enterprises is launching a PR campaign to counter our claims, and I'm hearing rumors about their intention to file defamation suits against anyone involved."

Alison felt a wave of frustration wash over her. "They're trying to shift the narrative and intimidate us into silence. We have to counter their tactics, and quickly."

"Agreed," Finn chimed in, moving closer to join the conversation. "This is exactly what Dr. Grant warned about—a preemptive strike designed to discredit us. We need to stay steadfast."

As the three of them strategized, the uneasiness surrounding their movement began to thicken, and the words of community members echoed in their minds. Doubt, apprehension, and fear intermingled in whispered conversations that haunted the air. Would this fight put their livelihoods at risk? Would standing up against a powerful organization only serve to deepen divides amongst their friends and supporters?

"The community needs reassurance," Tommy spoke up, clearly reflecting his own concerns. "We need to remind them that what we're doing is for the greater good. We can't let them oversell their viewpoint."

Alison nodded, determination mingled with apprehension surging within her. "Let's give them a reason to unite behind our message. We should organize an open forum where anyone can voice concerns. If we can create an environment where fears are acknowledged rather than whispered away, we can rekindle solidarity."

As they moved through the details of the gathering, the weight of the impending storm outside mirrored the emotional turmoil surrounding them. Reports streamed in about Coral Reef Enterprises' intimidation tactics, making rounds on social media and sending ripples of fear through the community.

When the time for their open forum arrived, Alison stood with shared anticipation and dread. The community center was packed again, filled with those who were drawn by the urgency of the moment. But a palpable tension clung to the air, whispers of un-

ease swirling as their previous unity dissolved into uncertain fragments.

"I want to thank you all for coming," Alison began, her voice
steady despite the tumult within. "This gathering is a chance for
us to address the fears that have surfaced and reaffirm our commitment to the reef and each other. We're all facing the same
storm, and it's essential we weather it together."

As she spoke, there were subtle hints of dissent among the
crowd—some faces wore expressions of worry while others flashed
signs of strength, illustrating the conflicting emotions swirling
within.

"Are we really ready to take on such a powerful organization?"
someone called from the back. "What if they retaliate? We've all
seen their influence. It could hurt our businesses!"

"True, but abandoning the cause is not the answer!" another
voice countered, a familiar face of support. "Standing up for the
reef is standing up for ourselves—we can't let intimidation dictate
the futures we want for our families and this community."

Alison felt her heart pound, grateful to see voices stirred by resilience amidst uncertainty. "We're here to advocate for the ocean,
for everyone who relies on it—not just for our businesses, but for
our environment, our ancestors, and generations to come. But if
you're feeling afraid, we are here to embrace that fear as a community."

Just then, a group of local business owners stepped forward,
their expressions mixed with fear and resolve. "We've heard the
threats and intimidation, and we're worried," said David, a voice
she recognized. "But we don't want to abandon the fight. We want
to find a way to support you without risking our homes. Can we
work together?"

Finn stepped forward beside Alison, an unyielding sense of
strength radiating from him. "Listen, everyone, fear is a powerful
tool—but it can also be manipulative. If we rethink our strategy, we

might find ways to empower each other while still pushing back against Coral Reef Enterprises."

As the room filled with murmurs and debates, Alison caught sight of a shadow moving toward the back entrance. It was Dr. Grant again, seeping in unnoticed as conversations reached a fervor. Her breath caught in her throat; the threat of his presence hung ominously in the air.

"Are you here to intimidate us again, Dr. Grant?" she called out, her voice steady despite the unease rippling through the crowd.

"No, Alison," Dr. Grant replied, his tone smooth but laced with condescension. "I'm here to remind you of the reality you're facing. This circus with the community will not change the facts. You could unintentionally harm the ecosystem you claim to care for, all in the name of a misguided campaign against Coral Reef Enterprises."

"What do you mean?" Alison demanded, confronting the unexpected challenge. "The only thing damaging the ecosystem are the practices you refuse to acknowledge!"

"Perhaps," Dr. Grant replied, his eyes narrowing. "But look at this gathering. It's fractured already. If you cannot align your community, what makes you think you can hold the line against us? We're not just a powerful corporation; we're tied into the fabric of this town. And we can assure you—attempting to publicly discredit us will have grave consequences."

Alison felt the tension swell as uncertainty rippled through the crowd. Whispers began to circulate, fragments of fear threatening to seep into their resolve. Would Coral Reef Enterprises succeed in changing the course of their fight simply by sowing seeds of doubt?

"This isn't about you!" Finn interjected, stepping forward, emboldened by the crowd's gathered strength. "This is about the coral, the community, and the future of our home! We won't let you manipulate this narrative any longer!"

As the energy in the room shifted, allies turned toward each other, questioning their initial reactions and emotions. The confrontation had created a fracture in their unity, but they stood poised, ready to confront the challenges that lay ahead.

"Together, we need to remain committed to our cause, regardless of the noise surrounding us," Alison urged, her resolve strengthening amid uncertainty. "Let's ensure we create a solid framework for standing up to Coral Reef Enterprises—one that holds true to our mission and amplifies the community's voice."

Dark clouds loomed outside, skimming dangerously close to the town, echoing the uncertainty still circling their discussions. But among the fissures forming, a renewed spirit flickered—the possibility of finding their footing together on this precarious path.

Alison felt a surge of hope amidst the brewing storm. This was not merely about fighting a powerful organization; it was about protecting their community, their environment, and their futures. They stood on a precipice, where shadows of doubt threatened to draw them into darkness; but together, they would confront it.

With every heartbeat echoing in solidarity amidst the tension, Alison knew they must remain resolute in their purpose, ready to navigate the treacherous waters ahead as a unified force. The path before them might be fraught with challenges, but they were bonded by the unwavering determination to safeguard their reef—a fight that would only strengthen their resolve. Together, they would weather the storm and rise above.

~ Fourteen ~

The storm that had loomed over Cairns finally broke, unleashing sheets of rain that pounded against the earth and painted the town in shades of gray. As the downpour cascaded down from the heavens, Alison sat in her apartment, staring out at the tempestuous skies. The weather mirrored the emotional turbulence within her; just as the dark clouds swirled and coalesced, fears and doubts churned in her heart.

It had been a week since their last gathering, and although they had faced down Dr. Grant and Coral Reef Enterprises with determination, uncertainty gnawed at her insides. The fissures that had emerged among the community still cast doubt; fragile alliances threatened to fracture, and the whispers of dissent raised questions about the strength of their movement.

"I can't shake this feeling that we're on the edge of something big—something dangerous," Eva said as she entered the apartment, shaking water droplets from her umbrella and closing the door against the wind. "I've heard the same rumblings you have. People are anxious."

"That's an understatement," Alison replied, her voice strained. "It feels like each day we're trying to navigate treacherous waters while the very foundations we've built are beginning to erode."

They set down their drinks at the small table littered with documents, and for a moment, silence enveloped them. Outside, the storm raged, reinvigorating the fear that had begun to tighten like a noose around their resolve.

"Is there any word from Tommy?" Eva asked, piercing through the quiet. "He was supposed to gather information from his contacts."

"No, not yet," Alison said with a frown. "He was concerned about the threats Coral Reef Enterprises posed. I wish he'd reach out. We need him now more than ever."

Just then, the ringing of Alison's phone shattered the silence. She glanced at the screen, her pulse quickening. It was Tommy.

"Hey, are you alright? What do you have?" she answered, her heart racing in anticipation.

"Alison...It's not good," Tommy's voice came through, strained and breathless. "I met with one of my contacts today. They mentioned that Coral Reef is ramping up efforts to discredit you all. They're trying to fuel unrest within the community. I overheard some plans to create chaos—to pit business owners against activists in order to weaken your support."

Alison's stomach dropped at the revelations. "What do you mean chaos?"

"The plan is to employ local supporters to spread misinformation about the movement. If they can get whispers of dissent or fears of financial ruin started among business owners, they could fracture any alliance formed. It could break the momentum you've built," Tommy explained, anxiety edging his tone.

"And if that doesn't work," Tommy continued, his voice grim, "I heard they might resort to more extreme measures."

"What kind of extreme measures?" Alison felt a chill run down her spine.

"Threats, intimidation...even deliberately sabotaging events or resources connected to the movement. They want to instill fear in anyone daring to speak out," he said, his tone urgent and broken.

Alison shared a worried glance with Eva, the weight of his words echoing in her mind. "We can't allow them to fracture our resolve. We need to gather the community and let them know what's going on," she asserted, her voice steely.

"We can't wait," Tommy replied, panic creeping in. "You need to be careful. If they're watching, they'll go after the leaders first."

"I'm not backing down. If we let fear control us, we're giving them power," Alison resolved, determination flooding her veins. "But we have to be strategic. I can't allow the momentum to falter."

"We need to be sharp about our messaging," Eva added, her expression reading the gravity of the situation. "This could be the moment when negotiating our alliances could come into play, balancing dialogue and confrontation."

"Then we strategize, and we act fast," Alison said, the urgency igniting within her. "We need to communicate with our allies and re-establish trust among the community. We don't have time for fear to splinter our mission."

As the storm continued to rage outside, Alison felt the wave of urgency surge as they began planning their next steps. That night, their war room was filled with brainstorming ideas—heading toward the front lines, armed with their evidence and the resolve to confront whatever chaos Coral Reef Enterprises would attempt to create.

But the uncertainty of Tommy's warning remained buried in her mind, a chilling reminder of the fragility that now surrounded their mission. She understood that they were charting dark waters, navigating treachery and deception which forced them to dig deep and safeguard their shared cause. They couldn't allow the darkness within to overshadow the light they sought to illuminate.

As the downpour drummed against her window, she thought of Mark—their mission to fight for the reef was never about fear but about resilience and a shared legacy of hope. It was those very values that would buoy her spirit even as the storm swirled beyond her doorstep.

Determination set her resolve hard, and by morning, she would stand on the precipice of action—ready to confront the storm and cast light on the truth, even as they navigated through the swirling shadows of deception attempting to ensnare them all. Together, they would rise against the tide, even in the face of their opponents' darkest ploys.

As dawn broke over Cairns, the storm that had battered the town was beginning to clear, leaving behind a fragile calm that belied the tumultuous days ahead. Alison rubbed her tired eyes and stared out at the remnants of rain-drenched streets. The sunlight poured through the clouds, illuminating the path ahead like a promise of new possibilities. But beneath the promise, the undercurrents of doubt and betrayal continued to swirl.

After the unsettling confrontation, whispers of division lingered in the air—rumors that Coral Reef Enterprises had begun targeting their supporters, using intimidation tactics to instill fear in the hearts of those who would dare to stand with Alison and her team. Yet, they had resolved to remain steadfast, and Alison knew the time had come to gather their strength once more and reaffirm their commitment to the reef.

With the community's resolve still unsteady, Alison and Eva organized a meeting at a local pub. It would be a more relaxed atmosphere, a place where people could voice their concerns without the heaviness of a formal gathering weighing on them. They hoped engaging in open and candid discussion would help rebuild the bridges that had begun to falter.

As the evening waned, individuals trickled into the pub, a kaleidoscope of faces—some familiar, some new. The warm ambiance enveloped them, and as Alison surveyed the crowd, she could feel the pulse of support still alive within each person. They were willing to rally together, no matter the obstacles they faced.

"Let's create a comfortable space for discussion, something that invites honesty," Eva suggested, scanning the room. "The more people we can draw in, the better."

"I agree," Alison replied, trying to suppress the anxiety bubbling inside her. "We need to remind everyone why we're here and ensure they feel safe expressing their concerns. That's the only way we can re-establish trust."

Once the crowd settled, Alison stood up to address the group. "Thank you all for coming tonight. We know the past few weeks have been challenging, and rumors have clouded our conversations. We gather here as a community not just to discuss our concerns, but to ensure our cause remains united."

The crowd nodded, but Alison could see uncertainty etched across many faces. She pressed on, "I want to invite anyone who feels uneasy about our movement to share their thoughts. Your concerns are valid, and they matter. We need open communication, especially in turbulent times."

One of the local fishermen, Carl, slowly raised his hand. "I've been hearing the rumblings about Coral Reef Enterprises retaliating. People are scared to speak up. The fear of job loss is real, and I worry about how standing against them could impact our livelihoods."

Alison nodded, understanding the weight of his words. "This is about more than just us. But if we cower in fear, we risk losing everything—our reef, our community, and our integrity. We need to confront the difficult times together, supported by the truth."

The crowd murmured in agreement, but Alison could feel the trepidation still lurking beneath the surface. As they continued the discussion, voices began to share anxieties—some suggested a compromise, while others held fast to the need for direct confrontation. It was evident that while they remained united in purpose, the path ahead was layered with complexity.

As tension crackled in the lively atmosphere, Sarah finally stood up, bringing silence across the room. "I've heard that Coral Reef Enterprises has been amping up their efforts to intimidate anyone who speaks out," she said, her voice steady yet containing an undercurrent of fear. "But if we allow ourselves to be swayed by threats, we'll lose sight of why we're here."

Dr. Samuel Grant's name finally crept into the discussion, drawing murmurs of concern. "He has his hand in many local ties," one attendee remarked. "If we're considering action against Coral Reef Enterprises, we should also consider that he's a cornerstone of their framework here in Cairns."

"Maybe it's time to confront him directly," Eva suggested, a spark igniting within her. "If we can lay out our findings and press him for transparency, we can expose nervousness in their camp. We could shift that narrative toward owning their responsibilities."

Alison felt a twinge of hesitation beneath the boldness of the plan. "It could be dangerous, though," she warned. "Dr. Grant has influence. If we approach him, he may use it to undermine us or rally opposition. What if we become entangled in a web of further deception?"

Just as uncertainty crept in, a voice emerged from the back—Finn. "Perhaps this is what we need to discover our true alliances. Approaching Grant could either strengthen our resolve or reveal who in our midst is truly on our side. It's a risk, but sometimes revealing shadows can be illuminating."

The crowd echoed thoughts of agreement and concern, each member wrestling with vulnerability and possibility. And just as she thought they were reaching a solid consensus, the door swung open, revealing an unexpected arrival: Lucas.

He stood there, wild-eyed and breathless. "I overheard something you all need to know!" he exclaimed, his urgency slicing through the discussions.

"What is it?" Alison urged, an instinctive sense of caution wrapping around her heart.

"I heard from journalists that Coral Reef Enterprises prepared to go public and downplay our findings. They're planning to release statements claiming you're just a handful of misinformed citizens looking for attention," Lucas said, his voice strained. "If this goes through, it could destroy our credibility before we even get a chance to present our evidence!"

The pub bristled with alarm, murmurs rising again as Alison clenched her fists, anger mixing with frustration. "They can't silence us. We have the truth on our side!"

"But they have the power of manipulation," Finn chimed in, his voice low but steady. "We need to ensure we present a united front, share our evidence before they can seed doubt."

Alison felt her heart race as she absorbed the implications of what Lucas had relayed. The threat of retaliation was becoming dangerously real, but so was the urgency of pushing forward before the organization could twist the narrative. "We must act now, with clarity."

"Then let's organize a press conference, strategically timed to coincide with their anticipated announcement," Tommy said, his expression determined. "If we can release our findings simultaneously, we can control the conversation before they hijack it."

As they strategized, Alison felt the tension in the air begin to shift again, uncertainty threatening their resolve. Each new revelation stirred doubt, and it was clear that the fight ahead would require more than just passion; it would adjust to the reality of malicious connections, both seen and unseen.

That evening, as they finalized their plan and steeled themselves for the battle ahead, Alison knew they were tiptoeing on the edge of revelation. The darkness surrounding their fight had grown deeper, shadows twisting around every decision they made.

But she also recognized a flickering light within their re-solve—a reminder that in their unity, they could confront the storm that loomed over them. The truth may be buried beneath layers of deception, but together, they would dig deeper and un-earth every detail necessary to reclaim their narrative.

As Alison breathed in the cool night air, she felt the weight of what they were beginning to uncover, layers of deceit that had long obscured the truth threatening their community and the reef. They would weather this storm. They would not back down.

With each heartbeat, she vowed to illuminate the darkness, and she could sense that together, they would rise above the looming pressures threatening to drown their cause. United, they would forge a path toward hope and truth, ready to confront whatever swells awaited in the waters beyond.

~ Fifteen ~

Alison sat at the edge of the community center, her heart pounding as she looked over the last-minute preparations for the press conference. The atmosphere buzzed with nervous energy; their mission was reaching a critical juncture, one that could either fortify their movement against Coral Reef Enterprises or plunge it into further chaos. Determination coursed through her veins—she had waited too long to introduce the evidence that lay bare the organization's deceptions.

"Are you ready?" Eva asked, her eyes filled with a mix of excitement and worry as she joined Alison at the table. "This is it."

"No turning back now," Alison replied, though a note of apprehension underscored her words. "We have everything lined up; we just need to stick to our message."

"Right. We need to convey the urgency and importance of exposing Coral Reef Enterprises for the fraud they've been perpetrating," Eva said sternly. "We can't afford to be sidetracked by their retaliatory actions or any attempts to mask the truth."

Alison watched as Finn and Tommy gathered their final materials and connected with supporters filing into the room. Her heart thrummed with anticipation, a cocktail of thrill and trepidation that had become strangely familiar over the past weeks. They were prepared, but more than that, they were ready to stand united against the tides of corruption threatening their community.

As the clock ticked closer to start time, the gathering began, buzzing with energy and hope. The seats quickly filled as local

journalists and concerned citizens settled in, their expressions reflecting a mix of eagerness and anticipation. Alison could feel the
weight of their collective attention as she stood at the podium,
gripping her notes tightly.

"Thank you all for being here today. We stand as a united front
for our community and our reef," she opened, scanning the room
and locking eyes with familiar faces that offered silent support.
"Today, we will delve into the evidence we've gathered about the
practices of Coral Reef Enterprises—information that reveals the
reality behind the organization's façade of environmental altru-
ism."

As she continued, her voice rang clear, delivering charts, testimonies, and visual documentation that highlighted the organization's malfeasance. The room absorbed each revelation with gasps
and murmurs—the tension palpable as incredulity washed over
the audience.

"And as we expose the truth, we have to consider the impact on
our community," she emphasized, her heart racing as the crowd
leaned forward. "We've heard threats of retaliation, of business interests being protected above the integrity of our ecosystem. But
what good will it do if we sacrifice our environment for momentary security? We must forge a new path together—one that allows
for both economic growth and the security of our reef."

The crowd erupted into applause, voices of support swelling
throughout the room. But Alison could sense a shift in the atmosphere—a momentary hesitation as O'Reilly and Dr. Grant entered
the room, a stark contrast to the camaraderie building around her.
As their presence filled the space, the energy abruptly shifted, tension crackling in the air.

"Let's not pretend this is anything but a misguided attempt to
stir chaos," O'Reilly announced, his tone sharp, eyes narrowing at
Alison. "What you're offering is nothing but conjecture, geared to

rally the crowd for your vindictive purposes. You continue to misrepresent our organization."

Alison forced herself to remain calm, though doubt flickered in her mind. "O'Reilly, the evidence we've gathered speaks for itself! The data shows the stark realities of mismanagement and lies that have gone unchecked. It isn't conjecture; it's the truth!"

Dr. Grant stepped forward, his demeanor unwavering. "To continue this public humiliation without basis is reckless. It puts the future of your businesses in jeopardy."

Voices rippled through the crowd, uncertainty creeping into the supporting members around her. Alison felt the tension rising once again, the fragile solidarity threatened by the looming presence of Coral Reef Enterprises' representatives.

But before she could respond, Finn stepped up beside her, a newfound intensity radiating from him. "We're here because we care about the future of this community. Intimidation has kept us silent for too long, and we will not return to that state! We must hold you accountable if we want a healthy reef!"

With each supportive cheer that echoed through the crowd, the scales began to tip. Individuals rallied, drawing strength from the bravery displayed in front of them. This was their moment to push back against the waves crashing against their purpose.

"Your attempts at discrediting our findings will no longer deter our fight!" Alison asserted, letting determination seep into her voice. "You can claim we're misguided, but truth is an anchor in the storm. We're standing up to protect our environment and our community! Nothing can mask the reality that if we stay silent, we lose everything."

With that proclamation, a wave of applause and agreement swelled, and for a moment, collective defiance rippled through the room. The stakes were clearer, the shared values igniting resilience in the hearts of those gathered.

O'Reilly's expression shifted to a scowl as he realized the energy had turned against them. "I warn you now! Pursuing this 'truth' of yours will have grave consequences! You're treading on dangerous ground."

"Dangerous ground?" Tommy exclaimed, stepping forward. "You've already tread far beyond what can be called responsible with your actions. We are here to protect the reef, not to bury our heads in a false narrative!"

As the audience rallied, Alison felt a surge of hope amidst the chaos unfolding. They had begun to expose the warped connection between Coral Reef Enterprises and the shadowy threats that had hovered over them. The room now hummed with resolve, and determination coursed through them, anchoring them against the oncoming storm.

But just then, the door swung open once more, revealing yet another unexpected figure—an older, distinguished member of the community who had not shown up earlier in the discussions. He stood with a look of concern etched onto his face, and the room fell silent when he entered.

"Wait," he said, raising a hand. "I've been hearing the rumors and discussing with others about the escalating tensions. We can't let fear disrupt our purpose." His words carried a weight that rippled through the crowd. "We have a history here that doesn't have to end in conflict."

Alison locked eyes with him, sensing an opportunity. "Can you help us? We need your voice to clarify to the community what's at stake. We can't let manipulation dictate our actions."

The room took a collective breath as the man nodded, stepping further into the gathering. "I've seen how Coral Reef Enterprises has swayed public opinion before, all while claiming to protect our interests. I want to stand with you and ensure our voices aren't drowned in the noise of intimidation."

A wave of applause erupted, igniting a fresh vigor within the group, showcasing that even amidst the rising storm, alliances could grow anew as trust began to be restored.

As the meeting continued, discussions evolved, cementing the resolve that while pressures mounted, betrayal and conflict didn't need to define their path. They could face the tumultuous waters ahead, united in purpose and fortified by newfound alliances.

That evening, as the gathering concluded, Alison felt a sense of relief wash over her—a recognition that even as darkness sought to divide them, the light of hope and solidarity could shine through.

Riding upon the renewed momentum, they prepared to take their fight to the next level, ready to expose the corruption within the walls of Coral Reef Enterprises. Together, they would navigate these turbulent waters, determined to unveil the truth hidden beneath the deceptive layers surrounding them.

The days slipped by with a heightened sense of urgency as the community in Cairns braced for the next phase of their fight against Coral Reef Enterprises. The adrenaline from the recent gathering fueled Alison and her allies, but the shadows of threats loomed larger than ever. Every interaction began to feel charged with the potential for both unity and division, as whispers of doubt continued to circulate around town.

As the sun began to set on the evening of their press conference, Alison could feel the weight of anticipation settling in her chest. They had gathered all the evidence they needed to present—a culmination of testimonies, data, and insider information that, if successful, could expose the dark underbelly of Coral Reef Enterprises. The community was poised, ready to witness the unveiling of the truth that had been buried for far too long.

At the entrance of the community center, she spotted Finn, his expression tightened with a blend of determination and apprehension. "Are you ready for this?" he asked, scanning the crowd gathering outside.

"I have to be," Alison replied, the urgency reflected in her voice. "We've worked too hard to let fear dictate who we are. Today is about empowerment—about revealing the reality behind the façade Coral Reef Enterprises has maintained."

As they made their way inside, Alison felt the charged air greet them—a mix of hope and uncertainty that echoed off the walls. People filled the rows of chairs, anticipation hanging thick around them, and as the room came to life, she felt the swirling emotions unify into a singular purpose.

Once they took the stage, Alison's heart raced as she surveyed the audience. "Thank you all for being here today. We gather not just to share our findings, but to reclaim our narrative," she began, her voice steady. "Today, we will expose the truth about Coral Reef Enterprises and the tactics they've used to manipulate public perception."

With each slide projected behind her, illustrating the evidence of corruption, financial misconduct, and misleading practices, Alison could sense the audience lean in closer, piquing their interest and stirring doubts.

"This information is important," she continued, her voice growing stronger as she delivered the evidence gathered. "Coral Reef Enterprises has disguised their mismanagement behind a veil of environmental advocacy, but it is the community that bears the consequences."

There were gasps and murmurs throughout the room as the crowd absorbed the revelations. It was clear their eyes were being opened, and each piece of evidence acted as a thread to weave them closer together united in a fight for the truth.

"Additionally," she added, pausing as tension filled the air, "we have gained inside knowledge from those who once supported Coral Reef Enterprises but have realized the extent of their deception. This reveals how intertwined local business and politics have become with their corrupt practices."

As Alison continued to lay out what they had discovered, Finn watched intently, pride swelling within him. The strength she exuded seeped through the crowd, binding everyone together in their shared mission.

But just when it seemed momentum was fully on her side, a figure broke through the back of the room—O'Reilly, flanked by a few strong supporters. His presence cast an immediate shadow over the conversation, his voice slicing through the discussions like a knife. "This is all a farce, distorting the integrity of Coral Reef Enterprises. You're spreading misinformation for your gain, not the community's!"

His anger reverberated through the crowd, and Alison could feel doubt creeping back in. The rhetorical chess game they were engaged in was evolving.

"Do you stand by the manipulation so intricately woven into your practices?" Alison shot back, fueled by determination. "Your disregard for transparency is what's at stake here, O'Reilly! You can't silence the truth just because it's inconvenient."

But O'Reilly pressed on, striving to twist the narrative. "And what about the impact on our local economy? Are you willing to risk jobs and stability for your idealism? You're painting a picture that doesn't reflect reality!"

In that tense moment, Finn stepped forward, his expression fierce. "If we let fear dictate our choices, are we protecting the community or merely preserving a status quo that allows for exploitation? We have a responsibility to ensure that future generations can experience a thriving reef."

The crowd erupted into applause, rallying behind Finn's fervent plea. Encouraged by their support, Alison felt a swell of hope ignite within her. They could reclaim their narrative, but the presence of O'Reilly continued to cast a long shadow over their gathering.

"Look around you!" O'Reilly shouted, still trying to assert dominance as he motioned toward the audience. "You think this is a community? You're creating divisions. You're risking it all for an ideal without considering the consequences!"

Alison clenched her fists, feeling the weight of his words—but she wouldn't let fear paralyze her cause. "No, we are unmasking the truth! This isn't just an ideal; it's our reality. Ignoring the consequences of Coral Reef Enterprises' actions is what puts us at risk. We have to rise together, demanding accountability, because if we don't, we have nothing left."

The cheers and applause that erupted from the audience reflected a unified spirit, refocusing their collective intent. With each passionate voice that rallied behind Alison, she felt the tides shift once more—their commitment strengthened, fueled by the realization that they were standing against manipulation and deceit.

Yet, somewhere in the periphery, Alison sensed a shift as well. As powerful allies gathered, divided by the ideologies of safety versus confrontation, she felt the thread of trust begin to fray just enough to create concern.

Once O'Reilly retreated from the front lines, Alison took a deep breath to regain her composure and address the crowd yet again. "We have come together because we believe in protecting the reef, but we must also protect one another. Collaboration instead of hostility is what will cultivate a thriving community, allowing us to take action on multiple fronts."

As the meeting drew closer to conclusion, the restless murmurs that had threatened to erupt earlier turned into discussions about unity. They began drafting ideas about forming a coalition that represented both local business owners and environmental advocates, emphasizing a collaborative approach to tackling the very real issues at stake regarding the reef.

While connections were forged and alliances reaffirmed, Alison couldn't shake the nagging feeling that not everyone at the table was entirely invested in their cause. Distrust lurked in the shadows, and she couldn't help but consider who among them may be tempted to betray their united front.

As she stepped off the stage, Alison felt the adrenaline surge through her—part exhilaration, part anxiety. They had faced Coral Reef Enterprises head-on and emerged with renewed strength, but the battle was still only beginning.

She glanced at Finn as he joined her. "You were amazing up there," he said, pride shining in his eyes.

"Thanks, but I still have a sinking feeling that we need to draw those cracks closer together—before they turn into gaping chasms," she replied, her tone now serious.

Finn nodded, understanding the depth of her concern. "We have the evidence now, and we can stand as one community. But I agree, we have a long fight ahead of us. We can't afford to underestimate our opponents."

Alison felt grateful for Finn's unwavering support and conviction. They needed to brace themselves—not just for the input from Coral Reef Enterprises but for any betrayals lurking within their own ranks.

With the warmth of community behind them and the cold presence of challenge ahead, Alison steeled herself for the battles to come. The truth was out there, waiting to be uncovered, and together, they would navigate the turbulent waters ahead prepared to expose every malicious connection that threatened to undermine their mission for change.

~ Sixteen ~

The days following the press conference were a whirlwind of activity, as the community propelled forward with renewed energy fueled by the revelations they had unveiled. But alongside that energy simmered an undercurrent of danger—an awareness that Coral Reef Enterprises was poised to strike back as they sought to protect their interests.

Alison felt the weight of their mission pressing down on her shoulders, the urgency propelling her forward as she delved into their findings and began organizing further action. But there was a feeling of trepidation in the air, as if the ground beneath them could shift at any moment, pulling her deeper into murky waters filled with deceit.

"Where do we go from here?" Finn asked, his tone steady as he leaned across the table strewn with notes. They had gathered yet again at the community center, the sense of unity necessary to navigate the chaos beyond their walls booming between them.

"I think we need to prepare for Coral Reef Enterprises' counteroffensive. They've shown their hand already, and now we need to make ours just as strong," Alison replied, her determination clear. "We won't let fear or intimidation stop us."

Tommy nodded in agreement. "We should continue to reach out and solidify community support. We need to ensure that every voice is heard and that no one feels isolated. If we embed ourselves deeper in their trust, we'll stand a better chance when we confront the threat."

As they mapped out their next steps, uncertainty loomed larger than ever. Fear was still a potent force, and whispers of dissent reverberated from the shadows. Just as excitement flickered, an unexpected knock on the door echoed through the room, pulling everyone from their serious undertakings.

"I'll get it," Eva said as she stood up. She opened the door to reveal an unfamiliar woman, her expression serious and eyes scanning the room.

"Are you Alison?" the woman asked, her tone cautious.

"Yes, that's me," Alison replied, intrigued and slightly wary.

"I need to talk to you. It's about Coral Reef Enterprises," the woman continued, her voice low and urgent as she stepped inside. "I have information that you need to hear."

"More intel?" Finn asked, glancing sideways with interest. "This could be crucial."

The woman hesitated, looking as if she were weighing the decision. "I need to be clear: this could put me at risk. If I'm seen talking to you..." She trailed off, the implications hanging in the air.

"We'll ensure your anonymity," Alison promised, her heart racing at the prospect of crucial information. "What do you know?"

The woman took a deep breath, steadying herself as she leaned in closer. "There are connections between Coral Reef Enterprises and local politicians—deals being made under the table. They've been manipulating the public narrative for a while now, and it runs deep."

"What do you mean?" Tommy asked, his attention riveted on the stranger. "How deep?"

"Deep enough that if you push this too hard, they could expose your team personally and attempt to discredit all of you," she revealed, her voice trembling slightly. "I have copies of documents that show illicit connections and backdoor agreements. They're paying off politicians, funding campaigns to counter anyone who stands against them."

Alison felt the breath catch in her chest. "If we could get our hands on those documents, it could change everything. We need proof."

"I understand the stakes," the woman continued, her expression one of defiance. "But the moment you release anything, they'll start digging into all of you. They've already got private investigators probing the community watching for weakness, searching for anyone who gets too close. They'll weave a net deeper than you can imagine."

"Who are you?" Finn asked, suspicion cloaked in curiosity. "What's your connection to this?"

"I used to work with the organization," she admitted quietly, her voice tinged with regret. "When I realized the extent of their deception, I knew I had to leave. I've been gathering evidence in case anyone stands up to them."

Alison hesitated, feeling the gravity of the moment pressing against her consciousness. "If we promise to keep you safe, can we see that evidence?"

The woman nodded, her expression hardening with determination. "I'll share what I have. But I can't stay long—it's too risky for me to be seen here."

Just as she spoke, a shadow moved outside the window, catching Alison's attention. "You need to get out quickly!" she urged, her instincts kicking in. They didn't need to draw attention from Coral Reef Enterprises or their supporters.

"Wait," the woman said, her eyes darting back and forth. "I have these documents secure, but I need time. I'll reach out soon."

"Meet us here," Alison instructed, her tone urgent. "We can create a more secure plan of action so we can unveil the truth without putting you or ourselves at risk."

The woman nodded, retreating cautiously as she left the community center. As Alison watched her go, the adrenaline coursed through her veins. They finally had a potential source of concrete evidence—it might be the very thing they needed to expose Coral Reef Enterprises for all their deceitful practices.

But uncertainty loomed with every moment, fear creeping into the embers of hope igniting. If this connection could put them at greater risk, it made the very mission more precarious.

As the group reconvened, Alison shared what they had learned about potential connections between the organization and local politicians—a narrative that could reveal how the tentacles of power intertwined within the community. "We have to tread carefully," she warned, feeling the weight of her words. "But if we expose these connections now, it might shift perception in our favor."

"Then we should gather our team and prepare to strike," Tommy suggested, his resolve solid. "We can't sit back and let this go unnoticed."

The pulse of anticipation coursed through them as they realized that the truth they had sought for so long was just within reach. But lurking in the shadows was the uncertainty of danger, and doubt threatened to erode their collective momentum.

Undeterred by fear, they began outlining their plans, forming strategies that allowed them to navigate the murky waters ahead carefully. They would not allow the storm brewing around them to deter their course.

As night fell, Alison stood at the harbor once again, the echoes of the meeting ringing in her ears. She could sense the darkness surrounding Coral Reef Enterprises deepening, layers of deception thickening with every new connection unearthed. But she also felt hope ignite within her—she had allies, a community standing firm beside her.

Despite the treachery the organization would resort to, she tightened her resolve. They would confront whatever chaos awaited them with clarity and courage, ready to expose the truth buried deep within the shadows. Together, they would rise against the tide, ready to reveal the depths of corruption threatening both their cause and their community.

The evening of the gathering arrived, and Alison could feel the weight of anticipation mixed with anxiety. The community center buzzed with activity as people filed in, eager to hear the latest updates and discuss their strategy against Coral Reef Enterprises. Each face carried the reflections of hope, determination, and uncertainty—the culmination of weeks spent navigating treacherous waters.

As she organized her notes one last time, Alison glanced over to where Eva and Tommy were engaging with community members. Conversations flowed like waves, crashing against the shore of doubt that had previously threatened to pull them under. But alongside that spirit of unity lingered the unmistakable tension that had been growing shadows of uncertainty that once again threatened to split their purpose.

"Are you ready for this?" Finn asked as he approached, his expression a mix of concern and support.

"I'm as ready as I can be," Alison replied, meeting his gaze with a firm resolve. "We need to stick to our plan, stay focused, and not let their intimidation distract us."

"We've accomplished so much already," he said, his voice reassuring. "No matter how it feels, every voice in this room matters, and together, we can push against the tide."

As the meeting commenced, Alison took a deep breath, stepping up to the front of the room. Her heart raced as she surveyed the faces of the community; they were ready to support their collective fight for the reef.

"Thank you all for coming tonight," she began, her voice steady despite the heightened emotions swirling around her. "We've gathered not just for updates, but also to reaffirm our commitment to protecting our environment, our community, and our shared future."

Applause erupted, and for a moment, Alison felt the warmth of solidarity wash over her. But the underlying tension remained, and she could feel the weight of people's scrutiny as she launched into the updates regarding their findings on the connections, they had uncovered between Coral Reef Enterprises and local players in politics.

"We're at a pivotal moment," she continued, her determination rising. "We've amassed evidence that proves the organization's misleading practices. It's time to reveal the truth and ensure accountability for those who have perpetuated these lies."

As she presented the documents showcasing the deeper connections and financial discrepancies, Alison felt adrenaline surging through her. She could see the crowd leaning in, absorbing the revelations with a mix of shock and outrage.

But just as she began to delve into the most critical parts of their findings, the door creaked open again, drawing her attention. Dr. Grant and O'Reilly entered, their expressions steely and resolute. The atmosphere in the room shifted immediately, apprehension creeping back like a tide pulling at the shore.

"Interrupting a community gathering now?" Dr. Grant called out, his voice cutting through the air like ice. "How charming."

"Surprised to see you here," Alison replied, her heart racing but her voice unwavering. "I thought you were too busy trying to spin public perception."

"Let's be clear," O'Reilly retorted, pushing his way toward the front, positioning himself directly across from Alison. "You're doing nothing more than sowing discontent and spreading unverified lies. This isn't transparency; it's an attempt to incite chaos."

"You can't ignore the truth!" Alison countered, feeling the crowd rally behind her with newfound confidence. "We hold evidence proving that Coral Reef Enterprises has engaged in unethical practices. We deserve answers!"

Dr. Grant stepped forward, the tension palpable as he met her gaze. "Your impatience clouds your mind, Alison. You're grasping at shadows—you're delving into waters where you don't truly understand the consequences."

The audience shifted, anxious whispers rippling through them as doubt threatened to bubble up once more. But Finn caught Alison's eye, a calm reassurance radiating from his steady presence.

"Dr. Grant, this is not a time for condescension," Finn said, stepping forward. "This is a time for accountability. You may hold power, but we hold the truth. You can't intimidate us into silence."

Alison felt the energy snap into focus, a united force ready to confront the threats looming above them. "If you want to speak about consequences, I can assure you that denying the damage being done to our reef will have repercussions—far deeper than any financial pursuit you defend," she declared, her voice lifting above the mounting tension.

Gradually, murmurs began to erupt, voices rising in affirmation as others echoed their sentiments—reinforcing that they wouldn't be silenced.

O'Reilly scoffed, but uncertainty danced in his sharp gaze. "You're naïve to think you can dismantle years of work built on foundations of trust and collaboration. If you pursue this vendetta, you'll find yourselves isolated before you know it."

"Isolated?" A voice came from the crowd, drawing attention to a group of local business owners standing strong. "You mean we'd be isolated from the corruption that's been neglected for too long? No, we want to stand with those fighting for truth!"

The applause that followed filled the room with renewed energy—powerful and invigorating. The tide was continuing to turn, shifting momentum in their favor as the community definitively chose sides.

Dr. Grant's face tightened as if struggling to maintain his composed facade. "By coming here, you only serve to undermine any remaining goodwill we could have," he admonished.

"Goodwill doesn't mean turning a blind eye to the truth," Tommy responded, stepping forward defiantly. "Goodwill comes from honesty and accountability. Power that hides behind false narratives is what ultimately crumbles."

In that moment, the crowd erupted into cheers of approval; the energy surged between them, fortifying their resolve. The tension pulsed and crackled, creating a fierce determination to stand united against the challenges that lay ahead.

For the first time, Alison could see fractures forming within the representatives of Coral Reef Enterprises. They were becoming less united themselves, discomfort brewing in their ranks as the audience rallied behind their cause.

As the back-and-forth intensified, it became clear that the community had taken a stand. The shared commitment to protecting the reef had turned into a definitive uprising against the deceptive organization that had once held them hostage.

In that pivotal moment, Alison realized that their movement wasn't merely a face-off against a corporation—it was a battle for truth, for integrity, and for the community itself. They had tangled with shadows but were ready to expose the light illuminating their cause.

With the crowd behind her, Alison looked Dr. Grant straight in the eye, a newfound strength etching itself into her voice. "We won't be intimidated, and we won't give in. We're shining a light on the truths that you've buried, and you can't drown us out any longer."

As the night wore on, Alison felt a surge of exhilaration wash over her. They had turned the tide, navigating the deceptive waters with resolve and unity. The truth would soon spill out like the ocean—their determination and strength carrying them forward into the fray.

With the shadows of fear pushed back, a new dawn awaited them, illuminating the path ahead. And together, they would unveil the depths of corruption threatening their home and ensure that the voices of the community echoed across the waters, unwavering against whatever waves sought to drown their cause.

~ Seventeen ~

The energy in Cairns still thrummed with the aftermath of their latest gathering, but as Alison stepped into the community center, she felt an unsettling mix of excitement and tension. The confrontation with Coral Reef Enterprises had empowered some, but the lingering doubts that had emerged during the discussions were threatening to fracture the solidarity they had worked so hard to cultivate.

Alison rounded the corner into the main hall, where Tommy and Eva were already deep in conversation. The atmosphere was quiet yet charged with anticipation—a potent reminder of the stakes they faced. If they wanted to translate the momentum from the gathering into tangible results, they would need to tread carefully.

"Alison!" Eva called out, her voice brightening as she saw her approach. "We've been reviewing the responses we received from the press conference. There's a lot of buzz around town—people are starting to talk."

"That's good," Alison replied, her determination steadying her nerves. "But we need more than just buzz. We need the community behind us for this next step. We can't rely on fleeting attention; we need action."

Tommy glanced up from his notes, an intensity in his gaze that reflected the urgency of their mission. "I've been in contact with some of the business owners who expressed doubts. It seems like a few of them might still be swayed to join us. We need to consolidate that support before Coral Reef has the chance to drown our voices."

"Exactly," Alison agreed, her heart racing at the thought of rallying those fractured connections. "We need a solid plan to reach out effectively and assure them that standing with us is in the best interest of their businesses—and the community."

Just then, a voice calling from the back caught their attention. It was Sarah, her expression serious as she gestured for them to gather. "Guys, I think we need to talk," she said, her tone urgent as they approached her.

"What's up?" Alison asked, sensing the tension beneath her words.

"I've heard troubling news," Sarah began, her demeanor serious. "Some individuals have started to question the validity of the evidence we provided at the last meeting. They're questioning whether we truly have the right foundations to stand against Coral Reef Enterprises. It feels like cracks are beginning to form again."

Alison's heart sank at the thought of their progress slipping away. "What do you mean? Who's questioning us?"

"Some of the people who attended the last meeting, including a couple of business owners who initially voiced support," Sarah clarified. "They're worried that we're pushing too hard and that we might end up hurting everyone in our community. The concern is that this may lead to retaliation from Coral Reef Enterprises."

"Ugh, this fearmongering from Coral Reef is exhausting," Eva snapped, frustration creeping in. "They're trying to manipulate everyone into being complacent. We gathered strong evidence; why can't people see the truth?"

"Because fear is a powerful weapon," Tommy interjected, running a hand through his hair. "And for people who don't understand the depths of Coral Reef's deceit, it's easier to retreat into the illusion of safety."

Alison felt a surge of determination rebuilding within her. "We can't allow this to continue. We need to bring everyone to-gether—safely— to reinforce our mission and assure them of our resolve."

"Maybe we can offer a workshop or a discussion session to break down the evidence for everyone's understanding. We need to clarify why these revelations matter to our community," Sarah suggested, her focus sharpening.

"That's a brilliant idea," Alison said, excitement bubbling to the surface. "If we can illuminate the connections—both personal and environmental—this could empower our supporters to push back against their own fears."

As they brainstormed ideas, Alison felt something shift in the air—a renewed sense of purpose. She was determined to ensure that this gathering would bridge the fears dividing their commu-nity and illuminate the path forward.

The plan quickly took form: they would host a series of work-shops emphasizing transparency and collaboration, underscoring the importance of the evidence they had gathered while encour-aging community input. People could bring their doubts, share concerns, and collectively empower each other to rise against the tide of deception.

That evening, as she finalized the details and sent out invita-tions, a familiar unease washed over Alison. The storm clouds from the previous days lingered on the horizon, a visual reminder of the potential chaos that lay just beyond their reach. But she had faith in the community's resilience—she knew they could inspire hope, even amid uncertainty.

Just then, her phone buzzed. It was a message from Finn: *"I have an idea for a follow-up article. I think we can use the buzz from the workshops to bring more attention to our fight."

Alison's heart swelled. Community engagement could not work in isolation; they needed resources to amplify their voices. "Yes!

Let's get our stories out there and show the community that we're serious," she texted back excitedly.

But even as hope surged within her, a nagging worry sparked in her mind. What if their efforts only drew Coral Reef Enterprises more into the fray? What if their concerns became a target for retaliation, further deepening divisions in their community?

Two days later, the workshops commenced amid uncertainty but also excitement. The first session drew a crowd eager to engage, eager to debunk the rumors swirling around them. As Alison stood at the front, the energy in the room was contagious—the scent of determination filled the air, igniting a spark in everyone present.

Together, they broke down the evidence piece by piece, guiding them through the complexities of the financial reports and highlighting the core truths that tied it all together. Conversations flowed, questions emerged, and slowly, the collective understanding began to grow. Allies were reaffirmed, lighting a fire that ignited the bonds they needed.

But later that afternoon, just as the success of the first workshop settled over the community, a chill swept through Alison's stomach when she heard an unexpected knock on her front door.

Opening it slowly, she found a figure standing there—a familiar face that sent a wave of shock rushing through her.

It was Lucas, and this time he bore an expression of urgency mixed with concern. "We... we need to talk," he said, glancing around as if the walls had ears.

"What's going on?" Alison asked, her heart racing as she stepped aside to let him in.

"They're planning something—Coral Reef has people watching you," Lucas revealed, anxiety evident in his voice. "I've seen them lurking near your home, trying to catch you off guard."

A wave of dread washed over Alison, the intensity of the situation crystallizing in her mind. Was Coral Reef Enterprises truly digging deeper, willing to throw their weight around to intimidate them further?

"Do you have proof?" Alison queried, her voice urgent.

"I've seen faces I recognize—some of them tied directly to the organization. I just thought you should know!" Lucas explained. "They want to deconstruct everything we've built together. They'll stop at nothing to see you and your friends fail."

Alison felt a storm brewing inside her, a knot of fear tightening around her heart. "We can't let this happen," she said, voice steady. "We have to prepare ourselves against whatever they throw at us."

Lucas nodded cautiously, his eyes flickering with concern. "But you need to be vigilant. I overheard talk about using insidious tactics—public controversy, smear campaigns... Anything to undermine your credibility."

A shiver ran down Alison's spine as she absorbed the words. They were walking a precarious line, and if Coral Reef was willing to resort to intimidation, they would need to be more adaptable than ever.

As Lucas left, Alison's mind raced with paranoia and determination. She turned back to her notes, the gravity of their situation weighing heavily on her.

"If they think they can divide us," she said aloud, her resolve hardening, "they don't know who they're dealing with. We'll turn the tide against them—together."

Alison felt the embers of resilience flicker within her, knowing that amid the growing shadows, a group bound by purpose and conviction stood ready to face whatever the organization threw their way. They had found unity against the currents of adversity, and she would ensure that the truth would not be buried for long.

In the days ahead, they would rise stronger, embolden each other, and weave together the threads of their fight into an unbreakable net resisting the storm that sought to tear them apart.

With courage igniting their path, they would navigate through this treacherous maze, determined to unveil the depth of Coral Reef Enterprises' deceit. The fight for the reef continued, and Alison could feel the tide shifting, ready to unveil the truths buried beneath the surface.

The heavy rain had finally given way to a calm drizzle, the clouds reluctantly parting to reveal a slate gray sky. As Alison stood on her porch, the air felt fresher, a cleansing of sorts after the chaos and upheaval unleashed in the past few weeks. But the turbulence had revealed more than just challenges; it had illuminated the strength of the community that surrounded her.

In the wake of the recent workshops, momentum had begun to gather once more, echoing the resilience of Cairns' citizens ready to stand united against Coral Reef Enterprises. Still, Alison felt the weight of uncertainty pressing down on her—a reminder that while they had weathered the storm, the aftermath presented its own challenges.

Earlier that morning, she had sent out a call to the community, urging anyone who had stood with them to come together for a debrief. The goal was clear: to discuss the next steps and reinforce their collective commitment in the face of adversity. They had to remain a cohesive force, ready to meet any retaliation that awaited them.

As attendees started trickling into the community center, Alison found herself exchanging nervous glances with Finn, who sat nearby. "This feels like a crossroads," he remarked, his expression equally determined and uncertain. "We've built momentum, but the question is whether we can sustain it against any further pushback."

"Agreed," she replied, swallowing hard against her anxiety. "But as long as we stand united, I believe we can weather the storm. If we have each other, we're stronger."

The gathering began to fill with familiar faces—those who had supported their cause from the start, individuals who had become companions in the fight for the reef. As they settled into the chairs, the warmth of camaraderie enveloped the room, filling the atmosphere with resolve.

"Thank you all for being here," Alison began, her heart steadying as she faced the group. "It's been a challenging few weeks, but we've come together in remarkable ways. Today is about regaining our footing and reinforcing our commitment to ensuring Coral Reef Enterprises is held accountable for their actions."

The crowd nodded, an unmistakable energy humming through them as they expressed their support. "Let's continue to wear our voices as badges of honor," Eva chimed in, her passion infectious. "What we're doing matters—it matters to the health of our reef and the future of our community."

"Don't underestimate the strength we've built," Tommy urged. "One voice might be silenced, but together, we present an unbreakable front. We've come too far to let fear or deception divide us."

As discussions flowed, they traversed strategies: how to amplify their movement through social media campaigns, foster collaboration among local businesses and artists, and create opportunities for everyone to share their stories. But as voices rose with fervor, Alison could feel a lingering tension crackling beneath their discussions—an uncertain relationship with trust began to resurface.

"Alison, there are still some who have decided to side with Coral Reef Enterprises," one of the local artists spoke up, a concerned expression crossing her face. "We can't ignore the growing counter-narrative."

"Trust is fragile, and I can't help but feel that some people are quietly bracing for the fallout," another voice added, drawing murmurs of agreement throughout the audience. "What if they target those of us who remain?"

The worries were palpable, and as the room surged with concern, Alison felt an unexpected whirl of emotions swirl within her. She wanted to rally everyone together, but unaired fears had begun to nestle back into the cracks of their solidarity.

"I understand there are fears—legitimate ones. But we need to remember the strength of our purpose and how far we have come," Alison affirmed, searching the crowd's faces for reassurance. "If we let those doubts reign, we risk becoming exactly what Coral Reef Enterprises wants—a fractured group that can be easily manipulated."

As she spoke, she felt the weight of her resolve harden. "This fight is not just about the reef—it's about standing firm in our values as a community. The truth we have gathered will ultimately prevail if we don't turn against one another."

A slow murmur of acknowledgment rippled through the crowd. It felt as if they were on the cusp of a turning point, the tide of support steadily drifting back in their favor.

"I believe in this community," Finn said, standing up beside Alison. "Who we are demands that we rise above intimidation. We have stories to tell, and those stories belong to every single person here. Let's make sure we honor that."

Together, they began discussing tangible strategies to solidify their message while remaining vigilant, ensuring that their unity would not be shattered. They spoke openly about what Coral Reef Enterprises might attempt and how they could bolster their connections rather than allowing fear to drive them apart.

Later, as the gathering came to a close, Alison could feel a renewed sense of optimism swelling within her chest. They had addressed the storms that threatened to divide them and emerged stronger, ready to take action.

As they prepared to leave, a familiar figure approached Hank, the fisherman who had spoken so passionately about protecting the reef. "Thank you for leading us," he said, his eyes filled with conviction. "I know the waters are murky and uncertain, but I believe we can reclaim our narrative if we stay united."

Alison felt a swell of gratitude. "That's the spirit we need to embrace," she said, her heartwarming at his words. "Together, we are a force to be reckoned with."

As she walked home that night, the clouds began to part, revealing a starlit sky twinkling overhead. It was a calm that soothed her spirit, reminding her of the beauty that lay ahead even in the face of doubt.

Resolving to remain steadfast, she clutched the folder of evidence against Coral Reef Enterprises close to her chest. They had the power to unveil the myriad truths that had been hidden beneath layers of deception—truths that could rise to the surface if they continued to navigate the turbulent waters ahead.

With trust rekindled and a community robustly supporting her, she knew they were poised to confront Coral Reef Enterprises with determination and purpose. The storm they faced might test their resolve, but the network of connection that now flourished within them would help them emerge, stronger than ever, ready to protect what truly mattered: the reef and the future they all aspired to build together.

~ Eighteen ~

The sun dipped low over Cairns, casting a warm golden hue across the community center as it reflected a sense of new beginnings and hope. After the intense gathering where fear had begotten dissent, a renewed sense of unity had slowly carved its way back into the hearts of the people. In the days following that emotional confrontation, Alison had witnessed the community come together in extraordinary ways—rebuilt alliances and engaged conversations that were once fractured began to weave themselves back into a cohesive tapestry of resilience.

Alison took a deep breath as she prepared for an evening meeting—this one focused on reinforcing their collective purpose while presenting the evidence they'd gathered against Coral Reef Enterprises. She felt a sense of calm wash over her; her nervousness had transformed into a determination that had become the driving force in her life. They stood firmly at a junction, ready to confront the gathering tides of deception.

As she arrived at the center, she spotted familiar faces flowing through the front doors—friends and supporters who had steadfastly rallied against the forces that sought to divide them. Tommy was already gathering materials at the front, while Eva animatedly spoke to a group of attendees. The flickers of hope ignited by confidence filled the air, banishing any remnants of doubt that dared to linger.

"Hey, everyone!" Alison called out as she entered, her voice filled with enthusiasm and determination. "Thank you all for coming. Today, we'll delve further into our findings and equip ourselves for the actions that lie ahead. Together, we will stand united to shed light on the truth and protect our community."

The crowd responded with applause, their attention focused on Alison as she positioned herself at the front of the room. She felt the warmth of connection flow through her, reminding her that they were not isolated in this fight—far from it. They were a collective force for change, ready to confront whatever lay ahead.

"Let's bring up Finn and Tom," she said, motioning for her allies to join her by the podium. "We need to reassess our approach and prepare for the next steps against Coral Reef Enterprises. Our mission to reveal their malfeasance is just beginning."

As they outlined their strategy, Finn took the opportunity to share insights he had gathered regarding Coral Reef Enterprises' recent public maneuvers. "They've been releasing strategic counterstatements, attempting to redirect the narrative," he explained, his tone serious. "If we're going to press our advantage, we need to capitalize on the community's sentiments and ensure we frame our findings before they can recover."

Just then, a couple of local journalists entered, cameras at the ready, eager to document the gathering. Their presence energized the crowd, a reminder that the movement was beginning to draw attention beyond their immediate community.

"Perfect timing," Alison said, feeling a renewed sense of determination surge through her. "We can be proactive about our message. The more we can highlight the connection between Coral Reef Enterprises and the damage to the reef, the more we take control of the narrative."

The meeting progressed, and as conversations flowed, Alison felt the collective spirit of determination swell around them. Members of the community—artists, fishers, families—spoke passionately about why preserving the reef mattered to them. Each story illustrated a personal connection to the ocean, rekindling the fire within every individual gathered.

Amid the impassioned exchanges, Sarah stood up, her voice rising above the murmurs. "We need to ensure our message is as clear as possible. If we're going to confront Coral Reef, we need to make it known what's at stake—not just for ourselves, but for the health of our children and future generations."

Alison nodded, feeling the depth of Sarah's conviction. "Exactly. Our fight is for something bigger—it's a legacy rooted in our commitment to this land and its resources. And while they may attempt to undermine us, we will expose the truth they've tried to bury."

As the evening wore on, the energy shifted from anxiety to anticipation, camaraderie enveloping the crowd. They were building momentum, preparing to present a united front at the next press conference—a powerful message to remind everyone of the stakes involved and the truth they would unveil.

After everything they'd built, Alison felt an unmistakable tide rising reflections of hope and strength moving through the community, a vibrancy she had envisioned for so long. Just as the meeting began to wrap, the door swung open and a new face entered, Lucas, looking more anxious than ever.

"Sorry to interrupt," he said, his voice strained. "But there's something important you need to know."

"What is it?" Finn asked, his demeanor sharp with concern.

"They're watching you. A couple of people I overheard in town have been reporting back to Coral Reef Enterprises. They aren't happy about what's happening, and there are whispers that they are preparing to take legal action against anyone involved in your movement," Lucas explained, his urgency palpable as he bore the weight of the information.

The room fell silent, the electric energy dissipating as the flicker of fear resurfaced. Alison's heart raced; the stakes had escalated once again. "How far are they willing to go?" she asked, her voice steady even as churned anxiety threatened to seep through.

"Enough to ensure their narrative prevails," Lucas replied. "If they can discredit you, divide you, or scare you into silence, they'll do it. They're desperate."

Alison felt the room shift; doubt and worry rippled among the attendees like waves. But amid the growing anxiety, she felt the urgency intensify. "We can't allow intimidation to fracture our resolve," she insisted, her voice unwavering and strong. "This only heightens the importance of what we're doing, and we must collectively support one another. We stand together, undeniably, and fear cannot dictate our actions!"

"We need to reinforce our commitment," Eva said, her voice rising in agreement. "If they think they can silence us, they'll only bolster our resolve."

Slowly, the hesitant whispers transformed into murmurs of agreement, gaining volume—each member of the community reflecting a glimmer of determination, no longer shrouded in doubt. They had faced storms before, but this was another sowing of seeds; their unity forged with intent and resilience could withstand the onslaught of intimidation.

With the meeting now focused on reinforcing their solidarity, Alison felt the excitement building again shaping it into a force that would propel them forward, unmoved by threats. Together, they could navigate any treacherous waters and emerge victoriously.

As the crowd began to disperse, Alison looked out at the faces filled with purpose and intense resolve. She could already sense the tides shifting with their unwavering strength; they were a community awakened and alive.

This was about more than just exposing the truth—it was a testament to fighting against the very essence of fear and exploitation threatening to tear their home apart. Standing united, they were ready to confront whatever challenges lay ahead, casting light on the secrets lurking beneath the waves, ready to protect their cherished reef at all costs.

As she stepped out into the cool evening air, extraordinary determination surged through her, compelling her onward. The fight was beginning to take shape, and she was resolute—together, they would weather any storm that arose, standing firm against the currents of darkness as they cast their eyes toward a brighter future for their reef and their community.

The days after the tense meeting at the community center hung heavy with anticipation as Alison and her allies prepared for the impending press conference. The storm of emotions swirling within her combined remnants of fear, hope, and determination. Each evening felt like a fragile thread, stretched taut by the weight of their impending confrontation with Coral Reef Enterprises.

But amid this chaos, another quieter battle raged within her heart—the emotional echoes of losing Mark. His absence still reverberated through her life, amplifying the friendships they had forged together and the longings that had burgeoned into something deeper, especially with Finn.

The morning of the press conference arrived, clear and bright, yet Alison felt an unsettled knot twisting in her stomach. As she stood in front of the mirror, she caught her reflection—eyes wide with resolve, but they sparkled with hints of anxiety. Would she be able to honor Mark's memory amidst all this turmoil?

At the community center, the air buzzed with energy as attendees arrived, eager to join the fight for their reef. Finn was already there, organizing materials and chatting with the gathered crowd, his cheerful demeanor radiating a warmth that couldn't help but ease Alison's nerves. As she approached him, he looked up with that familiar smile, momentarily dissipating the storm of emotions in her chest.

"Hey," he said, leaning against the wooden table. "You look ready to take on the world."

"Just trying to channel my best Mark impression," she replied with a faint smile, shaking off the somber undertones of her thoughts.

"I think you've already got him beat," Finn said, his gaze softening. "Whatever happens today, remember—our community stands behind you. You've rallied everyone for a greater purpose."

"Thanks, Finn. That means a lot." She paused, contemplating the unspoken emotions that lingered between them. "I—I've been thinking about everything we've been through and how you've been by my side. I appreciate your support."

"Always," he replied, brushing his fingers gently against hers, a connection sparking between them. "This fight is personal for all of us, and I'm grateful to be doing this together."

As the tension of their moment hung heavily, Tommy's entrance broke the spell, his energy punctuating the atmosphere. "Hey, team! They're starting to fill the room; it's almost showtime," he said, glancing around the bustling community center.

With a deep breath, Alison followed Tommy and Finn into the main hall where the crowd had gathered. Hearts raced with anticipation, and the buzz of discussion filled the air. She knew they were here not just to present evidence but to weave a narrative—a tapestry of connection, urgency, and emotional resonance.

Standing at the front to kick off the press conference, Alison felt the weight of everyone's eyes upon her, emotions swirling like the waters of the reef they sought to protect. As she delivered the introductory remarks, her voice steadied—she spoke about the urgency of protecting the reef for future generations, recalling Mark's belief in love for the ocean and its power to unite. The heartfelt declarations rose like waves, carrying determination through the crowd.

As the conference progressed, Alison presented their carefully collected evidence of corruption within Coral Reef Enterprises. Sharp images flashed across the screen, depicting environmental degradation alongside testimonials from local fishermen, artists, and families. Murmurs of shock rippled through the audience.

"It's important to remember that this fight isn't just about the reef; it's about all of us—our lives, our stories, our very futures," Alison reiterated, her heart beating with fervor.

Suddenly, just as she began to present critical documentary evidence, a voice rose from the back of the room—O'Reilly, who had been monitoring their meeting again.

"This is nothing, but a smear campaign disguised as a press conference," he shot back, his tone brimming with contempt. "You're just failing to understand the intricacies of business and the economy that sustains us."

Alison felt frustration bubbling up within her as uncertainty began to wrap around the crowd. Would Coral Reef Enterprises succeed in redirecting the narrative?

"Understanding doesn't obscure accountability," Finn countered, stepping forward beside Alison. "What we're revealing is rooted in facts and witness accounts. You can't hide behind walls of privilege any longer! That crushing weight beneath the water is suffocating the very essence of our homes."

With the audience stirred, Alison forced her gaze back to O'Reilly, unyielding. "You may try to manipulate this narrative, but we're here to reveal the truth. We will not be silenced like so many before."

But before they could regain control, a figure stepped forward, a member of the local fishing community—Peter, an older man who had long shared a connection to the sea. "Alison, I appreciate your passion, but I'm worried," he said, his voice wavering. "What if we're wrong? If we step too far, we could lose everything. People will turn on us!"

"Peter, I understand your fears," Alison replied, feeling the tension settle in the air. "But silence is not an option. We must bring light to these issues. Our community deserves to stand together against corruption—every business and every livelihood matters."

The crowd buzzed with whispers, uncertainty swirling like the clouds out of reach of the sun. Just as things began to settle into a fragile calm, a flash of news media stepped in, cameras rolling with intent; their presence only heightened the stakes.

"Does anyone care to comment on the accusations being leveled at Coral Reef Enterprises?" one reporter asked, adjusting their lens under the dim lights.

Alison took a deep breath, steeling herself. "We are here to address the facts and the emotional testimonies that illuminate Coral Reef Enterprises' disregard for our community and the reef. Unity is our strength, and we demand answers!"

Suddenly, a familiar face emerged among the media—a local journalist named Kate, known for her sharp insight and willingness to challenge the powerful. "What is your position on the backlash that has stirred among local businesses? How do you plan to restore trust with those who feel alienated by this movement?"

Alison felt her heart quicken; the questions were pivotal, aimed at exposing her team's vulnerabilities. "If we distance ourselves from the need for honesty, we lose the trust of everyone involved. We're not just fighting for our narrative; we're fighting for every person who relies on the reef—those businesses included."

The crowd erupted into applause as support surged through the hall, and Alison heartened by their force began to feel a sense of triumph rise. But still, the specter of doubt lingered; would the community remain united after this moment?

As they wrapped up the press conference, filled with fervor and emotion, Alison felt the weight of everything slip onto the floor as the audience drifted away. But amid the pride of their battle, she felt it—a creeping layer of treachery woven through the support of the townsfolk.

That evening, while reviewing their notes, Alison received a text from an unknown number: *"We know what you're doing. You'll regret exposing us."

A chill raced down her spine, fear gripping her heart. The storm they had faced was not just external; an insidious threat had begun to take root within their movement—betrayals emerging from those who claimed to advocate for positive change.

"Our search for truth has begun to rattle cages, and not everyone will play nice," she mused aloud, sharing what she had received with Finn and Eva.

"We can't lose our footing now," Finn replied, determination lighting his eyes. "We need to focus on strengthening our resolve, open the channels of communication, and identify anyone who seeks to undermine us from within."

The situation was precarious, but Alison knew that they couldn't allow fear to dictate their positions. Together, they would continue to dig deeper, uncovering the truths that lay just beneath the surface.

As the night settled around them and the looming storm clouds outside continued to darken the sky, Alison felt the strength of the community pulse around her. They would rise against the turmoil, ready to face whatever awaited them—each heartbeat a reminder of the connection that anchored them in their fight for the reef's future.

With the dawn of their next battle on the horizon, she resolved to unveil not just the malicious connections that threatened their mission, but also to confront any treachery that sought to tear them apart. Together, they would push beyond the currents of vulnerability, ready to emerge stronger on the other side.

~ Nineteen ~

The sun rose on Cairns, casting its golden rays over the shoreline like a promise of hope. After the tumultuous days filled with confrontation and hints of treachery, Alison awoke feeling resolute about the path that lay ahead. The bruising exchanges with Coral Reef Enterprises had shaken the community but had also ignited a fierce determination within them.

Today was pivotal. They had planned a public forum, intended not only to rally their supporters but also to ensure their voices reached every corner of Cairns. The emotional scars of past meetings still lingered, but with each step they took toward greater unity, they were learning to confront uncertainty together.

Alison and Eva arrived early at the community center to set up, glancing at the materials they had prepared. Banners reading "United for the Reef" adorned the walls, alongside stunning artworks of the coral that had become a focal point of contention. With colorful displays capturing both the beauty and the fragility of the ocean, the atmosphere felt rich with potential.

"Do you think we'll get a strong turnout today?" Eva asked, adjusting a banner while glancing out of the window.

"I hope so," Alison replied, a mixture of hope and anxiety bubbling beneath her words. "After everything, we need to reassure people about what we're fighting for. The truth matters, and we have a chance to show the community just how impactful their voices can be."

Just then, Finn entered, his expression brightening when he spotted them. "Good morning! Looks great in here! Are you guys ready to ignite some change?"

"Absolutely," Alison said, feeling a flicker of excitement at the thought of him being by her side. "Everyone needs to gather and see that our movement is far more important than the whispers of doubt circulating through town."

As the hour approached, the room began to fill with familiar faces—community members who had once stood on the fringes of the movement, now stepping forward to engage. Conversations flowed like the tide as people mingled, every exchange solidifying their collective resolve to stand united against Coral Reef Enterprises.

When it was time to begin, Alison took her place at the front, heart racing but steadying her voice. "Thank you all for coming out today! As we proceed into this forum, let's remember why we're here. We stand together, not just to protect our reef, but also to protect our community's future."

As she spoke, Alison could see the light rekindling in eyes that had been dulled by fear. "Today, we will share the latest findings and developments in our fight against Coral Reef Enterprises, and we'll discuss how we can continue to make the truth known."

The atmosphere in the room stirred as she introduced the first speaker, Hank, who had always had a deep connection to the ocean. He shared his story, speaking passionately about his family's history of fishing and how he had witnessed the ecosystem's decline firsthand.

"I've seen these waters give life to my community—and I've seen them suffer," he said, his voice resonating through the audience. "We owe it to future generations to understand the role corporations play in our stewardship of the ocean."

With each speaker sharing their experiences, the tide of emotion surged—an undercurrent of shared empathy spun through the room. Alison could sense the unity forming, hearts swelling with a shared purpose, ready to confront Coral Reef Enterprises as one.

As discussions continued, Alison felt a renewed confidence grow. They had lit a fire in the community, one that could not be extinguished. However, past fears began to surface; doubts crept in about how far they were willing to push against the organization.

Just as the atmosphere reached a high of camaraderie, Sarah stood up, her expression reflective. "What happens if we push too hard? What if Coral Reef retaliates more viciously? We could find ourselves in a deeper hole than we're in now."

As murmurs of agreement rippled through the crowd, Alison stepped forward, her heart pounding. "We cannot allow them to dictate our actions with threats. If we stand divided, we grant them power over us. But if we stand united in our truths, our collective strength will overcome any backlash."

A ripple of hope surged across the audience, and soon they were impassioned, voices rising in support of Alison's call. This was the energy they had been building toward—a community refusing to sit idly by, determined to fight against those who exploited their love for the reef.

Just then, a familiar face burst through the door, breathless and visibly shaken—it was Tommy. "I just heard something dreadful," he said, scanning the crowd with wide eyes. "Coral Reef Enterprises is planning to discredit us via the media, starting with accusations of wrongdoing in regard to how we've organized our events. They intend to throw us under the bus, and I overheard them discussing smear campaigns."

"What?!" Alison felt a wave of anger and worry rise within her. "They're preparing to manipulate the truth to protect their interests?"

"Yes," Tommy said, his voice strained. "They're looking for any opportunity to discredit our movement and fracture our unity, even going as far as to accuse us of trying to harm their business interests. They're framing this as a pursuit of their legitimacy, but it's lies."

The air grew thick with silence, each face reflecting the impact of Tommy's words. Fear cascaded through the room like a tidal wave, threatening to shift the atmosphere once more. Alison felt the tension threaten to unravel everything they had worked for.

"We can't let them get away with this," Eva asserted. "We have to pivot quickly! If they're planning this kind of offensive, we need to be ready to combat it head-on; we need to build narratives that counter their potential claims."

With murmurs of agreement rippling through the room, Alison felt a flicker of resolve spark within her. "Then let's fortify our narrative! We know that standing up for the reef means standing united. If they wish to throw mud at us, we'll gather our resources and ensure they understand that we are resilient in our cause."

As discussions heated, voices raised, mirroring the storm brewing outside. A sense of chaos erupted amidst the call for strategy, but together, they formulated a plan. They needed to leverage their allies and engage further with the press, pushing back against the tides that threatened to deconstruct their movement.

As the forum came to a close, Alison felt a renewed sense of purpose instilled within her. They wouldn't cower in the face of their adversaries; instead, they would rise together. They would champion the cause that had brought them together—the protection of the reefs, their community, and their truth.

All the while, she sensed the frayed bonds of trust beginning to strengthen again, knowing that their fight had harnessed something greater than fear—a pulse of hope crystallized among them.

With the night slowly closing in, the clouds overhead began to break apart, revealing stars that twinkled against the dusky sky—a glimpse of the resilience they sought to embody.

In this moment, standing shoulder to shoulder with her friends, Alison felt a wave crashing over her—a surge of strength revealing what lay ahead. They would weather the storms together; the tides would turn, and with each wave that rolled in, they would guard against the darkness that sought to consume them. United in their efforts, they would illuminate the hidden truths, determined to expose Coral Reef Enterprises for the deception lurking within their depths. Together, they were unwavering, ready to face whatever unfolded in tides of tomorrow.

The atmosphere in Cairns continued to shift as the community remained on high alert in the wake of the press conference. While Alison and her team had made incredible strides in rallying support for their mission, the backlash from Coral Reef Enterprises began to creep into their lives like a rising tide. Despite the outward appearances of solidarity, an unseen tension curdled beneath the surface, threatening to unearth long-held grievances and unresolved traumas.

Alison knew she couldn't let fear drive a wedge between them. She focused on maintaining alliances, knowing well that her allies were experiencing their own struggles alongside their collective fight. As she navigated through the remnants of the storm that had been called into their lives, she began to sense shadows lurking even among her closest companions.

Late one evening, Alison found herself at the community center again, poring over spreadsheets filled with research notes and testimonies that she hoped would expose the true nature of Coral Reef Enterprises. She flipped through dozens of pages, piecing together evidence they had gathered. But the mental toll began to weigh heavily, a grind of emotional heartache that threatened to crumble her resolve.

"Hey, you," came Finn's warm voice as he entered the room, breaking through her focused solitude. "You've been at it for hours."

"I can't seem to focus," she replied, glancing up at him. "There's just so much we need to put together before the next community meeting. I feel the weight of expectations pressing down on us."

"You can't take it all on yourself," he said, settling beside her at the table. "This needs to be a collective effort. We're all here for each other, and if you need a break, we can review this together."

Alison appreciated his support but felt a distant pang—a longing that burned deep within her. How could they truly help each other while forging a path through their emotional turmoil? "Thanks, Finn," she said softly. "Sometimes it's hard not to feel the burden of everything."

"What are you thinking? Talk to me," he urged, concern evident in his expression. "You're not alone in this. You've got all of us caring and rooting for you."

As their conversation progressed, Alison grappled with the emotions rising within her about the very real connections forming around this fight—specifically the stirrings of something deeper between her and Finn. Would it be wise to pursue those feelings amidst the uncertainty surrounding their lives?

But her own thoughts were interrupted as she received another message—a text from Tommy, fraught with tension. *"Meet me in the old dockyard; I have something urgent to discuss."

"I need to go," she said, almost instinctively. "It's Tommy. He wouldn't reach out unless it was important."

"Are you sure that's wise?" Finn asked, hesitation threading through his tone. "Given what's been happening, I don't want you to walk into a trap."

"I understand the risks," she replied, feeling the weight between them crackle with unspoken feelings. "But I have to find out what's going on. I won't let fear dictate my actions. I promise I'll be careful."

"Let's go together," Finn offered, standing up with determination. "I'd rather stay close than let you face something alone."

As they made their way toward the old dockyard, Alison noted the shadows deepening with the onset of dusk, a foreboding reminder of the turbulence that had unfolded in their fight. They arrived to find Tommy waiting, his expression tense, edges frayed, standing at the edge of the dock where the ocean lapped softly against the wooden beams.

"What's going on?" Alison asked as they approached, concern knotting in her stomach at the sight of her friend.

"I overheard something earlier today," Tommy said, his voice laden with urgency. "There's talk of certain individuals from Coral Reef Enterprises actively seeking to investigate the key players in our movement. They're not just trying to discredit us—they're digging into our backgrounds."

Alison felt her blood run cold. "What do you mean 'investigate'?"

"They've hired private investigators—people who are looking for weaknesses, personal stories they can manipulate to turn the tide against us," Tommy revealed, his eyes darkening with concern. "I think they want to expose our vulnerabilities, use personal information against us, to discredit the movement."

"Damn it," Alison whispered, anger bubbling inside her like molten lava. "They're desperate enough to send people after us?"

"They think they can intimidate us into silence," Finn said, his voice unwavering but filled with intensity. "This isn't just about protecting their organization; it's about silencing everyone willing to stand against them."

Tommy nodded solemnly. "We need to tighten our ranks, assess who in our circle can be trusted. The last thing we need is someone spilling our secrets or stalling our momentum."

Alison felt torn, realizing the fragility of loyalty and trust that had once formed the very foundation of their mission. This new knowledge weighed heavily upon her—a reminder that even those who had stood by them might be tempted to turn against one another under the threat of personal scrutiny.

"We can't let them win," she insisted, feeling the thread of urgency growing again. "But we have to be smart and strategize in a way that protects us without letting fear dictate our actions."

"I think it's time we approach this from a different angle," Finn suggested, his brow furrowed in thought. "We need to think beyond our local community—get outside perspectives, activists or environmentalists from outside Cairns who know the risks involved. They may provide insight on how to combat Coral Reef Enterprises effectively."

As they discussed the plan for the evening, Alison stewed over the implications of what they had learned. The fight they were waging was becoming more complex, infiltrated with shadows of betrayal threatening to undermine their goal.

With resolve, they decided to reach out to longer-established networks, environmental campaigners whom they trusted but had not yet engaged. They would bolster their cause with shared information and experiences, protect themselves against the shadowy forces surrounding them while illuminating the paths toward transparency.

But even as they plotted next steps, Alison grappled with the emotional storms that swirled beneath the surface. This wasn't just about the fight for the reef. It was about trust, hope, and the bonds of friendship that had forged between them. The turbulent waters would require careful navigation, and reaching out to those farther afield felt like both an opportunity and a risk.

As they wrapped up their discussion and ventured out into the cool evening air, the dim light of the docks flickered before them, a reminder of the uncertain path they had chosen. But together, they would face whatever shadows lay ahead, ready to expose every hidden truth lurking in the depths.

With the ocean swirling around them, Alison felt invigorated, her heart steadying as they pushed forward, determined to keep their mission intact against the undercurrents of fear that threatened to sweep them under. The fight was far from over, and amidst the darkness that loomed, they would discover new allies and fuel their resolve to stay anchored to the cause. Together, they embraced the tides of tomorrow with renewed strength, ready to navigate whatever storms awaited them.

~ Twenty ~

The sun sank below the horizon, casting the skies of Cairns in a warm tapestry of oranges and purples, a stark contrast to the turbulent emotions roiling within Alison. It had been a whirlwind of activity since the last gathering, as they worked tirelessly to prep for their next press conference, gathering allies, reaffirming connections, and continuing to dig deeper into the web of deceit surrounding Coral Reef Enterprises.

However, beneath the layer of excitement and determination was the parallel current of loss she'd yet to fully acknowledge. Mark's absence loomed large in her heart, and as the fight for the reef surged ever forward, she felt the growing ache of unresolved grief tugging at her spirit. The pressures of their activism intertwined with the emotional scars left by his passing, creating an almost unbearable weight.

"Hey, you alright?" Finn's voice broke through her reverie, concern etched into his features as he approached her in the community center.

"Just thinking," she replied, forcing a smile. "About everything. The stakes are high right now."

"I know. But remember why we're here," he said softly, coiling closer to her side. "We need to stay focused on the goal—exposing the truth about Coral Reef Enterprises and standing up for this community."

Alison nodded, appreciating his reassuring presence, which had become a steady source of strength. Yet she couldn't shake the feeling that something was still shadowing them—a tension that weighed heavily as they pressed forward.

Their upcoming press conference was only a day away, and she wanted to ensure they were fully prepared. But amid preparations, her thoughts kept drifting back to Mark—his laughter, his passion, and the bond they had shared—something that was becoming hard to articulate, especially in light of the growing connection between her and Finn.

"Let's go grab a coffee and take a moment," Finn suggested, sensing the shift in her energy. "We could use a break before heading back to strategize."

As they made their way to the café, Alison remained silent, contemplating how to unpack her emotional turmoil. Finn walked beside her, his presence comforting yet amplifying the mix of feelings that bubbled within.

Once they settled into a quiet corner of the café, Finn peered at her with gentle curiosity. "Alison, what's really on your mind?"

She hesitated, feeling a wave of vulnerability wash over her. "It's just... everything feels so intense right now," she finally admitted, her voice barely above a whisper. "The fight feels monumental, but sometimes it's hard not to feel the loss we've all endured. Mark's absence is still overwhelming for me. It's like I'm fighting for something he cared about so deeply, but I miss him every day."

Finn's expression softened, understanding flickering in his eyes. "I get that. We're all feeling the void he left behind. And I can't help but feel that the bond we've forged in his absence—through our shared mission—makes me acutely aware of what we've lost, too."

Her heart swelled as Finn spoke, his honesty resonating deeply. "The struggle brings us closer, but it also forces us to confront our feelings about what we've lost," he continued, his voice steady.

"You're not alone in this, Alison. I've been grappling with those emotions too."

Suddenly, a wave of warmth washed over her. The connection they had cultivated had become richer with layers of shared pain and hope—a bond of understanding evolving right in front of them.

"But it also means we're finding strength in each other," Finn added, his gaze intense yet comforting. "And we can keep pushing forward together. Mark would want us to honor his memory, not just through words but through action."

Alison felt tears sting her eyes as the emotions she had been holding so tightly began to surface. "I'm scared that embracing those feelings will distract me from the mission. It feels selfish to focus on loss when there's so much at stake for the reef."

"It's not selfish," Finn replied gently, reaching across the table to grip her hand. "It's human. We're dealing with loss while also forging a path for the future. We shouldn't have to compartmentalize our emotions. It's okay to feel both grief and strength; that's where our power comes from."

In that simple gesture, Alison felt a flicker of comfort and hope ignite within her, illuminating their shared journey. They were navigating the complexities of grief together, and with each conversation, their hearts knit together through shared understanding.

But even as they sat there, savoring the warmth of connection, Alison couldn't shake the weight of uncertainty looming ahead. Would their efforts to expose Coral Reef Enterprises draw a line of fire that could hurt the very community they sought to protect?

When they returned to the community center, Alison resolved to address the emotional undercurrents in the upcoming press conference. She would acknowledge the pain and loss they felt—speak openly about Mark to honor his legacy while using the strength of their mission as a unifying force.

As the night deepened and the moon cast a silver glow over the center, she gathered everyone together for a final strategy session before the press conference. With the air thick with promise, she felt the energy surge anew, strengthening the bonds of hope.

"Tomorrow, we will stand in our truth," she declared, her heart resolute. "We will rise as a community, united not only in the fight for the reef but also in remembrance of the friends we've lost along the way. Mark's passion lives in every one of us now, and together we can channel our grief into transformative action."

As they shared in that moment, the remnants of loss began to weave into a powerful tapestry of resilience, beauty, and strength. With every heartbeat echoing in solidarity around them, Alison was ready to face whatever lay ahead—not just for Mark, but for the reef and the future they all vowed to protect. Together, they would declare their mission, navigate the storms, and rise to shine through every shadow that dared to cross their path.

The morning light streamed into the community center, illuminating the space where the press conference was to take place. Alison stood at the podium, her heart pounding with a mix of anxiety and determination. Today was crucial; it was the moment they would unveil the evidence gathered against Coral Reef Enterprises and confront the shadows of deception that loomed over the reef and their community.

The atmosphere around them was electric, filled with the anticipation of supportive voices and watchful eyes. Journalists had arrived, eager to report on the unfolding story, and local citizens gathered to hear their case. But under the surface of excitement was an undeniable tension—a shared understanding of the risks involved, still unyielding to the horror stories of retaliation that had been whispered in the days leading up to this moment.

"Thank you all for being here today," Alison began, her voice steady and clear as she addressed the crowd. "We gather not just to shine a light on the truth but to honor the future of our community and our cherished reef."

As she continued, she felt the energy of the audience ripple around her, feeding off her determination. "Each of us has heard stories of decline and destruction; we've witnessed firsthand how the actions of Coral Reef Enterprises have affected our marine ecosystems. Today, we will present the evidence that shows we deserve better. We deserve transparency, accountability, and a commitment to preserving the environment."

With her heart racing, Alison launched into the presentation, detailing the piles of evidence they had meticulously gathered. Images flashed across the screen, depicting the grim realities of coral bleaching and the mismanagement that had plagued the organization for too long. The room filled with murmurs of disbelief and murmurs of anger as the facts began to wash over them.

Throughout the presentation, Alison shared snippets of personal accounts—the fishermen whose lives had been altered by the changing tides, artists who had drawn inspiration from the beauty of the reef, community members whose hopes for a sustainable future had been dashed. Every story added weight to their mission, each testimony echoing with shared purpose.

When she finished, the applause that erupted around her was electric—an affirmation that reverberated through the hall. But just as she felt a swell of confidence, the door swung open, interrupting the celebration.

Dr. Grant strode in again, flanked by O'Reilly, a condescending smile gracing his features. "I see you've gathered quite a crowd," he remarked, his voice unwavering. "But I think it's time to clarify a few things."

"What do you have to say, Dr. Grant?" Alison said, passion surging through her. "Do you wish to challenge the evidence laid before us?"

"Challenge?" he scoffed, stepping forward, an icy glint in his eyes. "I think you misunderstand the situation. What you've presented is not only misleading but also a distortion of the truth. You claim to care for the community, yet here you stand with a story crafted to malign the very organization that has worked to support it."

The crowd responded with a murmur of disbelief, rallying around Alison's determined stance as a feeling of solidarity began to surge. Just then, however, O'Reilly interjected, attempting to shift the narrative back toward fear. "What you're doing here is a claim of reckless endangerment. Your allegations could have serious repercussions—not just for our organization, but for every business that relies on it."

"I can assure you," Finn said, stepping up to stand beside Alison, "that it is not reckless to speak the truth. The consequences of silence are far more devastating. We have a right to our voices and an obligation to protect our reef!"

As the confrontation escalated, Alison could feel the stakes intensifying; the tension filled the air, pushing the crowd's energy to its breaking point. But beneath the surface of anger and resolve flowed a current of vulnerabilities—a shared fear that their efforts would only lead to retaliation that could destroy their cause.

Dr. Grant stepped back, eyeing the crowd, his expression shifting. "You may feel empowered today," he said, voice low and filled with menace. "But I can guarantee you that the fight you're waging will bring consequences that ripple far beyond what you intend. People will and can lose everything they risked by aligning themselves with you."

The crowd reacted, voices rising in protest, but Alison felt her own emotions bubble over—a concoction of grief, determination, and anger. "We will not see our community turned against one another because of a corporation that seeks to exploit our resources," she shouted. "We must hold the line against fear!"

There was a moment of palpable tension as the audience stood anchored in their resolve. No amount of intimidation would silence them.

"Let's see how long your bravado lasts when winter hits," Dr. Grant warned before turning sharply to leave, his expression a mix of frustration and acknowledgement that the tide was beginning to shift against him. O'Reilly followed closely behind, their retreat signaling a temporary defeat that left the community buzzing with excitement.

As the crowd slowly settled, Alison felt a surge of gratitude. "You, see? You just faced Coral Reef Enterprises together! Your voices matter, and the truth will ripple out to reach those who deserve to know it!"

Cheers erupted again, the applause igniting a fervent energy. But in the back of her mind, Alison couldn't shake the unease that lingered. The confrontation had not only unveiled the truth within the walls of the community center; it had confirmed that the storm was far from over.

In the days that passed, as they continued mobilizing support and sharing their message of truth, whispers of doubt remained, casting a shadow that sometimes warped their unified purpose. But Alison drew strength from each interaction, knowing that no matter the difficulties ahead, together they would rise against whatever tides threatened to pull them under.

As they prepared for their next community forum, Alison resolved to unearth every fragment of truth and shore up the foundations of their support. They would galvanize their resolve against the deceptive currents of Coral Reef Enterprises, determined to unveil the depths of their corruption.

Amid the darkness that sometimes fogged her mind, Alison felt a flicker of hope as they pushed back against shadows of betrayal—every accusation, every revelation, and every voice woven together to create an unbreakable bond and a movement ready to illuminate the truth buried deep in the waters they fought to protect.

~ Twenty One ~

As the dawn broke over Cairns, light spread across the town like a promise renewed. The vibrant hues of orange and pink painted the sky, illuminating the horizon and filling Alison with a sense of revitalization. After weeks of intense confrontation and threats from Coral Reef Enterprises, the community gathered for an additional forum, ready to unfurl their collective resolve in the pursuit of truth.

The scent of salt and the sound of waves crashing against the shore wrapped around Alison as she made her way to the community center. She felt a renewed sense of purpose sizzling in her veins; the time for weakening doubt and fear had long passed. Today was about clarity and strength—the chance to not only reveal the depths of their findings but also to remind the community of the ties that bound them together.

As she arrived, the atmosphere buzzed with energy—a mix of conversations and laughter fluttered through the air. Familiar faces filled the seats, support reflecting back at her like sunlight dancing on waves. The tenderness of their shared mission vibrated through every interaction; with each smile and handshake, Alison felt hope surging through her.

"Right on time!" Finn exclaimed, his sunny disposition palpable as he drew her into a warm embrace. "We're all set for the forum today. Everyone is fired up!"

"Awesome! I think this community needs this energy," Alison replied, her own spirits lifting as she prepared to face the crowd.

"We've got a lot to cover, and I want to make sure we address anything that lingers from previous meetings—especially after the chaos we faced."

With a sense of mutual understanding, they went over their agenda and tactics one last time, solidifying their stance as a unified front. As the crowd settled in, Alison stepped confidently to the front, surveying the sea of familiar faces—community members, friends, and supporters—all eager to witness the next wave in their fight for the reef.

"Thank you for coming today! It's heartening to see so many caring faces ready to protect the future of Cairns," she began, her voice steady as she addressed the room. "Today, we're not just unveiling our evidence against Coral Reef Enterprises—we're building a coalition for change and accountability."

Cheers erupted, invigorating Alison's spirit, fueling her determination. She launched into their findings, the evidence collected over weeks now ready to be unveiled with clarity and purpose. Images flashed on the projector screen, depicting the stark realities of the coral's decline alongside the disparity between what Coral Reef Enterprises reported and the truth.

"Every face in this room matters! Every story we share strengthens our mission!" she emphasized, weaving together threads of hope. "We are not alone in this fight. Together, we can push change through transparency and accountability."

As she spoke, Alison could see the community's eagerness grow, faces lighting up as each piece of evidence captured their hearts. Her words resonated deeply as she painted a vision, a brighter future for both the reef and Cairns itself—a world where support stood untarnished against the shadows of fear.

Yet, as the energy in the room surged, she glanced at the corner, where Lucas sat with an expression that seemed troubled. The worry etched across his face reminded her of the whispers of dissent that had broken through unity in previous discussions.

"Lucas," Alison called out, the crowd falling into a thoughtful hush. "Are you okay? Is there something on your mind?"

With the attention of their gathered supporters fixed on him, Lucas stood slowly, uncertainty clouding his features. "I want to believe in this movement, but I'm still struggling with the idea of retaliation. I'm worried about the risks that come with exposing Coral Reef Enterprises, especially after what I overheard. It seems they'll stop at nothing to discredit us."

"I understand that fear," Finn said, his voice infused with empathy. "But we must overcome it. Distraction and intimidation only empower them further. We have to stand firm in our convictions."

Alison felt the room shift, understanding rippling through the crowd as people confronted their own fears while rallying to Finn's words. She stepped forward, intent on bridging the gap between their concerns and their shared mission. "If we let fear dictate our actions, they win. But if we face this storm together, we can transform that fear into resilience."

With murmurs of agreement rising through the audience, Alison sensed the tide shifting back in their favor. They had faced the uncertainty before, and the threads of their unity began to weave themselves back together stronger this time, more fortified than ever.

After the presentations concluded and moments of connection built upon the evidence were shared, Alison looked out at the crowd, her heart swelling with gratitude. "We're standing on the precipice of a new horizon—a collective movement filled with the promise of change. Together, we can offer more than just resistance; we can provide a vision that cultivates hope for our reef and each other."

The applause that erupted felt electric, excitement pulsing through the room as they stood in solidarity, ready to forge ahead. They had begun to reclaim their narrative, fortified against the backlash that had threatened to tear them apart.

Finally, as they closed the meeting, Alison could feel a renewed sense of purpose settling all around her. People began to share their stories, and connections flourished among attendees, each testimony illuminating the shared light they brought to their mission.

The storm clouds that had once gathered now seemed to part as new alliances formed, revealing the clear promise of what lay ahead. They had become stewards not just for the reef, but for one another—a collective force alleviating the shadows of doubt that had once threatened their unity.

Walking home after the gathering, Alison felt the wind whip gently around her, carrying the scent of rain-soaked earth and the promise of new beginnings. She was reminded that it wasn't just the evidence they had gathered that mattered, it was the spirit of the community standing behind her that proved unshakeable.

With her resolve strengthening, she understood that they stood at the brink of transformation—a movement poised to thrive against the tide. Together, they would challenge Coral Reef Enterprises while navigating the waters ahead, ready to cast light on every hidden truth that lay submerged beneath the surface.

As she lay her head on her pillow that night, the echoes of hope and community filled her heart. Tomorrow would bring new challenges, but with each heartbeat, they were ready to rise with the sun—united for the reef, for each other, and for a future painted in hues of resilience and unwavering love.

The morning sunlight spilled through the window of Alison's apartment, illuminating the stacks of notes and documents scattered across her dining table. The press conference had been a turning point, but she was painfully aware that the foundation they had built, strong as it seemed, remained fragile. The impact of their revelations had stirred the community, and while many rallied behind them, doubt still lurked in the shadows, waiting to unravel their progress.

Over the past few days, Coral Reef Enterprises had amplified its public relations campaign, and Alison had witnessed whispers of dissent reemerge from the community. Business owners who had once stood firm were starting to sway, feeding into the fear that emerged after O'Reilly's threats had echoed through their ranks.

"Are we doing enough to address these concerns?" Eva asked, joining Alison at the table as she glanced over the notes. "I can't shake the feeling that we're losing traction among our supporters."

"It feels like every time we gain ground, the organization finds a way to pull us back down," Alison replied, a sense of frustration lacing her words. "We need to counteract their narrative carefully, or we'll lose the members we've worked so hard to unite."

Alison's phone buzzed, and she quickly grabbed it, her heart racing as she read a text from Tommy: *"Meet me at the docks. Important, trust me."

"What is it?" Eva asked, noticing her sudden tension.

"Tommy wants to meet at the docks," Alison said, her stomach twisting in anticipation. "He claims it's important."

"Do you think it might be another tip about Coral Reef?" Eva mused, her brow furrowed.

"We won't know until we get there," Alison replied, feeling the heaviness of apprehension settle over her. "Let's head out and see what he has to say."

The drive to the docks felt longer than usual, the air thickening with unease as thoughts raced through Alison's mind. What could Tommy have uncovered this time? Would it signal the tipping point in their fight against their adversaries, or would it only deepen the complications they faced?

As they approached the old dock, she noticed the dark clouds beginning to gather overhead, mirroring her unease. Dread settled deep within her chest as they parked and joined Tommy near the edge of the water, his face drawn and weary.

"Thanks for coming," he said, glancing around to ensure they were alone. "I've heard some frightening things."

"What is it?" Alison pressed, the urgency palpable in her voice.

"I've been speaking to some contacts, and they've been keeping an eye on the motivations of Coral Reef Enterprises," Tommy explained, his eyes darting nervously. "They might be planning to take even more drastic measures than we initially thought."

"What do you mean by drastic?" Eva asked, concern flickering across her face.

"They're looking into ways to compromise our integrity—by digging into our past, our connections, and any dirt they can find. They aren't just targeting individual members, but the entire coalition," Tommy revealed, anxiety evident in the way his hands shook.

Alison felt her heart drop. "Are they really that desperate?"

"More desperate than ever," Tommy replied gravely. "They'll stop at nothing, and if they can find anything in our backgrounds, they'll use it as ammunition to discredit us."

Alison tightened her jaw, anger flaring within her as she processed the implications. "This is a blatant attempt to sow fear and distrust among allies. They want to fracture our community and undermine everything we've built!"

"We can't let them intimidate us," Eva added, her voice firm but quaking beneath the weight of their predicament. "This could jeopardize our entire movement."

"Right. But we need to be strategical about how we respond," Tommy suggested. "To turn this fear into toughness, we must solidify our core group—everyone needs to understand what's at stake and how we should prepare for whatever comes next."

As the three of them brainstormed defensive measures and plans for protecting their movement, the clouds overhead grew darker, filling the sky with a growing sense of impending storm. The heaviness in the air mirrored the gravity of their discussions, and Alison felt the pressure mounting, both from within and from the outside.

Just then, a familiar figure emerged from the shadows—a man approached them at the docks. It was Lucas, his face taut and distressed. "Alison! Tommy! Eva!" he called, rushing toward them. "You need to hear this!"

"What's going on?" Alison asked, noting the urgency in his tone.

"I overheard some fishermen talking—saying Coral Reef Enterprises has sent people to infiltrate the meetings. They're gathering intel, making sure they know who's involved and who they can sway against you," Lucas explained, panting slightly from having rushed over.

"Holy—" Tommy's voice trailed off, disbelief flooding his features. "They're really trying to drown us out, aren't they?"

Alison felt the chill of impending reality wash over her; it was becoming clear that Coral Reef Enterprises was willing to play dirty. "They want to strip away our foundation of trust and solidarity."

Unsure of what to do next, the trio looked at one another, vulnerability creeping into the corners of Alison's determination. The stakes were getting higher, and any misstep could have repercussions that would ripple through the community.

"We've got to be more proactive," Eva said firmly. "We have to strengthen our ties, draw the lines where they cannot intrude."

"Right," Alison agreed, her heart racing as urgency coursed through her. "We can't let them find cracks in our foundation; we need to reinforce those bonds, remind everyone that Coral Reef Enterprises is the real enemy. And if we have to, we'll shine a light on their actions."

With newfound resolve, they discussed how they could safeguard the integrity of their movement, planning outreach to solidify connections and reinforce the community's support. They would fortify defenses while sharing their message more boldly, ensuring that the tide remained at their backs.

But even as their cohesive strategies formed, Alison wasn't fooling herself—darkness loomed beyond the edges of their plans. They had entered a treacherous game, one that would require more than passion; it would demand unity, vigilance, and unwavering courage.

As they parted ways that evening, Alison felt the storm rising inside her, both external and internal. They were ready to face whatever paths unfolded, united against the forces that threatened to tear them apart, ready to navigate the turbulent waters toward a brighter future for their reef and community. Together, they would reclaim their narrative and expose the truths buried beneath the surface, no matter the cost.

~ Twenty Two ~

The sky was a brooding gray as Alison stood atop a rocky outcrop near the beach, gazing out at the turbulent ocean. Waves crashed against the rocks below, sending splashes of saltwater into the air like nature's own battle cry. It mirrored the tumult within her heart—a mix of determination and fear as they braced for whatever Coral Reef Enterprises might unleash next.

It had been a week since their last community meeting—a gathering that had opened up conversations but had also heightened tensions surrounding their fight. Though they had fortified their mission and inspired many, Alison sensed that cracks in their support still lingered, driven by the onslaught of threats and whispers generated by the organization.

That afternoon, Alison had asked Finn to join her at the beach for a moment of reflection and strategy. "I need to clear my head," she texted him earlier. "Meet me at the cove?"

As the sound of footsteps approached, she turned to find Finn emerging from the dunes, his expression warm but serious. "Hey there," he greeted, his voice cutting through the damp air. "Nice to see you out here. How's the planning going?"

"Still grappling with the persistent whispers of dissent," Alison admitted, her concern evident. "Even after all we've accomplished, I can't shake this feeling that someone's watching us, waiting for an opportunity to exploit any divisions."

Finn glanced at the crashing waves, taking a deep breath. "I know what you mean. Just yesterday at the market, I heard someone mention the backlash from Coral Reef. Some folks are genuinely scared about where this is headed. They're worried about losing contracts or friendships."

"Exactly!" Alison said, frustration bubbling to the surface. "It's infuriating. We're fighting to protect this community, yet fear has redrawn the lines."

Finn stepped closer, the distance between them narrowing. "Look, they can't intimidate us into silence," he added, his voice firm. "But it's going to take all of us to face down Coral Reef Enterprises. If we allow them to split us apart, we're playing right into their hands."

"I get that," Alison replied, heart racing as the tension thickened. "But how do we reassure those still hesitant? How do we prevent the cracks from deepening?"

"We keep pushing forward with our message," Finn said resolutely. "We show them that their fear is what truly divides us, and that our unity is our strength. We need to be open to dialogue and confrontation but also ensure that loyalty and trust become paramount in this alliance."

Alison could see the determination in Finn's eyes, a reflection of the strength she had come to admire so deeply. "You're right. If we reinforce trust among each other, we'll become an unbreakable force."

"I think we need to have a community outreach day—something that allows us to reconnect, to remind everyone why this fight is so important," Finn suggested, enthusiasm surging in his voice as he looked toward the horizon. "Let's create art, share stories, and keep the conversations flowing. It can feed our spirit and remind people of what they truly want to protect."

As they fleshed out their ideas, Alison felt a sense of excitement blossom within her, igniting hope once more. "Yes! An outreach day could be a great way to engage everyone, and it would show that we're dedicated to including their voices in this movement."

Just then, a sense of foreboding washed over her as she caught a glimpse of something shifting along the shore—a group of figures. It was the same cluster of familiar faces from Coral Reef Enterprises, mingling amongst the tourists that filled the beach, their laughter carrying in the wind.

"Look," Alison pointed discreetly. "Those are people from Coral Reef."

"What are they doing here?" Finn said, his voice dipping into a hushed urgency.

"I don't know, but we should find out. I'll approach them," she resolved, feeling both trepidation and determination ignite within her.

As they walked toward the group, the tension in the air thickened. The figures turned, and Alison recognized O'Reilly, flanked by a handful of supporters. They were deep in discussion, but once they noticed her presence, a chilling smirk spread across O'Reilly's face.

"What a surprise to see you here, Alison," he greeted, feigning pleasantness. "Enjoying the lovely weather? It's a nice change from the storms we had."

"What do you want, O'Reilly?" she retorted, refusing to let his sarcasm derail her focus. "We know you're trying to discredit us, and I won't allow you to undermine our mission."

He chuckled, glancing at his companions, who feigned interest. "Trust me, we have no intention of wasting our time. But your little movement is cute. Are you hoping to rally enough support to shake us down?"

Alison fought to level her gaze, not allowing his condescending demeanor to rattle her. "This is about protecting our community and the reef—not about intimidation or childish games. You'll find we're stronger than you think."

"Strength? Is that what you call these whispers of doubt among your ranks?" he replied, his tone dripping with poison. "We both know it won't be long before this whole charade collapses under the pressure."

"What are you talking about?" Finn interjected, stepping protectively beside Alison. "You're using fear and manipulation to disrupt our community. We won't let you succeed."

"I'm simply being realistic," O'Reilly replied with a disarming smile. "I'm willing to bet that the more you push, the more ease of dissent you create. It's only a matter of time before your newfound allies realize the consequences of this little crusade of yours."

Alison felt a knot tighten in her stomach, the implication of his words wrapping around her like a vice. The shadows of dissent had taken root, and it was clear that Coral Reef Enterprises was willing to use separation tactics to fracture their growing movement.

"Doubt me all you want," O'Reilly continued, raising his voice to command the attention of those in the group. "In the end, the truth of your weakness will all come to light. Watch as your organized chaos unravels."

With that, he turned away, a wave of casual dismissal in his gesture that ignited a spark of frustration within Alison. Behind her, she could sense a shift; they had realized the weight of their own impact and understood the depth of their mission.

When Alison returned to Finn, her heart felt heavy. Yet she felt a simmering determination arise from within, the dark clouds unable to extinguish their fighting spirit. "We need to unite. Whatever they throw at us, we must combat it together. We cannot afford to back down."

As they regrouped with Tommy and Eva later that evening, they faced the reality of unraveling tensions. "We need to act fast. Let's address the community directly and make it clear that Coral Reef Enterprises is trying to fragment our unity," Tommy suggested, his voice tinged with urgency.

"Yes, and we need to reinforce our allies, in fact, re-establish connections with merchants and families from the last few gatherings," Eva added, determination lighting her features. "If we lay a strong foundation of trust, they can't tear us apart."

The night wore on them, emotions heavy yet resolute, as they strategized a way forward. With the threat of Coral Reef Enterprises ever looming, they felt an urgency to counteract their methods through unwavering resolve.

As the conversations diffused, Alison felt the weight of what was at stake clear within her. The fragility of the community's solidarity could not be overlooked, but she had faith that they would confront whatever fate awaited them.

The next morning, the sun shone brightly, illuminating a new day and a renewed sense of hope. Together, Alison and her allies stepped into the fray, ready to navigate whatever storms awaited them. They wouldn't allow the shadows of doubt to undermine their mission; they would rise, united, and bring light to the truths hidden in the depths, determined to protect the beauty of their beloved reef against the tides of deception.

As the sun dipped low on the horizon, painting the sky in shades of deep orange and violet, Alison felt a sense of urgency ripple through her veins. The community center was bustling with activity as they prepared for the rally, a culmination of their efforts to safeguard the reef and expose the corruption within Coral Reef Enterprises.

Alison paced back and forth, a mixture of anticipation and anxiety swirling within her. The stakes felt higher than ever, and she was acutely aware that they stood at the precipice of change. Since the last confrontation, they had set forth to bolster their message and re-establish allies among the community—a mission that would require unwavering resolve.

As she glanced around the room, she could see the faces of those who had become part of this journey—a mixture of familiar and new supporters standing shoulder to shoulder, ready to fight for their cause. Finn moved through the crowd, passing out flyers and engaging in conversations, a spark of enthusiasm lighting his features amidst the tension.

"Are you ready?" he asked, stopping beside Alison and catching her eye. "The energy in here is incredible!"

"I hope it translates into something meaningful. This is our chance to shift the narrative," she replied, trying to contain her nerves. "We need everyone's voices to echo throughout the town tonight. If Coral Reef Enterprises thinks they can silence us, they're in for a wake-up call."

"Yes! Let's remind them that our movement is not just a whisper but a resounding chorus ready to carry for the reef," he affirmed, his voice strong.

As the crowd began to gather in the main hall, Alison noticed Sarah weaving through the throngs, her expression serious. "Alison!" she called out, catching her attention. "I've heard some unsettling news. There are rumors about Coral Reef Enterprises planning a counter-rally to undermine our efforts."

"What? When?" Alison's heart sank at the news.

"Tomorrow, they're attempting to gather their supporters to paint us in a bad light, claiming our movement is built on misinformation. They want to drown out our voices before we gain more traction," Sarah explained urgently.

Alison exchanged troubled glances with Finn and Eva. "They're willing to go to any lengths," Alison said, frustration bubbling within her. "We can't allow them to overshadow our message. This is our chance to expose their deceit!"

"Then we need to make tonight count even more," Finn added, resolve seeping into his tone. "We need to be louder, stronger, and more united. Every story shared tonight must weave together to create an undeniable narrative."

As the evening progressed and the crowd began to fill the auditorium, Alison stepped to the front of the room, drawing the collective attention of attendees. She took a deep breath, heart pounding, determined to guide them through this pivotal moment.

"Thank you all for gathering here tonight!" she began, her voice steady. "We stand together to raise our voices against the actions taken by Coral Reef Enterprises. Reports of their growing influence have surfaced claims that seek to undermine all we've worked for!"

As she spoke, the crowd responded with animated nods and murmurs, support invigorating the atmosphere. "Recent revelations have unveiled a pattern of deceit. Our community has experienced the very real impacts of their neglect and manipulation—our coral is declining, and if we don't act now, we risk losing it forever."

With every recounting of evidence, the audience reacted passionately, emotion rippling through them as stories interspersed with facts ignited a sense of urgency. The room pulsed with the echoes of their shared commitment, forging a bond of resilience that fought against the tides of intimidation.

Just then, a familiar face stepped forward—Hank, his voice filled with conviction. "I've fished these waters my whole life, and I've seen the devastation first-hand. We can't let fear silence the truth; this fight is about our very existence, and we deserve to know what's happening beneath the surface!"

With each story shared, Alison could see the tide beginning to shift, the fatigue of doubt washing away as the community rallied behind their shared mission. But just as the discussion began to flow seamlessly, a figure stepped to the back, arms folded—Dr. Grant had arrived to loom over the proceedings.

"Here we go," Finn muttered under his breath, tension creeping into his posture.

Dr. Grant raised his hand to silence the crowd, his authoritative presence commanding attention. "This charade will not be tolerated," he declared, stepping boldly to the front. "Coral Reef Enterprises has always acted with integrity, and any claims presented here are nothing more than fabrications designed to stir chaos."

The audience stiffened; unease enveloped the air as he attempted to undermine their efforts once more.

"Enough!" Alison exclaimed, stepping forward to confront him. "We have evidence rooted in truth, and we will not allow you to manipulate the narrative any longer. If you really believe in the integrity of your organization, why not open the books and allow for scrutiny?"

With those words, the crowd surged in applause, passion igniting as they rallied around her stance.

Dr. Grant's expression darkened, and he glanced at the faces surrounding him—shifting quickly from waving complaints to fortified resolve. "You, of all people, should know that accountability doesn't mean revealing every document to the public. This is a business that runs on trust, and you're jeopardizing that."

"What you're jeopardizing is the very essence of our community," Tommy interjected, stepping beside Alison. "We have a right to know how our resources are being managed. Your trust will mean nothing if the reef continues to decline."

As the words echoed around the room, the responses poured in—community members standing up, recounting stories of how their lives had been impacted. Each witness against Coral Reef Enterprises added another layer, weaving a tapestry of truth that illuminated the growing conflict.

Allies in the crowd began to share their experiences, each voice amplifying their collective fight. The respect for Alison surged as both Finn and Eva stood staunchly beside her, ready to engage in whatever confrontation awaited them.

But just as the audience began to shift into a rallying force against the darkness surrounding them, Dr. Grant suddenly took a step back, a cool smile forming on his lips. "This isn't over. You're simply making this storm deeper for yourselves, and I'll ensure that the media captures the truths we want to tell."

As he turned and walked away, tension hung thick in the air, uncertainty threatening to derail their momentum once more.

"Did he just imply they'd spread misinformation?" Eva said, confusion woven into her voice.

"Probably," Tommy said, frustration emanating from his presence. "We need to be proactive. We can't let them control the narrative."

As the crowd began to disperse, Alison could feel the unease settling in—a reminder that while they had found unity in their fight, darkness still loomed at the edges of their resolve.

Alison's heart sank; the fleeting moment of triumph was overshadowed by fear that Coral Reef Enterprises would manipulate the truth against them. They needed to prepare for the storm of misinformation that could begin to seep into the community and risk fractures in their movement.

With a stubborn resolve, she knew they would need to gather everyone once more, reinforcing bonds of trust and commitment before the tides shifted beneath them. Their efforts were not in vain; they had brought light to hidden truths, but the shadows still threatened to rise against them.

As she and her team regrouped later, Alison felt fierce determination alongside her allies. They would not yield to fear; instead, they would confront the lies that Coral Reef Enterprises sought to unveil. They would prepare to act with clarity and unity, ready to combat whatever storm lay ahead.

The horizon may be darkened, but she sensed that they had forged a bond strong enough to withstand the aftermath. Their resolve would guide them through the waves of deception, bolstered by a commitment to protect their reef—a journey only just beginning. Together, they would rise toward the dawn of new beginnings, prepared to unveil the truths lurking in the shadows and confront the challenges that awaited them.

~ Twenty Three ~

The day of the counter-campaign had arrived, and the atmosphere in Cairns was thick with anticipation as Alison stood outside the community center, watching reporters line up to capture what was expected to be a defining moment in their fight. Coral Reef Enterprises had scheduled a press conference of their own, and the stakes felt heightened—the battle for public perception had officially escalated.

Alison could feel the waves of anxiety wash over her as she linked arms with Finn, Sarah, and Eva, standing firm alongside the community that had rallied around them. They had spent countless hours preparing for this moment, gathering evidence and fostering connections to ensure their voices could collectively rise. But the tension simmering around the day felt almost tangible, threatening to unravel their hard-won progress.

"Are we truly ready for this?" Sarah asked, a hint of worry lining her brow as she surveyed the crowd forming outside the center.

"We've prepared for every angle they could take," Finn reassured her, squeezing her hand. "If they try to spin this in their favor, we'll counter with our own facts. The truth is on our side."

Alison nodded in agreement, her heart steadier with his words. "We have to remain vigilant. If anything distracts from our message, it'll give them an opening to manipulate the narrative."

As the minutes ticked down, the atmosphere began to crackle with excitement. News crews prepared their cameras, eager to capture the unfolding drama between champions of the reef and the representatives of Coral Reef Enterprises. The community had come together, united by their shared cause, and Alison felt grateful to be part of something so powerful.

At the forefront, the Coral Reef representatives, led by Dr. Grant and O'Reilly, stepped out into the spotlight. The crowd murmured as the tension heightened. Alison focused intently as O'Reilly approached the podium, ready to launch his attack.

"Thank you all for coming today," O'Reilly began, his tone smooth as oil. "Today, we defend Coral Reef Enterprises against unfounded accusations, which only serve to sow discord in our community."

Alison felt a flicker of irritation rising within her. Was he already attempting to spin the narrative? The crowd shifted uneasily, anticipation mixing with apprehension.

"We have always acted in the best interest of this community," O'Reilly continued, seamlessly weaving together statements designed to evoke sympathy. "It is unfortunate that a handful of misinformed citizens wish to disrupt our commitment to preserving the treasures of the reef they claim to support."

The murmurs among the crowd grew louder, agitation spreading as Alison could feel the frustration rising like a wave.

Before she could process her thoughts, Dr. Grant joined O'Reilly, his expression serious. "As a company rooted in research and advocacy, we value accountability—but that accountability runs both ways," he asserted, narrowing his gaze at the crowd. "We will not stand for a reckless campaign driven by misinformation."

Alison felt the collective anger of the audience rise as emotions began to simmer, anticipating the pushback from those she stood with.

"This is not about misinformation," Finn shouted, stepping forward, his voice filled with conviction. "This is about transparency! You speak of accountability, yet your organization has a track record of deceit! You're trying to sidestep the very real impacts your practices have had on this community!"

Alison felt the energy of their supporter's surge, emboldened by Finn's words. The crowd began shouting for justice, demanding answers and pushing back against the narrative being spun before them.

Seeing the enthusiasm around her, Alison seized the moment. She stepped up next to Finn, addressing the community with a fierce passion. "We won't allow Coral Reef Enterprises to manipulate our truths! Together, we have uncovered evidence of their deceit—financial misrepresentations and broken promises that directly affect our reef and our lives!"

"People deserve to know the truth!" shouted someone from the audience, fueling the momentum further.

Defiant cheers erupted, and Alison used this to her advantage, her voice growing stronger. "The lies have been buried far too long; we must bring them to the surface! The health of our community and the future of our reef depend on the choices we make right now."

As O'Reilly and Dr. Grant exchanged glances, it became clear their facade of confidence was beginning to crack—a realization that their carefully woven narrative might not hold.

"Don't be swayed by their antics!" O'Reilly shouted, trying to regain control. "Consider the livelihoods that would be jeopardized. This is reckless and harmful!"

"Well, what's truly harmful is the collapsing ecosystem that sustains us!" Finn shot back, his voice unwavering. "Our fight is rooted in protecting the environment that feeds the community itself. Standing back while unethical practices continue is far more damaging!"

The crowd erupted into applause, their voices uniting in a collective force of resolve—a sharp contrast to the tension that had threatened to undermine them just moments ago. They had recognized an undeniable truth, and it sent the atmosphere buzzing with energy and conviction.

For a moment, it felt as though they could ride this wave to victory. But just as the momentum surged, Alison noticed a flicker of regrouping among Dr. Grant and O'Reilly—an implied strategy taking shape behind their cleverly crafted smiles.

"Let's not lose sight of the bigger picture," Dr. Grant interjected, his voice calm but now laced with desperation. "This community has thrived because of the partnerships we've fostered, and it's important to understand the delicate balance we work to maintain."

"Delicate balance?" Alison echoed, incredulity gripping her words. "At what point do we prioritize profit over our ecosystem? A delicate balance means nothing if natural beauty continues to plummet!"

The atmosphere in the room intensified again, rising as people began to express long-held frustrations. Alison felt the weight of the moment shift, sensing the discontent in the air, while O'Reilly and Dr. Grant began to show signs of agitation.

"Enough of this nonsense!" O'Reilly shouted, hands balled into fists. "You're nothing more than an unorganized group of radicals trying to tear down the very fabric of this town!"

"We are not radicals! We are guardians of this community and the reef!" Tommy declared, stepping forward and signaling toward the crowd. "We demand the fostering of a healthy environment, not the continued destruction of our waters!"

The air crackled with energy as the crowd rallied behind Tommy, their voices rising to a fevered pitch. In that moment, it was clear the tide had flipped; awareness had become fire, igniting a collective determination to push back against the impending threats of Coral Reef Enterprises.

As Alison stood among her allies, conviction coursing through her veins, she could feel the echoes of truth solidifying around her—an irrefutable sense of unity that refused to bend to adversity.

But Dr. Grant, desperate to regain some semblance of control, stepped back, his voice cool yet sharp. "We will not let a small faction dictate the future of our community. You can hurl accusations but attempts to undermine our organization will lead to consequences you haven't considered."

"Consequences?" Finn spat, anger flashing in his eyes. "What, intimidation and fear? That's not going to work on us. We're here to expose the truth!"

The emotion in the room surged, as each person began to express their agreement, voices rising in a growing wave of determination. In that moment, Alison felt a renewed sense of clarity—nothing would hold them back from the revelations they sought.

In that charged space filled with raw energy, they found themselves forming not just a coalition against Coral Reef Enterprises but a collective voice willing to stand against manipulation and corruption, ready to navigate the turbulent waters ahead.

As the confrontation reached its peak, Alison glanced toward the corners of the room, the faces of supporters lit with resolve. Even as shadows loomed larger with the threats they faced, she felt the warmth of shared purpose pushing away the fears that had threatened to divide them.

The fight was far from over, but together, they stood at the precipice of change, ready to cast light on the truth and reclaim the narrative that had been drifting away from them for too long. United, they would push forward against the tides of deception, their hearts tied to the reef and the community they lovingly called home.

The days following the tense press conference were filled with a profound sense of anticipation and uncertainty within Cairns. Alison and her allies had bared their truths before the community, but now they faced the reality of Coral Reef Enterprises' retaliation. As the echoes of confrontation faded, the threat of discreditation loomed larger than ever, casting shadows on the community they had worked so diligently to unite.

Alison stood at the community center that evening, surrounded by scattered papers and fading light. As the hour drew near for their next strategic meeting, she felt the weight of responsibility pressing down upon her like the dark clouds overhead. They had unearthed substantial evidence, but as the fallout began to spread, sentiments of doubt surfaced once more.

Tommy entered first, his expression grave. "Have you seen the latest articles? Coral Reef Enterprises is already spinning the narrative to paint us as a fringe group with no real connection to the community."

"How deep do their connections run?" Finn asked, scanning the room, anxiety flickering in his eyes. "Are they pulling allies away from us?"

"Worse than we thought," Tommy replied, frustration etched in his voice. "They're leveraging their relationships with local businesses and the politicians who back them. If they can force enough doubt into the narrative, we risk losing any newfound trust we've built."

"Then we need to stabilize our support," Alison responded, her heart heavy with the implications. "We need something more than passionate speeches; we must truly address the fears of the community while presenting the irrefutable evidence we have gathered."

Just then, the door creaked open, and another familiar face entered—the woman who had approached Alison at the docks days earlier, her expression serious and intent as she joined their small gathering.

"I'm glad I found you," she said, her voice urgent. "I have more information that may help you navigate these turbulent waters."

Alison felt her heart race at the sight of her. "Thank you for coming. What do you have?"

"Things are escalating," the woman began, sharing the intelligence she had gathered. "I spoke to a few community members, and they mentioned how Coral Reef Enterprises has been trying to cut off any support from the local government. They're attempting to frame you as troublemakers who are harming Cairns' economy."

Alison exchanged worried glances with her friends. The organization had stooped to new depths, and the treacherous waters were only becoming murkier. "What can we do to counteract this?" she pressed.

"Your focus needs to shift," the woman advised. "Form alliances with local environmental organizations or non-profits that have the community's interests at heart. If you can secure backing from more established entities, it will add credibility to your cause and offer protection against accusations from Coral Reef."

"Great idea," Tommy said with a nod, realizing the importance of fortifying their position. "We need to create a coalition that presents a united front against Coral Reef Enterprises—something that includes trusted allies who can reinforce our assertions."

Over the next few days, Alison dove into reaching out to local organizations, driven by the knowledge that they needed allies—those who had long fought for environmental integrity and shared her values. She found support from established groups and activists who had long been champions of the preservation of Cairns' natural beauty.

As connections expanded and support began to swell, the atmosphere shifted. They started forging alliances that could bolster their campaign, an echo of solidarity solidifying around them. But as they pushed forward, a sense of unease still threaded through the community—an undercurrent of tension amplified by Coral Reef's continued manipulation.

In the days leading up to the coalition's first public event, Alison gathered with Finn, Tommy, and Eva. They were bent over a table, reviewing materials together—the weight of their evidence illuminating the path before them. Their unyielding commitment fused together, forming a foundation that felt increasingly resolute.

"We can't afford any missteps, especially given the state of unrest in town," Finn reminded them, his eyes serious. "The moment we show vulnerability, Coral Reef Enterprises will pounce."

"Right," Alison agreed, her determination resonating throughout the room. "We need to assess the strengths of our coalition and ensure that we're all aligned on our message. If we do this right, we can shift the momentum totally in our favor."

Just then, a familiar figure appeared at the door, and Alison's heart tightened. It was Lucas, his demeanor more somber than she remembered. "Alison, I need to talk," he said, urgency etched across his features.

"What's wrong?" Alison asked, sensing the weight of his words before he even spoke.

"I overheard something," he replied, stepping closer. "Coral Reef Enterprises is not just targeting you directly; they're trying to turn some community leaders against you. They're attempting to fuel divisions and distract from the messages that empower you all."

A sense of dread gripped Alison's heart, her mind racing. "Are you saying they're actively seeking allies to undermine our progress?"

"Yes," Lucas confirmed, his voice grave. "They have people infiltrating our gatherings, sowing distrust and generating narratives that pit members against one another."

Finn stepped forward, determination rising in his expression. "This is unacceptable! If they're using tactics like these, we need to confront them with a united front! Their influence can't over-shadow the community's commitment to the cause."

"Then we strategize," Alison declared, resolve hardening within her. "We'll address any fractures and ensure our message is loud and unwavering. No more whispers of dissent. We'll push back against any attempts to create chaos."

"Agreed," Eva said, her eyes bright with intensity. "We're stronger together, and we can counter their narrative by empha-sizing transparency and the power of our coalitions."

With purpose ignited, they worked long into the evening, each member rallying around the resolve to shield their movement from the impending storm. They would not allow misinformation to corrode their foundation; they would rise against the deceptive currents and fortify their standings with every ounce of strength provided by their alliances.

As the days twisted into nights and the tension escalated, Alison's heart raced with both fear and determination. The tide was changing, but so too was the complexity of their mission. She knew that they would need to walk carefully, an intricate dance of transparency and strength.

When the night of the coalition's inaugural event arrived, the community center buzzed with excitement. Familiar faces filled the hall, each imbued with a sense of purpose as they prepared to witness the unity that had been forged amidst turbulent times. This was not just an event; it was a declaration that they would no longer be silenced.

With her heart pounding, Alison stood at the front, ready to embrace the collective spirit within the room. Tonight, they would share their truth, honor their alliances, and shine a light on the shadows threatening their cause.

"Together, we will navigate these waters," she declared, the en-ergy invigorating the room. "We stand united in our mission to protect the reef, our community, and our shared future. Let today mark the beginning of a new chapter in our fight, one defined by courage, collaboration, and truth!"

As the audience erupted into cheers and applause, Alison felt the weight of her journey lift, knowing they had forged a path that would carry them into the future—together, ready to face the tides and conquer the storms. Their mission would not end here; it was merely the beginning of their story, one made of solidarity, resilience, and the unwavering truth of who they had become.

~ Twenty Four ~

The air was electric with anticipation as the coalition's inaugural event unfolded in the community center. The resonating energy from the gathered crowd filled the space as Alison stood at the forefront, her heart swelling with pride. They had come together after the chaos of past weeks—confronting betrayal, uniting against manipulation, and forging a path toward a brighter future for the reef.

As the evening progressed, stories were shared, each voice echoing the importance of preserving the ocean and the promises made to the community. The energy in the room felt like a tide rising, washing away doubts that had previously threatened to pull them under. Alison's spirits soared as she watched familiar faces rally together, all determined to transform their love for the reef into collective action.

But even amidst the surge of camaraderie, a sense of uncertainty lingered just beneath the surface. Though the gathering was flourishing with conviction, Alison couldn't shake the feeling that they needed to confront the undercurrents that sought to disrupt their unity. The whispers of fears crept back in, despite their shared commitment.

"Let's take a moment to reflect on why we're here," she said, addressing the crowd and holding her breath as their eyes turned toward her. "This is about our relationship with the reef and the future of our community. It's crucial that we move forward together, but we must be mindful of the potential fractures that still remain."

She could see heads nodding in agreement, yet she sensed the unease rippling through the audience. People felt the weight of their fears; the threat of Coral Reef Enterprises still loomed on the horizon. "It's vital that we maintain this unity," she continued, determination through every word. "If we want to challenge any existing narratives being thrust upon us, we must stand as one community."

The room buzzed with murmurs of discontent and renewed energy, the dynamic shifting as they engaged in open dialogue and shared their concerns. Individuals voiced their doubts, their business fears mingling with a desire for transparency that felt increasingly tangible.

As the crowd debated, a voice rose from the back. "But what happens when we push too hard? What if Coral Reef retaliates against the movement?" One of the older fishermen expressed, cautious but sincere. "These are things we must consider."

"Are we to remain complacent, allowing fear to dictate our actions?" another voice cut in, fueled with passion. "If we don't speak up and challenge Coral Reef Enterprises, we risk losing the marine life that has sustained us!"

The tension mounted as conflicting opinions rippled through the crowd, doubt threatening to unravel their newfound unity. Alison could feel her heart race, sensing the pivotal moment that lay before them. Would they choose the safety of silence or the risks that came with confronting the truth head-on?

Finally, Finn stepped forward, lifting his voice over the escalating debate. "Together, we have the strength to combat our fears. We must remember, in the face of intimidation, that we are in this together for the same cause. The tide of our fight should never shift in favor of fear. If history has taught us anything, it's that silence will only lead to more harm."

Alison felt the weight of his words settle in the room like an anchor, stirring hope amid the uncertainty. She decided to use the moment to remind them why they were gathered. "I know the ramifications are frightening," she reached out, her voice encouraging. "But we are here to reclaim our narrative, acknowledge our fears, and refuse to be divided. Together, we have the power to change the conversation."

As the discussions pivoted back toward solidarity, Alison sensed a shift within the audience—an understanding emerging from the tension's undertow. They were more than just supporters; they were a collective force fueled by shared values and an undeniable resolve to protect their community and the precious reef.

The gathering continued, increasing in fervor as emotions surged, stories resonating jolting sparks of commitment. The coalition began to solidify a platform, one anchored by the truths they had uncovered, casting light on the shadows that had long lurked amidst the tidal waves of manipulation.

But as the night drew to a close and attendees began to depart, Alison felt a mix of triumph and unease. While they had made significant strides in building solidarity, she knew an even larger force awaited them—a looming conflict with Coral Reef Enterprises that would test the fabric of the trust they had worked so diligently to weave.

That evening, before falling asleep, Alison reflected on the emotional tones that had been present throughout the gathering—all the heartbreak and resilience intermingled, creating a current of redemption that promised to carry them through.

In the quiet of her room, beneath the soft whispers of the night, she found her thoughts drifting to Mark—the inspiration behind their fight. Each day they pressed forward both honored his legacy and illuminated the path for her own aspirations.

With renewed determination, she vowed to navigate the tumultuous waters ahead, ready to face the challenges that Coral

Reef Enterprises would present. They had weathered storms before, and she felt empowered by the shared journey that lay before them.

With the dawn of another day approaching, Alison felt the undercurrents of unity marinate steadily within her. Each heartbeat echoed the stories that had illuminated their truths, promising that while the road ahead might be fraught with turmoil, their voices would stand together as a beacon against the darkness.

Together, they would rise, facing every obstacle before them, ready to unveil the depths of corruption and manipulation that stood against the heart of their community and the ocean they loved. United, they would forge ahead into the new horizon, strength unwavering in the face of adversity.

The days stretched on as the rallying cry for the reef echoed throughout Cairns. After the coalition's crucial gathering and the increased tension from Coral Reef Enterprises, Alison felt a sense of purpose flooding her life. The sense of unity forged with her friends and community had rekindled a fire within, yet beneath the surface of their shared fight simmered a more personal conflict—her deepening feelings for Finn.

As she busied herself with preparations for their next outreach event, Alison found her thoughts frequently drifting to him. The way he had stood by her side during the previous gatherings and how he believed in her mission made her feel safe amidst the chaos. There was a connection that had blossomed, yet it left her torn between the urgency of their fight and the emotions bubbling beneath the surface.

That afternoon, the sun hung low as Alison reviewed documents at the café where they had once gathered. The café buzzed with life, but she found it hard to concentrate, her mind racing as memories of her interactions with Finn swirled like warm eddies in her thoughts. Just then, the bell above the door chimed, drawing her attention as Finn entered, a wide grin lighting his face.

"Hey! You've been busy," he remarked, sliding into the seat across from her, his eyes shining. "How's the planning going?"

"Good, but I think we need to focus on reinforcing our relationships with the community," Alison replied, eager to shift back to their shared mission. "If we can keep people aligned with our cause, we can create a stronger front against Coral Reef Enterprises."

"Absolutely," Finn agreed, leaning forward, engaged. "We should reach out to those who haven't been fully involved yet. There are still whispers of doubt, and we need to minimize those."

As they discussed ways to strengthen their outreach, Alison could feel the familiar warmth spreading across her chest while their chemistry simmered. Moments lingered, filled with stolen glances and the electric connection that seemed to pulse between them. Every shared smile and brush of hands intensified the complicated stirrings of emotion within Alison—a tension that refused to settle.

"Do you think we'll really see a return to unity?" she asked, her voice quieter than she intended. "I know we can expose the truth, but what if we destroy trust in the process?"

Finn studied her with an intensity that made her heart race. "It's a risk we have to take. But the truth can ultimately rebuild trust. Corruption thrives in secrecy; by bringing everything into the light, we can forge stronger bonds, not only with each other but with our community."

"It's easy to preach that, but fear can be a strong force in people's lives," she admitted, the weight of doubt coloring her words. "What if we lose others in the fight?"

Finn leaned closer, earnestness glimmering in his eyes. "Alison, after everything we've overcome, we are on the verge of something that could change everything. But we can't let those fears control our actions. Our mission is built on truths, and honesty is the cornerstone of any relationship."

His words resonated within her, but amid the discussion of strategy, the emotional currents between them remained uncharted. Alison felt her resolve falter as desire lingered in the quiet spaces of their conversations, knocking against the weight of their ever-present tensions.

As they wrapped up their meeting and prepared to head out for a late lunch, a fleeting thought crossed Alison's mind—the notion of exploring her connection with Finn, yet both the conflicts of their fight and the gravity of their passion felt competing.

"We've got to keep moving," Alison finally said, her voice settling into determination as they left the café behind, backpacks slung over their shoulders. "We need to engage as many people from the community as possible."

The sun had begun to dip lower in the sky, painting their path in hues of warm gold—reminders of the beauty they fought for. But as they walked, a familiar shadow fell over them, a sudden chill in the air as they encountered Lucas standing at the edge of the street, his expression grave.

"Hey, you two," he said, his voice trembling slightly. "I just heard more news—I don't know how to say this, but Coral Reef Enterprises is ramping up their attacks against anyone associated with your movement. There are whispers about targeting press folks who've covered you, even going so far as to threaten legal action."

Alison felt a sinking sensation in her stomach. "Threatening who? We've done everything by the book!"

"They're targeting those who could potentially sway the narrative in your favor," Lucas explained, anxiety lining his voice. "It feels like they're coming after anyone who rocks the boat, and if you're connected to the upheaval..."

Alison's heart raced, anger bubbling up again as the shadows of manipulation threatened to tighten around them. "They're trying to intimidate us! They can't silence our message!"

Finn glanced at Alison, concern etched in his features. "This is getting serious. We need a firm response—something to counter any pushes against us."

Determined, Alison nodded, feeling the weight of her resolve return. "Then we prioritize solidifying our connections with the press. We'll approach them again and ensure they understand how Coral Reef operates. We need to build a fortress from truth."

As they prepared to defend their movement, a sense of urgency surged through Alison. She knew they wouldn't just stand by; they would counteract the tides that threatened to drown their mission. In their unity, they would expose the depths of Cornwall Reef's deception and the lengths they were willing to go in order to silence the collective voice that had begun to rise.

Later that evening, they gathered at the community center again, eager to share their findings and outline their next steps. As they strategized, the shadow of doubt that had tried to resurface gradually transformed into an unbreakable bond, an alliance fortified by shared purpose.

As Alison stood at the front of the room, a flicker of awareness passed between her and Finn. In that moment, the tumult within her heart quieted as she sensed that while the challenges, they faced were fraught with complexity, their growing connection didn't need to be a distraction; rather, it could be a source of strength.

With the community gathered around them, every heartbeat resonated within her—reminding her that this fight went beyond individual desires; it was about uniting in purpose and unwavering commitment. Bound by truth, they were ready to confront whatever awaited them, prepared to push back against the darkness that threatened their hopes.

Together, they would shape the narrative, rise above fear, and fight for the future they believed in—one forged by hope, resilience, and the undeniable bonds that connected their hearts in this turbulent journey. And even as challenges loomed large, they would navigate the waters ahead as allies and friends, steadfast in their mission to protect the reef and the narrative that belonged to them all.

~ Twenty Five ~

The atmosphere in Cairns felt electric, charged with anticipation as Alison and her allies prepared for what felt like a defining moment in their fight against Coral Reef Enterprises. The previous weeks had brought both triumph and tension—new alliances forged, but the threat of retaliation loomed heavily. As the press conference approached, Alison understood that they had exhausted almost every avenue; now, it was time to go public with everything they had uncovered.

Gathered in the community center, the room hummed with a mixture of excitement and apprehension. Local business owners, environmental activists, artists, and community members filled each seat, all drawn together by a shared purpose. It felt like a family affair, yet the weight of what was at stake hung over them like dark clouds gathering on the horizon.

Alison stood at the front, heart racing as she looked out over the crowd. "Thank you all for coming today," she began, striving to project strength through the uncertainty spiraling within. "We stand on the threshold of something immensely important—not just for ourselves, but for every person who relies on the health of this community and our beloved reef."

A wave of applause surged through the ranks, providing a spark of reassurance. "We've gathered evidence representing the concerns of our community about Coral Reef Enterprises and the threats they pose, not just to the reef but to our livelihoods as well.

Today, we confront the truths that have long been veiled in shadows."

As she reviewed their findings, the tension in the room seemed to shift, every person leaning in toward her words. Images flashed across the screen, revealing the stark realities—financial discrepancies, environmental degradation, and testimony after testimony from those who had seen firsthand the impacts of the organization's negligence. The collective realization of what Coral Reef had done created a palpable stir among attendees.

"The truth can no longer be buried, and we cannot remain complacent while deceitfulness thrives!" Alison declared, passion lighting her voice. "We owe it to ourselves, and we owe it to those who came before us to stand together and demand accountability!"

But just as momentum began to build within the audience, a familiar voice echoed through the hall—Dr. Grant had returned, flanked by several supporters from Coral Reef Enterprises. Alison's heart sank, tension ricocheting through the crowd as the atmosphere shifted once again.

"Excuse me," Dr. Grant announced, his tone smooth yet dripping with condescension. "This is nothing but a misguided witch hunt against a reputable organization that has dedicated itself to marine conservation."

"We're here because we care about the truth!" Finn shouted, stepping forward, his eyes blazing with conviction. The nervous energy in the room simmered, yet beneath their anger, Alison could sense a flicker of doubt—this encounter could be pivotal.

"Is it truth you seek?" Dr. Grant responded, raising an eyebrow. "Or is it the false narrative designed to get you clicks, views, and attention? You are treading uncertain waters, and once you dive in, it could have detrimental effects."

Alison felt the crowd twitch, wavering beneath the weight of his words, uncertainty threatening to bubble up once more. "You can't manipulate the narrative any longer!" she pressed, steadiness returning to her voice. "We have evidence that reveals your organization's hidden motivations. It's clear that you've prioritized profit over responsibility."

Just then, O'Reilly stepped up beside Dr. Grant, crossing his arms as he surveyed the crowd. "This is reckless, and it will harm your reputations in the community," he warned, his voice smooth but filled with veiled threats. "What you're attempting to ignite will only lead to reputational ruin—both for the individuals speaking out and for the local businesses supporting Coral Reef."

The crowd shifted uncomfortably, and for a heartbeat, Alison could see the doubts creeping back into their expressions. They had fought so hard for unity, only to have this provocative reminder of fear push against it.

"Wait," a voice from the crowd called out. It was Sarah, a fierce look in her eyes as she stepped forward. "We won't be intimidated into silence! We're not here for personal gain; we're fighting for our community and for the future of the reef!"

As Sarah spoke, an electric charge surged through the room, one that Alison had felt before. The crowd seemed to rally around her, agreeing and affirming their commitment to protect their shared mission.

"Your tactics won't work, O'Reilly," Finn added, his voice resolute. "Intimidation has no place in this fight. You may think you can scare us into submission, but we're fueled by truth!"

As the audience began to cheer in response to Finn's declaration, Alison felt the momentum shift once more. This was what they needed—their voices rising above the manipulative rhetoric of Coral Reef Enterprises, empowered by the very truth they sought to uphold.

"Let's focus on what this means for us. We're at a crucial juncture," Alison emphasized, rallying the energy in the room. "We need to ensure we're prepared to navigate the backlash. If they're willing to play dirty, we need to stand firm in our resolve."

Determined voices began to rise, united by a common goal: to reclaim their narrative and dismantle the corporate stranglehold that had ensnared them for far too long.

As the dialogue turned more proactive, Alison realized they were shifting back toward unity—rallying behind the truth they had amassed.

But then, just as the crowd began to regain its footing, a figure emerged—the woman who had previously approached Alison at the docks, her face pale and expression filled with urgency.

"What are you doing here?" Alison asked, concern sharpening her voice.

"I'm sorry to interrupt," the woman said, breathless as she reached their side. "I just learned something crucial—I overheard Coral Reef Enterprises talking amongst themselves about the next phase of their strategy."

All eyes turned to the woman, tension woven into every expression as they tried to grasp the implications of her words.

"They plan to launch a smear campaign, targeting you personally, Alison. They'll dig into your past, trying to use anything they can find to undermine your credibility," she warned, shaking slightly as she spoke.

A wave of dread swept through the room, the realization lingering in the air like an impending storm. With each word, it became clear that the battle against Coral Reef Enterprises wasn't just a challenge against an organization—it was a personal confrontation that could threaten the very core of their mission.

"What do you mean 'dig into my past'?" Alison felt her heart racing, fear coiling around her.

"I mean they want to expose anything that could weaken the community's trust in your leadership," the woman replied relentlessly. "Everything is on the table. They're going to turn those who are unsure against you."

Finn stepped closer to Alison, his face etched with concern. "We can't let this shake us. They may try, but we need to be transparent—our truths strengthen us."

"Transparency is paramount for our movement," Alison said, resolve flooding her system as she nodded. "We need to be vigilant and prepared. We'll tackle whatever comes our way, united as a community."

"Together," Tommy and Eva added firmly, their voices rising in solidarity. "Together."

But even as optimism began to trend upward, Alison felt the storm brewing around them. Knowing that the costs would be steep, she silently navigated her own emotions, preparing to confront not just the organization but the personal impacts it might have on her life.

As the meeting drew to a close, a sense of determination radiated throughout the crowd. They gathered together, aware of the challenges that lay ahead and promising to remain vigilant. But Alison understood that stepping into the spotlight could bring both external threats and personal struggles she had yet to face.

That evening, lingering uncertainties weighed heavily on her mind. She would need to confront not just the organization but the shadows growing closer—the remnants of her past that Coral Reef Enterprises might exploit.

With hope tinged with trepidation still bubbling within her, she knew now more than ever that they were bound for change. Together, they would face the tides of corruption, rising as guardians of their reef and champions of their narrative, determined to navigate the storm ahead. Together, they would bristle against the deceit lurking beneath the surface, ready to expose the truth and protect the future of their community and beloved ocean.

The atmosphere in Cairns had grown tense as Alison and her allies prepared for the moment that could reshape their fight against Coral Reef Enterprises. After weeks of encountering threats and navigating turbulent waters, they now stood at the threshold of unveiling the final pieces of evidence that could expose the organization's deception. Tonight was their chance to present everything they'd gathered—not only to the community but also to local officials and press, ensuring their message reached the largest audience possible.

With an air of purpose, Alison gathered in the community center for the much-anticipated press event. The room was a blend of excitement and anxiety, a palpable current that pulsed through the assembly of community members, journalists, and local activists. Each face reflected a mix of hope and determination, but beneath the surface, Alison could still sense the fragility that had settled in as a result of Coral Reef's strong-arm tactics.

"Alison, are you ready?" Eva called out, sensing the slight tremor in Alison's resolve as she studied the assembled crowd.

"Ready as I'll ever be," Alison replied, drawing a deep breath to steady her nerves. "Tonight is about unveiling the truth that lies beneath the surface—a truth we all deserve to see."

As the hours ticked down, attendees settled into their seats, and Alison felt a familiar sense of expectation ripple through the room. Just before they were set to begin, Finn appeared at her side, concern woven into his features. "How are you holding up?" he asked, his voice low.

"I'm anxious. But I'm also convinced we need to do this," she said, gratitude swelling in her chest for his unwavering support. "We've come too far to let fear get to us now."

As the press conference commenced, Alison stepped up to the podium with careful poise, scanning the audience filled with eager faces. "Thank you all for coming tonight. We gather here as a united force, standing firm in our commitment to protect our reef and our community," she began, voice steady despite the emotions swirling within.

With a swipe of her hand, she called up the first slide, images of the deteriorating coral flanking the walls of the community center. "Recent evidence has revealed that Coral Reef Enterprises has not only misrepresented their involvement but has also concealed critical financial dealings tied directly to our environment," she stated with resolve as murmurs of surprise surged through the crowd.

Sharing the evidence collected over the weeks—financial documents, testimonies from affected fishermen, and even insider accounts—the room seemed to respond, emotions simmering just below the surface. The crowd absorbed the information, each moment feeling like a battle cry echoing against the institution they were challenging.

"People of Cairns, I stand before you not just as an advocate but as a voice for our community," she declared passionately. "We deserve transparency, and we must hold those who exploit our precious resources accountable!"

The energy in the room shifted as support surged, fueled by the stories being shared. Each testimony unfolding carried the weight of their shared experiences—painful narratives woven from years of devotion to the reef and the community.

Yet just when the moment seemed to pulse with unity, a hand shot up from the back of the room. It was O'Reilly, a scowl on his face. "This is nothing but a fabrication! You think sensationalizing unproven claims will get you anywhere? You're destroying the foundation of trust within our community!"

Alison felt her heart race, knowing there would always be pushback from him. "We're not here to destroy trust—we're here to reclaim it!" she countered sharply, determined to face the challenge head-on. "If there's nothing to hide, why not be open about your financial dealings? Why not show the people they deserve to see what's at stake?"

Murmurs swept through the crowd, uncertainty dancing beneath the surface. Alison sensed the tide was shifting, and she needed to assure the audience that their fight was worth the risks they faced.

"Your tactics will not intimidate us into silence," she continued, rallying the support around her. "We've had enough of hollow promises and unchecked practices! If you're genuinely here for the community, it's time to show us!"

Once again, the applause erupted, shaking the walls of the gathering. Backed by Finn and the shared energy of those gathered, Alison felt a warmth igniting within her—a reminder that they were not merely standers by in this fight, but agents of change.

But then, as the energy surged, a sudden commotion erupted from the side. A group of locals had entered the gathering—seminal figures in their community who had remained on the fringes until now. They approached the platform, their expressions serious.

"We've been listening," one of them said, his voice steady. "This conversation is too important. We can't afford to let fear and doubt fracture our unity! If we're going to fight for the reef, we need to stand together."

Those words struck a chord, amplifying the energy in the room as others began to rise, expressions turning from uncertainty to solidarity. "Let us speak, too!" another voice called out, echoing the sentiment. "This is about all our futures."

As people stepped forward to voice their stories, the tides began to shift decisively. The crowd was no longer a mere audience; it had transformed into an empowered collective, ready to confront the looming threat of Coral Reef Enterprises.

Alison felt a wave of gratitude wash over her as she witnessed the community embracing the need for action and solidarity. Together, they could fortify their ranks, armed with testimonies and shared beliefs that would render Coral Reef's threats powerless.

Once the evening concluded, Alison knew that the path ahead would still be fraught with challenges. But as she looked into her friends' faces—Finn, Eva, and the community members who had stood strong—she could feel the weight of their collective energy shifting toward a formidable front.

They had turned the tide against Coral Reef Enterprises that night, securing a powerful momentum born of truth and unity. With the evidence laid before them and the voices of the community resonating in harmony, they were ready to push back against whatever retaliatory storm awaited them.

The moon hung high in the sky, illuminating the path forward. Together, they would navigate the turbulent waters ahead united by a shared purpose and an unwavering commitment to reclaim the future for their reef, their community, and the legacy they would build in honor of those who had come before them.

Alison knew the fight was just beginning, but as she stood amongst her friends, she felt an undeniable sense of hope, ready to confront both the obstacles and the darkness that lingered just beneath the surface. With every heartbeat of resolve echoing in the evening air, they were poised to shine the light of truth on the shadows, and together they would emerge victorious.

~ Twenty Six ~

The early morning light bathed Cairns in a soft golden glow, a welcome sight that felt like a harbinger of hope. But for Alison and her team, the events of the previous night lingered heavily. The community had rallied behind their cause, yet tensions with Coral Reef Enterprises reached a new climax, escalating the stakes of their ongoing struggle.

After the press conference, Alison had returned home, thoughts racing with the implications of what lay ahead. They had unveiled their findings and rallied the community, but O'Reilly's words about repercussions echoed ominously in her mind. What would Coral Reef Enterprises do next? How far would they go to protect their twisted narrative?

She gathered at the community center that morning with Finn, Eva, and Tommy, all three of them eager to discuss how best to address the situation. The atmosphere oscillated between the promise of momentum and the shadow of fear that had tried to seep back into their movement.

"Okay, we need to plan our next steps carefully," Alison said, her voice steady as she took a deep breath. "Reports of Coral Reef's retaliatory actions have already started to surface. We need to anticipate their moves and remain proactive."

"We've shown we can garner community support, even if some are still tentative," Eva added, her tone resolute. "But the whispers of doubt cannot take root again. We need to assure our allies that standing together is paramount."

"Let's also consider reaching out to some regional environmental organizations," Tommy suggested. "If we can gain their backing, it'll bolster our credibility and may draw eyes away from any potential smear campaign they might organize against us."

"Good point. We need to build a coalition that extends beyond our local reach," Finn chimed. "It'll help reinforce that we stand as part of a larger environmental movement, showing that this fight for the reef is shared across many communities."

Just as they began discussing the logistics of these efforts, a sudden voice interrupted—the voice of Lucas, who rushed into the room, a look of concern etched across his face.

"Guys, I need to talk to you," he said, his voice strained. "I've just learned that Coral Reef Enterprises is planning something—an event that might undermine everything we've worked for."

"What kind of event?" Alison asked, trepidation creeping into her tone.

"They're organizing a PR function—a major showcase claiming their commitment to the environment. They intend to present it as a direct response to the accusations you've been leveling against them," Lucas explained, anxiety palpable in his posture. "If they successfully reposition themselves as defenders of the reef, it could draw a lot of attention away from our message."

"Damn it," Alison murmured, frustration bubbling up. "They're manipulating their narrative again."

Finn stepped forward, his brow furrowed in thought. "We need to counter this proactively. If Coral Reef Enterprises is trying to distract the community with their showcase, we should plan something of our own, a counter-narrative that emphasizes facts over PR fluff."

"Yes!" Alison exclaimed, her heart racing at the thought. "Let's organize a community science day—something that showcases real data, real people, and emphasizes what we are truly fighting for."

"I love that idea," Eva said, her eyes lighting up. "We could host local experts and activists, have workshops that educate the community about the reef, and bring people together to actually participate in active restoration efforts."

"Exactly!" Tommy added, his excitement palpable. "Let's put Coral Reef Enterprises on the defensive. If we generate enough grassroots support and awareness, they won't be able to dominate the conversation. Let's show them how strong our community is together."

As they began to outline their ideas for the science day event, Alison felt a renewed surge of hope wash over her. They had faced countless challenges, but they could transform the tide in their favor—competing narratives could coexist, but the truth would cast the real light on the issues at hand.

Later that afternoon, in the bustling market, Alison and Finn met with several local environmental organizations. With conversations flowing, they drew enthusiastic responses, interested in collaborating for the community science day.

"I appreciate your commitment to inviting the community together," one representative said energetically, clasping Alison's hand. "When we stand together for the reef, we amplify the truth, and that resonates in ways that cannot be silenced. We're on board!"

As the meeting concluded, Alison felt renewed energy fluttering within her, a sense of progress washing over her amidst the excitement. But as they stepped out into the marketplace, Finn pulled her aside, voice low and earnest.

"Alison," he said, his expression serious. "There's something I've been meaning to ask. With all the chaos surrounding us, how are you managing everything? I see the pressure you're under."

The warmth of his concern stirred her heart, and she hesitated, a mix of gratitude and vulnerability rising within her. "I'm trying to keep the community moving while also reconciling my grief over losing Mark. It feels overwhelming sometimes—there's so much at stake, and I don't want to let anyone down."

Finn took a step closer, the intensity in his gaze compelling. "You've carried so much on your shoulders, but you're not alone. We're all in this... together."

As his words sunk in, Alison felt the shadows of doubt lift slightly, the connection they shared providing solace amidst the storm. She wanted to confront her emotions, to explore the bond that was developing between them, but the urgency of their fight remained at the forefront of her mind.

"It's just that... there's so much at stake, I don't want to let my feelings distract from what we're doing," she confessed, vulnerability lacing her words.

"Your feelings matter too, Alison," he said, sincerity radiating from him. "Navigating all this emotion is tough, and embracing what we feel only strengthens our efforts. Together, we can face both the community's fight and our personal connections."

The vulnerability in his voice struck a chord deep within her, igniting a warmth that spread through Alison. Their friendship had evolved into something more, and she felt it was time to acknowledge the feelings that had lingered between them.

As the sun began to dip behind the horizon, a sense of clarity settled in. The storm outside parallelled the tumultuous emotions swirling within her, but she found strength in knowing they were tethered together, navigating the depths of their shared mission and building something meaningful.

"Okay," Alison said, her voice steadying. "Let's call this a work-in-progress. But whatever comes next, I want to face it alongside you."

"Agreed," Finn nodded, a spark of understanding passing between them, igniting a sense of intimacy amidst the chaos around them.

With new resolve, they returned to the community center, the plans for the science day taking shape and bolstering the fortitude of their efforts. As they drove back into strategizing, Alison felt invigorated, the currents of unity pushing them forward.

Drawing strength from the warmth of community and the bond growing between herself and Finn, Alison knew that they would confront whatever challenges lay ahead. The fight for the reef was bigger than any single person—bathed in the light of truth, they would rise together against the tides threatening to overshadow their lives.

The morning sun may have shown warmth, but it was through the darkness, the challenges, and the heartstrings they would unite, forging a destiny intertwined with hope—ready to navigate the uncharted waters of tomorrow and whatever storms were still to come. Together, they would turn every tide, rise through every challenge, and protect that which mattered most.

The vibrant colors of dawn spilled over the horizon as Cairns awoke, stretching its arms toward the sun like a collective sigh of relief. After weeks of tension, confrontation, and the persistent specter of Coral Reef Enterprises looming over their community, a sense of resolve flowed steadily through Alison and her allies. The dawn symbolized a new beginning—a chance to reclaim their narrative and push forward with renewed vigor.

The day of the community science day had finally arrived, and the air was thick with anticipation. Alison spent the morning setting up tables, canvases, and displays that would showcase their findings and the community's collective efforts. There was an unmistakable energy buzzing through the crowd of volunteers as they prepared to educate others about the importance of protecting the reef—one of the anchors of their community.

As people gathered, the sight filled Alison with hope. Parents brought their children, friends came to support families, and artists displayed their work—all dedicated to the preservation of the reef. It was heartwarming to see the community come together, determined to demonstrate resilience in the face of adversity.

"Are you ready for this?" Finn asked, joining her at the center of the bustling activity. His smile held the bright light of determination, and she felt a steady sense of calm radiating from him.

"More than ever," Alison replied, her heart lifting. "Today is our chance to show what we're fighting for—this movement is bigger than any one of us."

As the forum began, they welcomed speakers who had an array of experiences and expertise to share. Local marine biologists, dedicated activists, and citizens who had witnessed the reef's shifting bounty stepped forward to lend their voices. Each testimony resonated with the crowd, echoing their commitment to protecting the marine ecosystem.

Hank stood at the forefront, recounting stories of thriving he had seen along the coast, as well as the decline that had ensued. "This ocean has given us life," he said, his voice rich with emotion. "We cannot let it slip through our fingers. We are the guardians of this environment, and in turn, we are guardians of our future."

With each presentation, the crowd leaned in closer, visibly moved by the shared experiences. Alison felt the energy rising—a powerful surge of solidarity. This wasn't just an event; it was a rallying cry that reinforced their commitment to the fight for the reef and the interconnected futures they all shared.

As the day wore on, they hosted workshops where community members could participate in hands-on activities related to marine conservation—learning about reef ecology, the importance of sustainable practices, and the pressing need for action. Laughter and chatter drifted through the air like melodies of hope, underscoring the strength in their collective resolve.

As dusk began to settle, casting a warm glow over the community center and the gathering, Alison stood at the edge of the activity, watching the joy unfold. She couldn't help but feel proud of how far they had come; the community bonded together in pursuit of protection rather than succumbing to the fear that had shadowed their movement just weeks prior.

When they gathered for closing remarks, Alison felt a wave of gratitude wash over her as the community listened intently. "Thank you all for being here today," she started, her heart swelling with emotion. "We stand united not just in this fight for the reef, but in our love for this community. The stories shared today reflect our interconnectedness, and it's a powerful testament to what we can achieve when we come together."

She paused, surveying the faces around her—filled with hope and determination. "The threats imposed by Coral Reef Enterprises will not distract us or deter us from our mission. We've shown that our voices matter; together, we can combat manipulation and deception."

Small clusters of applause arose around the room, voices rising in agreement. "If we've learned anything today, it's that our strength lies in unity—the more we come together, the better equipped we are to confront any threats."

As the night drew to a close, the attendees began to mingle, renewed spirits evident as laughter echoed in the air. Alison found herself chatting with an old acquaintance, a fellow business owner who had once stood on the fringes of their movement. "I've regretted not getting involved sooner," he admitted, sincerity in his voice. "Today opened my eyes. I'm in. I'll do whatever I can to support this cause."

A swell of happiness flushed over her—a reflection of the underlying strength the community had found. Alison felt they had shifted beyond fear; together, they had ignited a light of resilience, illuminating the path that lay ahead.

As the crowd slowly began to disperse, Finn approached her, a soft yet determined expression on his face. "You were remarkable today, Alison. You really brought everyone together," he said, admiration lacing his voice.

"Thank you," she replied, trying to contain the warmth blooming within her. "I couldn't have done any of this without all of you. You were all incredible."

Finn hesitated for a moment, uncertainty flickering in his eyes. "I wish I could have had the courage to open up sooner, amidst everything we've been through. But seeing you lead brought everything into perspective."

Alison felt her heart quicken at his admission. "And how do you feel about where we stand now?"

The pause hung between them like a breath suspended, fraught with possibilities. "I feel a connection I haven't been able to shake," he confessed, his honesty washing over her like a tide. "What we've built together—our shared purpose, the struggle, and everything else—it means more than brightening the future of the reef. It makes me realize how much this fight has come to mean."

"I feel it too," Alison said, emboldened by their shared truths. "The fight brought out everything within me, and while we navigate the chaos ahead, I want to confront my feelings too."

The air crackled with energy as they stood close, the evening light painting them in warm tones. But just before they could lean into that moment, Lucas returned, a look of trepidation on his face, pulling them both out of their shared gaze.

"Alison, you need to hear this," he said, urgency clear in his voice. "I saw someone lurking outside the community center earlier... someone looking for you."

"What do you mean?" Alison asked, the air suddenly thick with unease.

"Coral Reef Enterprises has eyes everywhere. They may see your growing influence and are trying to find a way to counteract it—by targeting you personally," he revealed, glancing around cautiously.

Alison felt her heart drop, the earlier warmth dissipating, replaced by the chill of dread. The comforts of the evening now tangled with the grim reality of their adversaries' employing threats and intimidation.

"We can't allow them to deter us," she said, her voice resolute, though she felt the tremors of fear still hovering nearby. "But we need to stay vigilant. Our unity is our greatest defense."

With renewed clarity taking shape in the room, she shared what she had learned, and the energy shifted again. Discussions erupted, strategizing about safety, communication, and bolstering defenses as a coalition formed—a reflex against the encroaching threat.

That night, as Alison returned home, the world outside felt charged and unpredictable. Shadows began to stretch across Cairns as daylight waned, reminding her of the challenges that lay ahead. Even as rallying cries echoed in her heart, the looming danger of Coral Reef Enterprises hung overhead, threatening to cast a pall over their fight.

But amidst the uncertainty, she felt a current of hope rising stronger than ever. The community's bond had forged a fire—in their struggle, they were becoming allies turned into family, ready to confront whatever darkness awaited. They would seek out the truth, keep the flame burning, and illuminate the shadows that Coral Reef Enterprises sought to manipulate.

With the dawn of new challenges on the horizon, Alison held tightly to the belief that together they would navigate the shifting tides, rise against the darkness, and forge a path to protect the reef that intertwined their lives in lasting connection.

~ Twenty Seven ~

The sun dipped low over Cairns, casting golden rays that danced upon the tranquil waters of the Coral Sea. Yet, beneath that shimmering surface, a maelstrom of tension brewed. Alison stood at the edge of the beach, the salty breeze tugging at her clothes while her thoughts swirled with the complexities of the battle ahead. The evidence she had gathered against Coral Reef Enterprises was damning, but she knew they wouldn't roll over quietly. They were playing for keeps, and the stakes had never been higher.

Gathering her resolve, she turned back toward her temporary home—a modest rental just off the coast. The familiar path was now a reminder of the tenuous grip she had on everything she held dear. Mark's death had ignited a fire within her, urging her on, but it also left a chasm of grief too deep to ignore. With every step, memories of their shared laughter echoed in her mind.

Inside, Eva was sifting through papers at the table, her brow furrowed with concentration. Alison's heart warmed at the sight of her friend. Despite the weight of their mission, Eva had been a beacon of support—her unwavering strength shining in the darkest moments.

"Hey," Alison said softly, sitting across from her. "How are you holding up?"

Eva looked up, a hint of worry flickering in her eyes. "I've been organizing the evidence, but I can't shake the feeling that they're planning something. The board met again last night, and I overheard whispers about 'cleaning house.' It could mean anything."

Alison took a deep breath, feeling the pressure mount. "We need to act fast. If they're tightening their grip, we have to expose them before they strike."

Just then, their phones buzzed simultaneously, and they exchanged wary glances. It was a notification from the local news app announcing an emergency meeting convened by Coral Reef Enterprises—a last-minute desperation moves to reassure the public amid rising scrutiny.

"We have to be there," Alison said, her pulse quickening. "They can't be allowed to dictate the narrative."

As she and Eva rushed to prepare, Alison felt an unease settle in her stomach. The stakes were higher than mere reputations; there was a very real threat that Coral Reef would resort to dangerous measures to maintain their power.

The atmosphere at the meeting was charged. Locals had packed the community center, their faces a mix of confusion and anger. Alison and Eva squeezed into the crowd, catching snippets of anxious conversations as they fidgeted, their anticipation palpable.

A tall, slick executive, Oliver Thatcher, stood at the podium—his polished demeanor contrived under the scrutiny of the community. He spoke of transparency and commitment to marine conservation, but Alison saw right through him. It was a performance, a smokescreen for the underhanded tactics lurking beneath.

As he droned on, a growing rumble of dissent emerged from the audience. People began to challenge him, voices rising in protest against their declining trust in the organization. Alison felt their frustration resonate within her, a mirror of her own turmoil.

Suddenly, a loud crash echoed in the back of the room. The crowd gasped as a group of masked individuals burst through the door, brandishing flash drives and cameras. "We're warning you, enough is enough!" one shouted, catching everyone off guard. "Coral Reef is running out of time!"

Alison's heart raced. This was exactly the chaos she had feared. Caught in the frenzy, she felt Eva grab her arm. "We need to leave. It's not safe here."

But before they could react, Oliver Thatcher shouted, "Security! Get these intruders out of here!" The atmosphere shifted dramatically, from defiance to panic as chaos ensued.

In the ensuing commotion, Alison's instincts kicked in. She couldn't let this moment slip away. She ducked under the flailing arms and pushed forward, determined to confront Thatcher. She had to expose him now, amidst the confusion and fear.

"Mr. Thatcher, how do you respond to the claims about your deceptive practices?" Alison called out, her voice cutting through the din. The room fell silent as every eye turned to her.

"Ms. Harper," he sneered, a glint of irritation flashing in his eyes. "This isn't the time for your antics."

"I'm here to ensure our community understands the truth about Coral Reef Enterprises!" she pressed, her voice steady. "You think you can manipulate us with false promises while you drown the reef?"

Silence lingered in the air, but the weight of her words reverberated. The crowd murmured, bolstered by her assertion. But Thatcher wasn't finished. "You will regret this, Alison. We have resources beyond your comprehension. This isn't a game you can win."

Just then, as the masked individuals were escorted out, the atmosphere shifted again, the tension setting like concrete. The realization of impending conflict hung heavy in the room. The battle lines were drawn, and they had awoken a tiger.

As the meeting adjourned in disarray, Alison turned to Eva, adrenaline flooding her veins. "We need to gather what we can.

They're cornered, and now more than ever, I trust we're on the right path."

But as they stepped out into the fading light, a chill skittered down Alison's spine. The terrifying reality of their fight lay ahead of them, and it would be a battle fraught with peril.

Tomorrow, the stakes would rise higher, and whispers in the wind would carry the truth they desperately needed to reveal.

The next morning brought clouds heavy with potential rain, mirroring the turmoil brewing in Alison's chest. As she poured herself a cup of coffee in the dim light of her kitchen, the events of the previous night replayed in her mind. The confrontation with Oliver Thatcher had stirred something deep within her, a fierce determination not only to uncover the truth but to protect what remained of her community and their precious reef.

Eva arrived moments later, looking equally determined but visibly drained. "I hardly slept last night," she confessed, sinking into a chair and rubbing her temples. "I can't shake this feeling that they're planning something big."

Alison nodded, understanding her friend's unease. "We need to stay ahead of them. Let's meet with anyone who might have inside information. We can't wait for them to make the first move."

They spent the morning reaching out to their contacts, orchestrating meetings with local fishermen, environmentalists, and even former employees of Coral Reef Enterprises. The goal was to piece together a clearer picture of the corporation's intentions and any potential schemes brewing beneath the surface.

As the afternoon slipped by, Alison felt a mix of hope and anxiety. Each conversation revealed a more complex web of corruption than she had anticipated, with murmurs of shady dealings and backdoor agreements slipping through clenched teeth. A disturbing pattern began to form, one that indicated the corporation would stop at nothing to safeguard their interests, even if it meant resorting to violent means.

At the pier, they met with Lucas, a local fisherman who had once collaborated with Coral Reef Enterprises on conservation projects but had left in disillusionment. His sun-weathered face spoke of years of hard work and betrayal as he leaned on his boat, casting wary glances toward the sleek modern vessels owned by the corporation.

"They're not in it for the reef's sake. It's about the money," Lucas stated, his voice low but emphatic. "I know they've been stockpiling resources, preparing for a big project under the guise of restoration. But it's a front, Alison."

"What kind of project?" Eva pressed, taking notes furiously.

"A mangrove restoration project. They claim it's about reviving the ecosystem, but I've heard rumors they're actually planning on building something—a new resort or even a luxury marina. They'll push locals out under the pretense of conservation, and they sound convincing, but it's just another way to exploit the land and water."

The weight of his words struck Alison like a punch. "That's why they want to control the narrative. If they can convince the community that their motivations are noble, they can keep us from opposing them."

Lucas sighed, raking a hand through his hair. "Just be careful, you two. They have eyes everywhere, and I'd hate to see you get hurt while you're poking around their business."

Dread seeped into Alison's heart. The precarious nature of their mission became all too clear. As they headed back to shore, the sky grew darker, mirroring their mood. The gathering storm was not just in the weather—it was in the very air they breathed, thick with uncertainty and danger.

Back at Alison's home, they pored over their notes, cross-referencing the information they had gathered. As they reviewed the details, the scattered pieces of the puzzle began to align. The urgency of their revelation pressed upon them.

Suddenly, Alison's phone buzzed, interrupting the quiet tension. It was a message from Tommy, her old friend and a fellow activist who had been investigating Coral Reef for months.

We need to talk. Meet me at the café on Main Street. Urgent.

"Tommy's found something," Alison said, excitement and trepidation battling within her. "This could be what we need to bring them down."

They hurried to the café, the faint sound of thunder rumbling in the distance. Once inside, they located Tommy sitting in a back booth, his brows knitted in concentration. "Thanks for coming," he said, glancing around before leaning closer. "I've gotten some intel about a shipment coming in tomorrow night—something big."

"What do you mean by 'big'?" Alison asked, her pulse quickening.

"They're bringing in construction equipment under the radar, most likely for that restoration project Lucas mentioned. I have an informant who works at the port. They're set to unload right around midnight."

"That's insane!" Eva exclaimed. "We have to get media coverage on this."

"We need hard evidence," Tommy said, urgency lacing his voice. "I need you both to come with me tonight. We can document everything, catch them red-handed. It could be our opening to expose them."

Fear and excitement waged war within Alison. The risk was high, but so was the potential reward. If they could capture undeniable proof, it would not just be their word against Coral Reef's; it would be an undeniable truth.

"We're in," Alison responded, adrenaline surging through her veins. "We can't let them win."

As they planned their operation, the first drops of rain began to fall outside, tapping gently against the window. Little did they know that the storm brewing above was reflecting the turmoil be-low as Coral Reef Enterprises prepared to take desperate mea-sures to protect their empire.

Tonight, they would walk into the eye of the storm—unset-tling, dangerous, and, perhaps, the only chance they had to turn the tide against a faceless adversary. As Alison looked outside, the gathering clouds foreboded change—strengthening her resolve while fueling the fire within. All that was required now was the courage to face what lay ahead.

~ Twenty Eight ~

The oppressive gloom of the storm settled over Cairns as darkness enveloped the town. Underneath the clouds, the atmosphere was thick with tension, a precursor to the conflict that loomed like a tide against the shore. Alison, Eva, and Tommy huddled in the shadows of an abandoned warehouse near the port, the scent of salt and impending rain in the air. The whir of the ocean waves beyond mingled with their anxious breaths.

"Remember, we're here to document everything," Tommy reiterated, glancing at the two women. "Stay close and stay quiet. We can't afford to be spotted."

Alison nodded, her heart racing. "I still can't believe we're actually doing this."

"We have to," Eva replied, determination etched on her face. "This might be our only shot to expose Coral Reef Enterprises for what they truly are."

Together, they crept closer to the dock where a series of large containers, marked with the logo of Coral Reef Enterprises, awaited unloading. The lights from nearby floodlights illuminated the area, casting looming shadows that made their hearts race. The sound of machinery echoed ominously in their ears, blending with the rhythmic drumming of raindrops starting to fall.

"Okay, there should be a small loading dock just up ahead," Tommy whispered. "That's where we'll set up. When the delivery trucks come in, we'll get the footage and then slip back out."

With hearts pounding, they moved silently toward the loading dock, crouching behind stacks of crates as the rain began to fall in earnest, soaking their clothes. The chill seeped through their skin, amplifying their adrenaline. They watched intently, the ebb and flow of their nerves riding the waves of anticipation.

Minutes turned into tense hours, and just as Alison began to doubt their timing, headlights pierced the darkness. Two large trucks rolled into view, rumbling to a stop just outside the unloading area. Her heart leaped into her throat as the figures clad in dark clothing emerged, barking orders at one another.

"Get the cameras ready!" Tommy hissed, positioning his equipment. Alison and Eva scrambled to follow suit, capturing every moment. The distant sound of thunder rumbled like the warning growls of a beast awakening.

As the workers started unloading heavy machinery—excavators and bulldozers—Alison's stomach twisted. She couldn't shake the feeling that this was more than just a construction operation; it was a direct threat to their community, to the reef she had fought to protect.

Just then, as the tension in the air reached a boiling point, one worker—a burly man with a scar running down his cheek—spotted something in the corner of his eye. "Hey! What are you doing over there?" he shouted, abruptly halting the operation.

A deafening silence swept over the dock, the air heavy with tension. The sound of machinery clanging fell still as eyes turned toward the trio hiding in the shadows. Alison's heart raced as the man began advancing toward them.

"Run!" Tommy called, urgency thrumming through his voice. In an instant, the three of them pivoted on their heels, sprinting back the way they came. The sharp thud of footsteps followed them, crashing through the rain-soaked ground.

"Don't let them get away!" a voice yelled, sending a crescendo of panic coursing through Alison's veins. Her pulse pounded in her ears as they dashed toward the trucks no longer concealed by shadows.

Alison didn't look back, but the sounds of commotion behind them intensified, and the unmistakable sound of something heavy crashing to the ground trailed them. Just as they turned a corner, a hand shot out from the darkness and caught Alison by the arm.

"Don't move!" a voice ordered, sharp and commanding. She froze, heart pounding against her ribs, desperate to break free but paralyzed by fear.

But instead of harm, she found herself face-to-face with a familiar face—Samuel Grant, the scientist from Coral Reef Enterprises, his expression a mixture of relief and urgency. "What are you doing here?" he hissed. "Were you following me?"

Alison shook her head, tearing her gaze away from his piercing eyes. "We came to expose Coral Reef Enterprises! They're planning to build—"

"I know," Samuel interrupted, glancing nervously toward the direction of the loading dock. "But you've walked straight into a trap. They're not just unloading equipment; they're eliminating loose ends."

"Loose ends?" Eva echoed, eyes wide. "What are you talking about?"

"Someone I know—someone far too close to the board—is ready to do whatever it takes to silence dissent, and that includes you."

Anger surged through Alison. "Why should we trust you? You're a part of this!"

"No—I'm not," he insisted, voice tense. "I was wrong for ever being part of their organization. They've twisted their original purpose for profit, and I couldn't stand idly by."

Horns blared from the dock, voices rose, and the chaotic shuffle of feet echoed against the night. The workers now knew they were being hunted, and the danger was rising rapidly.

"Look, if you want to stay alive and make sure your footage gets out, you have to trust me," Samuel urged, urgency thrumming through his voice. "Follow me. We can get to the east side of the docks and find a way out."

Before Alison could respond, a shout resonated from the shadows behind them, cutting through the chaos. "They're getting away! Grab them!"

In that moment, fear gripped the trio. The stakes surged higher, and they had no choice but to leap into uncertainty.

"Now, move!" Samuel commanded, leading them away from the path of danger. As they fled, the rain intensified, masking the sounds of their footsteps against the slick pavement. The world around them blurred, each beat of Alison's heart reminding her of their frailty in facing a well-armed adversary.

The hasty escape through the downpour became a blur of faces, breaths, and pounding hearts. But as they turned a corner, a chilling realization hit this wasn't just a fight for the reef anymore. It was a fight for their lives, and they were now trapped in the crossfire of corruption, with an uncertain future hanging precariously in the balance.

The rain had faded to a soft drizzle by the time Alison, Eva, and Tommy stumbled into a cramped side alley, panting and soaked through from head to toe. Samuel led them to a nondescript door at the back of an old building, its paint peeling and forgotten by time. He hurriedly opened it, glancing back toward the darkened docks as if expecting a chase on their heels.

"Inside, quickly!" he urged, stepping aside to allow them entry. They slipped into the dimly lit room where the musty smell of damp walls and rusting metal greeted them.

"What now?" Alison asked, her heart still racing from their close call. "Are we safe here?"

"For the moment," Samuel replied, securing the door behind them. "But we need to figure out our next move, and it's critical we stay silent about all this."

Tommy shook his head, disbelief flooding his features. "You expect us to trust you after all this? You just served them! You're part of the problem!"

Samuel's face darkened, and he stepped closer, lowering his voice. "I know I was, but I was naive. Coral Reef is shifting to a more violent approach to protect itself. They don't just want to silence dissent; they're actively hunting down anyone who gets in their way."

"But why should we believe you?" Eva countered, crossing her arms. "You had a chance to come forward before, but you didn't. You were complicit!"

Alison felt the tension crackle between them, each accusation resurfacing old wounds. The weight of their lives hung in the balance, and trust felt like a luxury none of them could afford.

"I understand why you're angry," Samuel said, his voice steady despite the chaos surrounding them. "But the fact is, I've seen documents proving that they're planning to not only exploit the reef but also dismantle anyone who stands in their way. That includes you three. You have to believe me if you want to stay alive."

"We need proof," Tommy said, his voice edged with skepticism. "And not just your word. We can't go public with half-baked ideas."

Alison sighed, exhaustion clawing at her thoughts. "If he's telling the truth, we need information that can back it up. Can you show us those documents, Samuel? We need something we can use."

Samuel hesitated, uncertainty clouding his features. "I can try, but I have to be careful. The board monitors our communications closely—my access is limited. But I might have something stored on my laptop back at my place."

"Then we go there," Alison said, firm resolve setting into her posture. "But we need to be smart about it. No more running into traps without a plan."

Samuel nodded, visibly relieved at their willingness to cooperate. "I know it's a risk but trust me to guide you. The last thing we want is to get caught again."

As they moved deeper into the old building, Alison couldn't shake the uneasy feeling in her gut. They were navigating a precarious path, and trusting Samuel felt impossibly risky. Yet if what he said was true, then he held the key to not just their investigation, but the fate of the entire reef.

Exiting the alley, they made their way through the wet streets toward the edge of town where Samuel's small apartment stood. The faint glow of lights in the distance was both comforting and treacherous, a reminder that they were still caught in the game played by the corporate giants.

The streets were eerily quiet, save for the rhythmic drip of rainwater cascading off rooftops. Alison led the way, glancing over her shoulder every few moments, attuned to the shadows that danced along the alleyways. Each step felt charged—a reminder that they were not just facing an adversary; they were entering the very heart of a conspiracy.

When they reached Samuel's apartment, he unlocked the door, ushering them quickly inside the cramped space that smelled faintly of coffee and old books. "This way," he instructed, guiding them to a makeshift home office in the corner.

As he powered up his laptop, Alison couldn't help but observe him. He was a man caught between worlds, grappling with the repercussions of his choices. Would he redeem himself, or would he lead them into another dangerous trap?

"Here it is," Samuel said, his fingers flying across the keyboard. As he pulled up a document, the screen illuminated a series of schematics and internal memos detailing the planned construction over the reef.

"This is it. They're moving to begin development next month," he said, urgency tinging his voice. "This exchange is scheduled to happen during a special gala that will distract the public. They're also planning to mettle with the records to keep it all under wraps."

Alison's heart sank as she read the details. "This is devastating. They plan to initiate everything under the guise of a conservation event. It's genius and diabolical."

"This isn't just about money; they're determining the future of our coastline, and they want it free of anyone who might challenge them," Samuel clarified solemnly.

"Then we have to act fast," Eva said, determination simmering beneath her unease. "If we can get this information out to the media before the gala, it will expose them."

"I can help with that," Samuel agreed, his confidence returning. "I can connect with journalists I trust—people who know how to handle this without making it seem like a personal vendetta. But first, I need that footage you captured last night."

"We'll share it," Alison promised, "but we need to make a plan. We can't be blindsided again. With what they're hiding, they'll do anything to protect their interests."

Just then, a sharp knock at the door sent a chill through Alison's spine. They exchanged frantic glances, adrenaline surging anew as the unexpected reality struck them like a lightning bolt.

"Who is that?" Tommy whispered, his eyes wide with fear.

"Everyone stay quiet," Samuel instructed, moving toward the door cautiously. The haunting realization that they were not just risking exposure but possibly their very lives filled the room with palpable dread.

Samuel paused, his hand hovering over the doorknob. "If it's them, we need a contingency plan."

Before he could finish, the door swung open, and a figure stood silhouetted against the streetlights outside. Rain poured down, obscuring the face of the newcomer, but an unsettling familiarity swept over Alison.

"Samuel, I know you're in there!" the figure called, voice steady but charged with a subtle threat.

Stunned silence filled the room, and Alison's heart sank as she recognized that voice. It was a voice she never expected to hear tonight.

It was Oliver Thatcher. The hunt had begun.

~ Twenty Nine ~

Alison's breath caught in her throat as the figure of Oliver Thatcher materialized in the doorway, a menacing silhouette framed by the dim glow of streetlights. The rain soaked him, but his presence seemed to steal the warmth from the room.

"Samuel," he said, his voice smooth but carrying an undercurrent of threat, "you know this is a dangerous game you're playing. You need to let me in."

Alison instinctively moved closer to Eva and Tommy, her heart pounding in her chest. Fear mingled with anger; the last thing she wanted was for Oliver to expose them—or worse, to force them into a confrontation they weren't prepared for.

"Stay behind me," Samuel whispered, lowering his voice as he stepped forward to meet Oliver, his expression a mix of defiance and tension. "This isn't your territory anymore, Thatcher. You can't just barge in here."

"Is that so?" Oliver's lips curved into a chilling smile. "You might want to rethink how far you've wandered off the path. I know who you're with. I know the plans you're making. And it won't end well for you."

Alison exchanged glances with Tommy and Eva, dread pooling in her stomach. She knew that Oliver was not one to back down easily, and his threats held a weight that indicated he was serious.

"Get out," Samuel said firmly, the resolve in his voice betraying the unease he felt. "We have nothing to discuss with you. This is over."

"You think you can simply walk away from this?" Oliver countered, stepping further into the room, the smell of rain mixing with the musk of tension. "You're in over your head, my friend. We both know I have resources at my disposal that you can only dream of. All it takes is one call, and this little operation of yours. Done."

As the two men squared off, Alison's instincts flared. She could see the cracks forming in Samuel's confidence, the uncertainty creeping into his eyes. She had to intervene before Oliver turned the conversation into a battle of intimidation.

"Thatcher, you're not going to intimidate anyone here," Alison asserted, stepping forward, determination doing its best to mask the fear grinding in her chest. "You may think you know everything, but you're wrong. We have proof that your organization is involved in unethical practices, and we're not afraid to expose you."

"Proof?" Oliver laughed, but the mirth didn't reach his eyes. "What proof? Anything that comes from you will be dismissed as an agenda. This is a game with larger stakes than personal vendettas, and you're woefully unprepared."

Before Alison could retort, he shot a glance over his shoulder at the still-open door, his demeanor shifting like a switch flipping. "But I suppose I've said too much. The last thing you want is to ruin your little gathering here by letting someone overhear."

"Overhear what?" Samuel challenged, taking a step closer, emboldened. "That you're chasing ghosts? That you're desperate to cling to a sinking ship?"

"They aren't ghosts, Samuel. You have no idea how real the stakes are," Oliver replied with a mix of anger and condescension. "You're playing with lives, including your own."

Alison shifted uncomfortably, weighing her options. If they pushed too hard, they could provoke Oliver. But if they retreated, they might lose their chance to gather information or assert any sort of strength.

"Let me make you a proposition," Oliver said, his tone suddenly more composed, calculating. "I can guarantee your protection—this meddling in affairs that are beyond you can end right here. Just walk away and forget what you've stumbled upon."

Samuel's eyes narrowed. "You think I'll sell out my friends for a hollow offer? We're not afraid of your threats, Thatcher."

"That's a dangerous attitude," Oliver countered, his smile tight. "I'd hate for something unfortunate to befall you—or worse, your friends here."

At that moment, the tension reached a boiling point, and Alison could feel the walls closing in. They needed to defuse the situation, and quickly.

"Oliver," she said, her voice steady but laced with urgency. "We're not afraid of you or your threats. We know what's at stake, and we're going to do everything we can to make your plans public."

He chuckled, the sound devoid of real mirth, and stepped back, a predator surveying his prey. "Your bravado is commendable, Alison, but this is not a romantic ideal. You're confronting powerful interests that spill blood to protect their secrets..."

As if his words were a dagger, Alison felt a chill creep up her spine. His insinuation hung palpably in the air, and she realized that they were way over their heads. If Oliver threatened violence against them, she had no doubt he would follow through.

"Remember this moment," Oliver continued, moving toward the door as if to leave, but not before letting his words linger in their minds. "You may have convinced yourself that you are crusaders for a noble cause, but the truth is ugly, and it rarely aligns with your moral compass. If you value your lives, you'll retreat before you attract the wrong kind of attention."

With one last, deliberate glance, he slipped out into the rain-soaked night, leaving a pervasive silence in his wake.

As soon as the door clicked shut, the air thickened with tension. Alison turned to Samuel, her heart racing. "Did you hear him? He's serious. They are willing to go to any lengths to protect their secrets."

"Of course he is," Samuel replied, his voice strained but resolute. "But we can't back down now. We've come too far."

"Are we really prepared for this?" Tommy asked, glancing at the door as if expecting Oliver to return. "What if he's right? What if we're getting ourselves into something much bigger?"

A heavy silence followed his question. "We have to take this risk," Eva finally said, clenching her fists. "If we expose them, we have the chance to disrupt their plans. We must keep pushing forward."

With a shared understanding, their eyes met, and Alison felt the weight of their consensus settle like a shroud over them. But beneath that resolve was an undercurrent of doubt—a realization that in the shadows, betrayal had already begun to bloom. The fight for the reef had transformed into a battle for their very lives, and they would have to navigate through the tangled web of deceit that threatened to ensnare them all.

The storm circling outside was nothing compared to the storm brewing within and around them. They couldn't falter now; the threat was more real than ever. But at what cost?

The relentless rain continued to drum against the windows of Samuel's apartment, a fitting backdrop to the turmoil swirling inside. Each member of the group seemed lost in their own thoughts, the gravity of Oliver's visit weighing heavily on their shoulders. It was clear: the stakes had never been higher.

"Are we sure about this?" Tommy broke the silence, his voice a mixture of doubt and concern. "We're facing an organization with resources and connections that we can't compete with. How do we know they won't retaliate?"

Alison glanced around the room, studying her friends' faces. The fire in Eva's eyes had dimmed, and even Samuel seemed uncertain. "I understand your fears, Tommy. I feel them too. But if we don't act now, we lose everything. We'll lose the reef and the community we've fought so hard to protect."

"What if we're the ones who pay the price?" Eva asked, her voice quaking slightly. "I'm not afraid of them, but I don't want to put us all in jeopardy for something that might just backfire."

Alison took a deep breath, trying to harness the strength she felt was waning in the room. "I get that, trust me. But we have something they don't—each other. If we stand united, we have a fighting chance. We're not alone in this; we have the town behind us, concerned citizens who also want to stop them. We can rally support."

"Rally support?" Tommy scoffed, frustration creeping into his voice. "We're up against a corporation that can crush anyone who stands in its way! They aren't afraid to use violence."

"Then we play it smart," Samuel interjected, his confidence gradually returning. "We'll gather our evidence and get it into the hands of reliable reporters and activists outside of Cairns—make sure it's public before the gala. If people see the truth, it increases the risk for Coral Reef Enterprises to strike back."

A grim silence settled over the group as, one by one, they nodded. The resolve was slowly building again, the embers of their determination reigniting.

"Alright," Alison said, firming her stance. "Let's pull everything we have together. We'll share the footage, and the documents Samuel has with every connection we have and ensure they're ready to publish before the gala. We'll distribute it online as well, even to outlets that may not love us, just to get it out there."

Eva clutched her notepad, nodding vigorously. "We can create a social media campaign to spread the word fast. If we can generate enough buzz, we might even draw in national attention."

"Agreed," Samuel replied, reassured by their growing camaraderie. "Let's meet with the fishermen, activists, and anyone willing to stand with us. The more voices we have, the harder it'll be for them to silence us."

With newfound vigor, the task at hand felt like a rallying point, a collective mission steeped in the courage of their convictions.

As they began to formulate a plan, a sudden, resounding crash echoed from the direction of the front door, snapping them out of their shared focus. They froze, exchanging terrified glances.

"Did you lock the door?" Alison whispered, dread coiling in her stomach.

"I did!" Samuel's voice trembled slightly as he moved towards the sound. "Stay right here."

In a whirlwind of motion, he opened the door cautiously, peering into the darkened hall. As he did, they heard voices, growing louder threatening.

"Keep it down, you idiots! Search every room!" a rough voice barked.

Alison felt her heart race again as she exchanged rapid glances with Tommy and Eva. Their retreat options were limited. There would be no escaping the impending threat. It was clear Oliver had sent someone after them, perhaps to retrieve Samuel or eliminate their potential for resistance.

"Hide!" Samuel whispered urgently, retreating just as a group of men spilled into the room, clad in dark clothing, faces obscured by hoods.

The trio scrambled into the adjoining bedroom, pressing themselves against the walls as they held their breaths, adrenaline coursing through their veins. Through a crack in the balled-up curtains, they saw the intruders search the living area, tossing over furniture and rifling through drawers.

"We have to get out of here," Eva whispered frantically, her eyes wide with fear. "There's too many of them!"

"They can't know we're here," Alison murmured, her mind racing. "If we can manage to slip out the back, we can make a break for it."

But as if on cue, one of the men shouted, "They must be in here! Check the bedroom!"

Panic surged through Alison's veins. "We need to distract them," she said, suffocated by dread yet fueled by desperation. "If we can cause a diversion, we can get away."

"Can you create noise?" Tommy whispered. "Like, get their attention elsewhere?"

Alison glanced around the room, her mind whirling as she spotted a heavy vase on a shelf beside the bed. She nodded, rushing toward it as the intruders moved closer.

"On three..." she whispered, anxiety sparking in her chest. "One, two, three!"

With one swift motion, she hurled the vase against the wall, the sound shattering like glass against the concrete. Startled by the noise, the intruders bolted towards the source, leaving the doorway unguarded.

"Now!" she hissed, motioning for the others to follow her out. They slipped past the threshold into the hall, heart pounding as they dashed down the dim corridor to the back of the apartment. In the distance, they could hear the muffled voices of the men, now confused and searching.

"Out the back door!" Tommy whispered fiercely, pushing them toward a small exit that led to a fire escape.

They rushed outside, rain pelting against their skin as they scrambled down the metal stairs, adrenaline fueling their urgency. Just as they reached the bottom, the echoes of yelling filled the air behind them, propelling them forward.

"Go, go!" Alison urged, leading the way as they rounded the corner of the building, the taste of fear and freedom mingling together.

They sprinted through the streets, the chaos behind them, and desperation pushing them forward into the night. Each footfall felt like a life-affirming declaration of endurance, a promise to push back against the shadows that threatened to engulf them.

As they reached a stretch of trees lining the outskirts of town, they slowed, catching their breath. Rain cascaded around them, soaking them to the bone, but it felt more like a cleansing than a burden—a reminder of their resolve to fight.

"We need to regroup, come up with a new plan," Eva panted, her hair plastered against her face, exhaustion threading into her voice. "We can't go back to Samuel's place; they'll be tracking us."

"No, we can't," Alison agreed. "But we also can't give up. We need to find allies and make sure our message gets out."

The storm around them raged on, a reflection of the tumult within. They were at the precipice of a battle that threatened everything they held dear, but they weren't ready to back down. With a renewed sense of urgency, they braced themselves for what lay ahead—their last stand against the forces that sought to silence them.

~ Thirty ~

As dawn broke over Cairns, painting the sky with hues of orange and pink, Alison, Eva, and Tommy found refuge in a small, secluded café at the edge of town. They huddled at a corner table, attempting to warm up with steaming cups of coffee while processing the events of the previous night. The world felt eerily calm, a stark contrast to the storm of emotions swirling within them.

"We can't stay in hiding forever," Tommy said, his brow furrowed with concern as he absently stirred his coffee. "Oliver will be looking for us, and if they catch wind of our plans to expose them…"

"We're not giving them that power," Eva interrupted, her voice firm. "We have the evidence. We just need to figure out our next move without compromising ourselves."

Alison opened her laptop, determined to press forward. "If we can coordinate a meeting with the fishermen and local activists, we can leverage their networks to get the truth out there. If combined, our voices will be louder than anything Coral Reef Enterprises can throw our way."

As they formulated their plan, Alison's phone buzzed, interrupting their discussion. It was a text from Samuel: "Meet me at the library. I have information we need".

"Samuel wants to meet," Alison said, feeling a mix of relief and anxiety. "We should go see what he found."

When they arrived at the library, an imposing building adorned with lush vines and shady trees, a sense of urgency filled the air. They pushed open the heavy oak door, the familiar scent of old books immediately wrapping around them. Samuel was waiting by a row of dusty shelves, a tense expression on his face.

"Thanks for coming," he said, glancing over his shoulder as if expecting someone to follow him. "We need to talk somewhere private. I have crucial information."

They followed him to a secluded alcove at the back of the library, hoping for safety amidst the sea of books. The sunlight streamed through the large windows, casting long shadows that seemed to stretch and twist like darker thoughts lingering in the air.

"Have you managed to retrieve anything?" Alison queried, anxiety tightening her chest.

Samuel nodded, pulling out a USB drive from his pocket. "This contains documents I managed to extract while keeping my access under the radar. It shows the extent of what Coral Reef Enterprises is planning and their connections to specific government officials. They're pulling strings to secure permits for that construction without proper oversight." He paused, glancing around once more. "But that's not all."

"What do you mean?" Eva asked, leaning in, intrigued yet wary.

"I found out that some scientists on their payroll have been falsifying reports about the health of the reef," Samuel continued, his voice low and urgent. "They're covering up data to make it look like everything is fine to gain public support. The reef's biodiversity is in critical danger, and they know it."

"Their motive is profit over preservation," Tommy interjected, disbelief lacing his tone. "They'll kill everything for dollars."

"Yes," Samuel affirmed, his voice steadier now. "But there's something else. This USB will expose not only their corruption but also details linking to the recent spate of accidents that happened to the dissenters—people who tried to speak out."

Alison's heart sank. "You mean... they might have been involved in those incidents? The accidents?"

Samuel nodded grimly, the weight of their plight settling heavily upon them. "If we can get this evidence out to the right people, it will become a catalyst for action—not just against Coral Reef but illuminating the dangerous lengths they'll go to sustain their interests."

"But we have to move quickly," Eva insisted. "The gala starts in less than a week. If we wait too long, they could bury this—literally and figuratively."

"Then we need to get this USB to the media," Tommy said, determination igniting in his eyes. "But first, we need to ensure our safety. If Oliver and his men recognize we've gathered this evidence, they'll come for us again."

"Agreed," Alison said, her mind racing. "Let's finalize our plan before anyone alerts them to our movements."

Suddenly, the unmistakable sound of footsteps echoed from the hallway outside the library, drawing their attention. They exchanged worried glances, instinctively stepping back into the shadows of the alcove.

"Quick, be quiet!" Samuel urged, pressing himself against the wall.

As the footsteps grew louder, Alison felt her heart thudding painfully in her chest. The door to the library creaked open, and her breath caught as a familiar figure stepped through—a figure she had not expected to see here.

It was Dr. Samuel Grant, the scientist she had met previously, but this time he wore a tense expression, a deep worry creasing his forehead. The moment he entered the alcove, his eyes flicked around the small room. "What are you doing here?" he asked urgently, closing the distance.

"Dr. Grant," Alison breathed, relief flooding her. "We were just discussing the allegations against Coral Reef Enterprises. We have evidence—"

"I know about the evidence," he interrupted, glancing around as though fearful of being overheard. "I need your help. My colleagues and I have been targeted, and I suspect they might try to take me out next."

"What do you mean?" Samuel asked, his brow furrowing with worry. "You're involved with them—how are you a target?"

"Because I've been gathering information too," Dr. Grant explained, gesturing to the three of them. "I realized too late how deep the corruption ran, and now they know I'm a risk. I need you to trust me; the material I've gathered can complement what you have and strengthen our case against them."

Alison's instincts flared. She needed to be cautious. "Why should we trust you? The last time we spoke, you were holding back important information."

"I get that," he said, desperation tainting his voice. "But I wasn't aware of the full scope of their plans, and now that I am, I can't just stand by and watch them destroy everything. The reef, your lives—it's all at stake."

Tommy frowned, still unsure. "How do we know this isn't a trap?"

Dr. Grant's gaze was intense, his expression resolute. "Because I've dedicated my life to studying and preserving the reef. I didn't realize how it would all spiral into exploitation and violence until it was too late. Trust me, if you're planning to expose them, then please let me assist. I can help."

The tension in the small alcove pulsed, a web of suspicion and possibility. Alison weighed her options, her instincts battling her hopes. "If we let you help, you need to come clean about everything. We can't risk our lives on half-truths or veiled intentions."

Dr. Grant nodded vigorously. "I promise. Everything I've learned, you'll have. I understand you're wary, and you have every right to be. But together, we can shift the balance of power."

Alison took a moment to observe the man before her. The fight for the reef was no longer just about evidence and exposure; it was about trust, alliances, and stepping into a maelstrom where danger lurked at every corner.

"Alright," she said, her voice steadied with resolve. "We'll work together. But we have to be smart. The more eyes we have, the better our chances."

As uncertainty loomed overhead like a storm cloud, Alison felt a flicker of hope ignite amidst the chaos—the realization that they were not in this alone. With the stakes monumental, their fight was transforming, and the shadows of betrayal could become pathways to redemption. They were standing at the edge of a reckoning, and with every fiber of their beings, they would take that step into the unknown together.

The atmosphere in the library felt charged with anticipation as Alison, Eva, Tommy, Samuel, and Dr. Grant huddled together in their makeshift strategy session. Each moment felt crucial; they were at the edge of a precipice, and the next steps they took could either lead to exposing the truth or plunging them deeper into peril.

"First, we need to consolidate everything we've gathered," Alison began, her voice firm. "Dr. Grant, can you provide us with the materials you've acquired?"

"Absolutely," he replied, pulling a small collection of documents from his satchel. "These include internal reports, communications between the board members, and evidence of falsified data regarding the reef's health from my lab. It's a mess of connections that leads back to Coral Reef Enterprises."

As he laid out the papers, Alison felt a sense of dread creep into her thoughts. Each document held the weight of the lives affected by the corporation's greed. "We'll need to cross-reference this with the data Samuel has," she instructed. "If we can build a coherent narrative, we can present a strong case to the media."

Eva leaned over the papers, her brow furrowing in concentration as she scanned the contents. "This is incredibly damaging. If we can publicize these discrepancies, it could create a tidal wave of outrage. We have to ensure its accurate so they can't discredit it."

"Right," Tommy added, urgency lacing his words as he perused the documents. "And what about a backup plan? If they discover we're onto them, they won't hesitate to come after us again."

Alison nodded, her mind racing as she considered their options. "We'll need to be smart about how we disseminate this information. I can write a press release summarizing our findings and the evidence we have backing it. Let's reach out to a journalist who has a track record of handling sensitive stories."

"Then we'll get the fallout rolling before the gala," Samuel said, determination rekindling the fire within their group. "The gala will be their grand distraction, and we can use that against them."

"They might be expecting this kind of pushback, so we need to get as many allies involved as possible," Eva suggested. "Let's approach the local environmental groups—get their support and help mobilize more people to raise awareness."

Just as they began to strategize, a new wave of noise filtered in from outside. The muffled sounds of raised voices pierced through the library walls, sending a shiver of apprehension through Alison and her friends. Instinctively, they moved closer together, glancing toward the heavy library door.

"Sounds like more than just a few people," Tommy whispered. "What's happening outside?"

Samuel stood and approached the door cautiously, peeking through the small window embedded in the wood. His expression shifted from curiosity to alarm. "It's a group of protesters—definitely against Coral Reef. They're rallying around something."

"Could this be a result of our earlier attempts to spread the word?" Eva asked, her heart racing. "What if they're here to support us?"

Dr. Grant frowned, "That's possible, but it's just as likely they could be puppets in Coral Reef's game. They might be redirecting attention away from their real issues."

The group fell silent, contemplating the implications. In this precarious moment, every choice felt heavier than the last.

"Let's not draw attention," Alison said quietly, trying to keep the group grounded. "If the protesters are being pushed away from the truth, we don't want to compromise our position."

"But we need to know what they're saying," Tommy argued, his gaze fixed on the door as chants echoed against the walls. "If they're bringing any real news to light, we can use that."

In a moment of resolve, Alison nodded. "I'll go take a look. If it seems like they're aligned with our cause, we can prepare to approach them for support."

She moved carefully toward the door, adrenaline thrumming through her veins. Opening it just a crack, she peeked out into the bustling plaza in front of the library, where a throng of people, holding signs and chanting slogans, filled the square.

"Save our reefs!" one sign read. "Coral Reef Enterprises: Lies and Deceit!" shouted another. Her heart raced at the sight; this crowd could be a pivotal force in their fight.

Just as she took a step back, her breath caught in her throat as she noticed a few familiar faces among the protesting crowd—a group of local fishermen and environmental activists she had worked with during the campaign for reef preservation. They were passionate advocates for the oceans and had faced intimidation from the corporation in the past.

"This isn't just a coincidence!" she murmured to the group behind her, excitement bubbling within. "They're here fighting for the same cause!"

"Go talk to them!" Eva encouraged, her eyes bright with hope. "This could turn the tide for us."

With a determined nod, Alison took a deep breath and stepped outside. The cool air hit her face, invigorating her resolve as she approached the gathering.

"Hey! Did anyone mention Coral Reef Enterprises?" she called out, raising her hands to command attention. The din of voices quieted as heads turned toward her.

She recognized Jeff, a local fisherman with years of experience and a wealth of knowledge about the waters. He stepped forward, eyes alight with determination. "Alison! We're rallying against Coral Reef's lies. They've been misrepresenting the state of our reefs for far too long!"

"I know," she replied, exhilaration thrumming through her veins. "We have evidence, and we need your support. The truth is out there, but we have to come together to make sure it's heard."

The crowd stirred, murmurs rippling through as people shared curious glances. "We need to act fast," Alison continued, passion fueling her words. "Our voices need to rise in unity, creating an undeniable force that will pressure Coral Reef Enterprises to back down."

"Count me in," Jeff said, and the crowd released a chorus of affirmations. "But we need to make this bigger—leaflets, social media, press releases!"

As the excitement mounted, a wave of renewed determination washed over Alison. With this newfound support, she felt hope returning, propelling her forward into the light of possibility.

Back inside the library, the group hastily began to organize, fueled by the synergy of shared purpose. They prepared pamphlets and documented their findings to distribute to the protesting crowd. They would not only fight but unite their efforts, an unbreakable chain sent to challenge the tightening grip of Coral Reef Enterprises.

Outside, as Alison and her allies prepared to take their stand, the rallying cries for change echoed louder—the truth was buried, but no longer unnoticed. Together, they would uncover it, fueling a movement that rippled through Cairns and beyond, rising against the tide of deceit that sought to drown them all.

~ Thirty One ~

As the sun dipped below the horizon, casting a fiery glow across the sky, the atmosphere outside the library crackled with energy. Alison stood at the forefront of the gathered crowd, her heart racing with a mix of hope and trepidation as the sea of faces turned toward her. The rally against Coral Reef Enterprises was swelling beyond her expectations, budding from a small assembly into a formidable gathering of passionate voices ready to fight for their reef.

Jeff had climbed atop a makeshift podium, bolstered by a stack of crates, and was rallying the crowd with powerful rhetoric about the threats they faced. The echo of his words resonated through the plaza, galvanizing others as they chanted slogans in solidarity.

Alison glanced back toward the library, where her friends were assembling materials and preparing pamphlets. Eva was coordinating with some local activists, while Tommy worked on capturing footage that would document the event. Amidst the chaos, the palpable anonymity of their fight morphed into a larger entity, each heartbeat resonating with purpose.

"Alison!" she heard a voice call out behind her, and she turned to see Samuel pushing through the crowd, his face drawn with concern. "I'm glad I found you. We need to talk—there's been a development."

"Is it about the evidence?" she asked, an uncomfortable twinge in her stomach. "Have they found out?"

"No," he said hastily, his eyes darting around nervously. "But we might have a mole inside our ranks. Someone tipped off Coral Reef Enterprises about our plans for this rally."

Alison felt a wave of nausea wash over her. "What? How do you know?"

"I overheard two guys discussing something in the coffee shop earlier. They were connected to Coral Reef, clearly gathering intel on these protests. If they've been monitoring us, it's only a matter of time before they decide to crush this demonstration, and anyone involved."

Panic surged through Alison's veins as she processed the revelation. "We need to alert the crowd. If there's a mole, we can't risk them sabotaging our efforts."

"No," Samuel urged, his voice low and intense. "If we panic now, it will only feed into their hands. We need to regroup, come up with a strategy that keeps everyone safe without igniting fear."

Alison nodded, swallowing hard against the sense of impending doom. She turned her attention back to the crowd, where Jeff continued to stir the spirits of the people. Tempered enthusiasm surged like a wave, but Alison knew there was a danger lurking just beneath the surface.

"Everyone!" she called out, raising her hands for attention. The crowd slowly quieted, turning expectantly to her. "Thank you all for being here tonight! Your passion and commitment to preserving our reefs is essential. However, I need to share something important. We must remain vigilant against any efforts to divide us."

A ripple of concern crossed the crowd as whispers spread like wildfire. "We can't afford to be complacent. There's a possibility that there may be those present among us who are not aligned with our cause."

"Who?!" a voice rang out from the crowd.

Alison hesitated, feeling the weight of their eyes pressing down on her, but she maintained her composure. "We don't know who is aligned with Coral Reef yet, but I urge everyone to remain united and watchful. Stay close to those you trust, and report anything suspicious to me or the local activists."

The crowd exchanged anxious looks, murmurs rippling through them. The air had shifted, the vulnerability of their protest now starkly evident. Yet amidst the looming tension, a strange sense of defiance began to materialize.

A young woman stepped forward, her fists clenched at her sides. "We can't let fear dictate our actions. They may try to intimidate us, but we're here for a cause that matters! We won't let them silence us!"

Applause and cheers erupted in response, rekindling a flicker of courage among the crowd. Though Alison felt the tremors of fear, she realized that the spirit of unity held tremendous power. One voice could create a ripple; together, they could unleash a tidal wave.

As she scanned the crowd, however, her unease resurfaced. What if someone truly was sabotaging their efforts? Could they really trust each other?

Samuel returned, now flanked by Tommy and Eva. "We've made progress with the pamphlets and media strategy," he said, though his expression remained troubled. "But we need to make sure the most crucial elements are prioritized. Let's get someone out to monitor the entrances and keep everyone safe."

"Good idea," Eva chimed in, her brow furrowing in concentration. "If we can keep eyes on the crowd, we can intervene if anything goes south."

"Have we considered talking to the police?" Tommy asked, visibly frustrated. "They might be able to provide protection for the rally."

"No," Alison interjected sharply, recalling earlier conversations. "If Coral Reef has connections with the local authorities, we can't trust that they'll act in our favor. We can't risk making this a target for those who want to undermine us."

The tension hung heavy in the air as different strategies were proposed, but as night descended, they had to act quickly. The crowd was growing restless, and the need for decisive action felt urgent.

"Let's divide into teams," Samuel suggested, his tone steady now. "We can assign people to monitor the entrances, look out for suspicious individuals, and keep a central communication channel open."

Alison felt a swell of resolve. "Agreed. Each person plays a vital role in ensuring the safety of this protest. The more people we have alert and aware, the less likely we are to be caught off guard."

As they finalized their plans, the rally continued to gather energy. With every passing moment, Alison found her fears abating, replaced by an invigorating sense of purpose. They were no longer just a small group battling an enormous corporation; they were a community ready to face whatever darkness awaited them.

But as she glanced toward the crowd, a sense of unease still lingered in her heart. The threat of betrayal hung like a shadow, waiting for the opportune moment to strike. She would have to be cautious, for beneath the facade of unity lay the potential for hidden dangers—a reality that could turn their battle into betrayal.

And yet, she felt it: a heartbeat of hope, a rallying cry growing louder with each passing minute. Together, they would expose the truth buried in lies, and in doing so, they would uncover each other, creating a bond of trust that could not be easily broken.

Whatever transpired, they would face it head-on, moving toward an uncertain future—together.

The energy of the rally swelled like the ocean tides, setting a rhythm of anticipation among the crowd. Alison stood at the forefront, her heart syncing with the chorus of determined voices chanting for the reef's preservation. The library plaza was overflowing with supporters, each banner and placard held high, carrying messages of unity against the corrupt grasp of Coral Reef Enterprises.

"Save our reef!" echoed through the air, a piercing keystone that rang in the faces of onlookers, passersby, and especially the local media, who had gathered to capture the historic moment. But beneath the surface of excitement, Alison felt an unsettling knot in her stomach—an awareness of the threats lurking just outside their collective optimism.

As the evening sky darkened, twinkling stars began to peek through the clouds, unfurling a tapestry of wonder above the tumult below. Alison glanced at her friends, each absorbed in their roles—Eva was at the frontlines, rallying the crowd, while Tommy documented the movement, capturing every moment through his lens. Meanwhile, Samuel and Dr. Grant coordinated with local activists, ensuring safety protocols were in place.

Yet despite their preparations, the apprehension of betrayal lingered like a shadow on the edge of their gathering. Alison remained vigilant, scanning the crowd for any sign of unwanted attention. And then she spotted him—Oliver Thatcher, standing off to the side, a menacing figure among the throngs of passionate voices.

"Samuel!" she hissed, elbowing him urgently as she pointed toward Oliver. "He's here!"

"What? Are you sure?" Samuel strained to see over the crowd.

"He's watching us," she replied, heart thundering in her chest. "He's not alone. He brought a couple of goons with him."

Dr. Grant turned, narrowing his eyes at the sight. "We need to alert everyone. If they're here, they might be planning something."

"Before we instigate panic," Alison said, holding up her hands, "let's keep our cool. We can't afford to give them a reason to disrupt us. Let's observe first. We need to know what they're planning."

With hearts racing, they kept their focus on Oliver and his associates, who appeared to be whispering amongst themselves, casting furtive glances toward the main stage. The tension twisted like a knife in Alison's gut. This wasn't just a protest anymore; it was paramount to a battleground.

Moments later, the speakers began to call for attention, and the crowd quieted down. A local environmental leader stepped up to the podium, her voice steady yet impassioned as she spoke about the dire condition of the marine ecosystem, urging the crowd to come together in solidarity.

Alison's breath caught in her throat as she glimpsed Oliver moving quietly, signaling to his cohorts. Suddenly, she sensed an abrupt shift in the mood—the crowd drew back slightly, whispering to one another uneasily, as if sensing the undercurrent of turmoil brewing at the edges.

"Move!" she suddenly shouted, her instincts screaming that something was about to go very wrong. Samuel and Dr. Grant were beside her in an instant.

"What's going on?" Tommy asked, his eyes darting between Alison and the crowd, confusion etched across his face.

"Down the sides!" Alison urged, gesturing toward the outskirts of the plaza. "We need to form a barrier around the stage before they create chaos!"

As the crowd began to murmur nervously, Alison sprinted ahead, rallying support among the activists to position themselves around the focal point of the rally. The movement transformed from cooperative heartbeat to frantic urgency, igniting the passion shared among the attendees.

Just as they established a perimeter, Oliver raised his voice, cutting through the unity of the moment with slashing bravado. "Do you really think you can mask the truth with your noise? This so-called corruption is nothing more than the grumbling of a few misguided souls!" He laughed, a sound devoid of humor, slicing through the feeling of solidarity.

Before anyone could respond, his goons surged forward, plunging into the gathered crowd. "Get back!" one of them shouted, shoving participants aside, churning the message of unity into chaos.

Alison's heart raced as she glimpsed Eva, pure determination written across her face as she stood her ground, calling for calm among the crowd. "Don't let them intimidate you!" she yelled, fighting to keep the momentum alive.

The crowd began to swell and push back against Oliver's representatives, who found themselves struggling against the force of solidarity. They were met with chants of "Save our reef!" and "We will not be silenced!" that resonated like thunder through the plaza.

"Stay strong!" Dr. Grant shouted at Alison's side. "The more united we remain, the harder it is for them to divide us."

Alison glanced at the crowd's tenacity, feeling a renewed sense of purpose amid the fray. But she couldn't shake the anxiety twisting within her. "What if this escalates? We can't have anyone hurt."

As if in response to her fears, one of the goons lunged toward the stage, swinging his arm at Samuels, who had emerged to defend Alison. In that instant, everything seemed to slow down; the widening eyes of the crowd, the rush of adrenaline, the chaotic surge of bodies—as fist met fist, the dark undercurrents of deception threatened to drown the spirit of the rally.

"Everyone! Back up! Form a line!" Alison shouted, trying to bring order to the eruption brewing before her.

Just then, a nearby police siren split the air, illuminating the chaos with flashes of red and blue. The officers arrived, but Alison's heart sank. Would they side with the protesters or Coral Reef Enterprises?

They quickly moved in, assessing the tumultuous scene as Oliver's goons began to retreat under the pressure of growing momentum. The officers moved cautiously, expecting trouble.

"Everyone, stand your ground!" a police officer called out, his voice steady. "We're here to maintain order. Step back, and let's calm this situation!"

"Calm down?" Oliver sneered, his eyes narrowing. "You're here to protect us—you all should be ashamed for protesting against a legitimate organization!"

A murmur of anger rippled through the crowd. "We are not afraid of you!" Alison shouted, raising her hand. "This isn't just about Coral Reef Enterprises. This is about our community, our environment, and who we choose to stand by!"

The police began to disperse the crowd into smaller groups, pushing Oliver and his men away amid the swelling emotion. But with every moment of division, uncertainty punctured through the hearts of the gathered. The police's presence didn't guarantee security; it was just another layer of complexity.

"Alison, look!" Samuel called, pointing toward the back of the crowd. "Media! They're capturing everything!"

Alison turned, witnessing cameras rolling and reporters frantically capturing footage of the chaos. This was a pivotal moment—the very thing they needed to draw attention to the lengths Coral Reef would go to dissuade the truth. If they could get the right coverage, perhaps it would amplify their fight to new levels.

But just then, as emotions surged and unity clashed against deceit, Alison felt her heartbeat heavily. Could they truly withstand the unfolding chaos? The hits they had endured already were marked by the shadows of betrayal. Still, with the camera lens trained upon them, they had to unite stronger than ever.

With every fiber of her being, Alison stepped forward as the crowd bashed against discord, her voice rising above the chaos. "This fight isn't just ours—this is for the generations to come, for every life interwoven with this reef! We will not back down!"

As her words rang out, a collective determination ignited a new chorus of chants. The tide was turning, but the flickering flame of commitment must persist; this was not merely a protest but a movement—the heartbeats of a united force rising against betrayal.

With courage reborn amid the surging tide, Alison knew that they would face the roaring waves together and expose the truth buried beneath the brush of greed and corruption. Even amidst chaos and uncertainty, the fight for the reef burned brighter than ever. Together, they would stand and face whatever trials lay ahead.

~ Thirty Two ~

The morning after the chaotic rally felt surreal, like waking from a tempest into calm waters. The sun poured through the window of Alison's temporary apartment, casting warm golden rays across the room and illuminating the remnants of their frenzied preparations. Despite the lingering adrenaline from last night's events, a blanket of exhaustion had settled in, wrapping around her like a shroud.

As she sipped her coffee, Alison stared out at the Coral Sea, each wave crashing against the shore reminiscent of the battles fought for its preservation. In the wake of turmoil, she found herself reflecting on the journey that had led her to this moment—how a simple investigative quest had morphed into a fight for their community.

Memories of her father flooded forth, tugging at her heart. He had been a passionate advocate for marine life and had instilled within her the importance of truth and accountability. Yet, his abrupt disappearance plagued her thoughts like a specter, haunting every decision and making her question the price of her inquiries.

"Alison?" Eva's voice broke through her reverie as she entered the room, reports in hand. "You should see this."

Alison turned to face her friend, curiosity piqued. "What's going on?"

Eva held out a folder, her face illuminated with urgency. "I've compiled the footage from last night. The media picked up everything—the chaos, your speech, the crowd response. It's going viral."

Alison's heart raced as she flipped through the pages, each screenshot and article detailing their fight splashed across headlines. "This could be huge," she breathed, astonishment mixed with a swell of pride. "This could put significant pressure on Coral Reef Enterprises."

"Yes, but we need to keep momentum," Eva replied, her expression serious. "We have to follow up and connect with potential allies, especially if they think we're gaining traction. We were lucky to catch the public's interest."

Realizing the urgency of their mission, Alison nodded. "Let's focus on reaching out to environmental organizations and grassroots movements. If we can link the information, we have with others who've been targeted, we can amplify this even further."

As they began drafting emails and messages to allies, the excitement of collective purpose reminded Alison of her father's teachings. He always told her that in pursuit of truth, unity was strength. And now they were standing on the brink of something monumental—not just for themselves but for the very future of the reef.

Just then, a knock on the door interrupted their focused energy. Alison exchanged a glance with Eva before cautiously peeking through the peephole. A recognizable face greeted her: Jeff, the local fisherman who had rallied alongside them last night.

"Hey! Everything alright?" Alison asked as she swung open the door, relief flooding through her.

"Is it true what I saw on the news?" he asked breathlessly, stepping inside. "You all really stood against Coral Reef Enterprises like that?"

"Yeah, we did," Alison replied, excitement simmering within her. "And it looks like we might have actually captured some attention."

Jeff grinned, a hopeful glint in his eyes. "I thought so! We need to capitalize on this energy. The fishermen are brewing. Everyone's talking about forming a coalition to hold them accountable. They can't keep lying to us and getting away with it."

Alison felt a spark ignite within her—a resurgence of the very determination that had fueled her quest for justice. "We should capitalize on it! If we can turn this momentum into a movement, we'll have the community backing us in ways we never imagined."

As they strategized, a quiet knock at the door pulled their attention again. This time, it was Samuel, his face drawn but animated with urgency. "Alison, Eva, we need to talk. It's about our next steps."

"Did something happen?" Eva asked, concern etching her features.

"I just came from a meeting with the local environmental council," Samuel replied as he stepped inside. "They're in full support of our cause. They've also offered to help connect you with larger environmental groups across the state."

Alison's excitement surged. "This could elevate everything we're trying to accomplish. We need every voice on our side."

Samuel's expression turned serious. "But there's more. While they're supportive, the council is hesitant to act publicly without verifiable proof of Coral Reef's misconduct. A paper trail, data, anything that can substantiate our claims."

"Let me guess—what they mean is hard evidence," Alison said, her heart sinking slightly. She had anticipated this hurdle but knew they could overcome it with the right resources. "We have gathered some, but we need to compile it into an irrefutable package."

"I can help with that," Samuel replied. "I have access to our lab's data on the reef and the recent changes. I'll include the discrepancies regarding the health reports, the data we've uncovered about project plans, and everything that links Coral Reef Enterprises to these fraudulent claims."

"Perfect," Alison said, determination coursing through her. "Let's gather everything we can and produce a comprehensive report that highlights Coral Reef's deceit. We will send this out and get other groups to verify our findings. This isn't just about now; it's about preventing future harm to the reef."

As they began to break down the components of their report, Alison felt her father's presence guiding her. Each piece of evidence and testimony could serve as a foundation for unearthing the truth. Yet—she also felt the echoes of their past, the frustration, the loss, and the sacrifices that had brought them to this precipice.

"Alison?" Jeff's voice brought her back to the moment. "Are you alright?"

She nodded, forcing a smile despite the weight lingering in her heart. "Just remembering how important this is—not just for us but for everyone connected to this landscape. We're not just fighting for ourselves; we're fighting for all those who came before us."

"Exactly," Eva added, her tone infused with hope. "This could be the beginning of something transformative—not just for the reef, but for the entire community. You're channeling your father's legacy, Alison. He believed in this fight, and so do we."

As the group set to work, a renewed sense of purpose seeped into the air, and Alison knew that the battle was far from over. They were on the brink of unearthing new truths, but the echoes of the past resonated with every step forward. It was imperative to keep pushing ahead—together—for the health of the reef, for her father's memory, and for the future they envisioned.

Ultimately, they were united by more than the cause; they were bound by a shared commitment to preserving what mattered most, even if the fight meant confronting the demons that threatened to engulf them.

And as they delved deeper into their task, Alison felt emboldened knowing that though the path ahead was fraught with uncertainty, every heartbeat of their combined efforts echoed for change. Together, they would stand resilient against the shadows, illuminating their journey with the promise of truth.

The following days were a flurry of activity as Alison and her allies delved deeper into their mission to expose Coral Reef Enterprises. In the cozy back room of the local café, tables became makeshift meeting spaces cluttered with papers, laptops, and half-empty coffee cups—epicenters of hope and determination where ideas intertwined in their quest for justice.

"Alright, everyone, let's keep the momentum going!" Alison proclaimed, her voice ringing with confidence as she addressing the assembled group. The café was buzzing with supporters: fishermen, environmentalists, and concerned citizens—all eager to contribute their voices to the fight.

"We've compiled a substantial amount of evidence," she continued, her gaze moving across the crowd, "but it's imperative to ensure it reaches the right channels. We need to connect with larger environmental organizations and local media to gain traction."

Samuel stood beside her, his laptop open, ready to share their findings. "We have documentation showing how Coral Reef has manipulated environmental assessments and neglected critical data regarding the health of the reef. If we can align our efforts with established environmental groups, it will add credibility to our claims."

Tommy chimed in, enthusiasm lighting his expressions as he captured the crowd's attention. "I've been in touch with a couple of journalists already. They're intrigued by our story. If we can furnish them with solid evidence, they could run a feature piece that would take us to a larger audience—possibly even national coverage!"

A ripple of excitement swept across the room as whispers of approval and determination sparked alive.

Jeff raised his hand, his brow furrowed in thought. "What about the fishermen? Can we organize a way to collectively voice our frustrations? The more fishermen we have on our side, the stronger our message becomes."

"Absolutely," Eva replied, her eyes sparkling with inspiration. "We could host a community event—something to draw people in, inform them about the situation, and unify everyone. A rally focused not just on complaints but on solutions, plans for restoration of the reef post-Coral Reef Enterprises."

"That's a great idea," Alison agreed, her heart racing at the thought of putting together an impactful event. "We can call it a Coastal Community Gathering or something. A place to share stories, experiences, and hopes for the future."

Samuel nodded in approval. "We could invite local artists to showcase their work that reflects what the reef means to them. Art has always been a powerful medium for evoking change; it could help rekindle the love people have for our oceans."

The group buzzed with excitement, enthusiasm reverberating through every corner of the café. They began brainstorming ideas: speakers who could address marine conservation, musicians to foster an uplifting atmosphere, and displays to educate attendees on the importance of preserving the reef.

"Let's not forget social media!" Tommy suggested, leaning forward. "We can create an event page, share updates, and get the word out. We need to ensure that it's spread far and wide."

With determination fueling their efforts, the group started assigning roles and responsibilities. Everyone contributed in some capacity, forming a tapestry of shared commitment to the cause.

As the day wore into evening, ideas flowed more freely, and connections were forged—new relationships blossoming among like-minded individuals united by a shared purpose.

As Alison watched the camaraderie grow, a warmth surged within her. She thought of her father's dedication to the ocean and how his work had inspired countless others—in the end, he had woven such a strong network, much like what she was witnessing unfold before her.

That evening, as they wrapped up their meeting, Alison stood back and admired the vibrancy of the group gathered together, exchanging stories and laughter. It was a sight she cherished—a community rediscovering its ties to one another and to the vital ecosystem threatened by greed.

"Thank you all for your dedication," she said, raising her glass of water in a toast. "We stand together today, and together, we'll push back against the shadows. We owe it to our children and our waters to fight for what's right."

Cheers erupted among them, a whirlpool of emotion swirling through the air. It was as if they'd collectively reignited a flame that had flickered for too long, breaking through the darkness that had lingered for years.

Suddenly, a thought struck her. "What if we also create a visual representation of our goals? We could weave together a banner featuring ideals, hopes, and the futures we want to see for the reef. Something we can display at the gathering."

"That's brilliant!" Eva replied, her eyes lighting up. "A visual embodiment of our mission—people will be able to add their thoughts or drawings. It'll illustrate just how interconnected we all are in this fight."

As they began discussing plans for the banner, Alison felt an electric sense of unity coursing through the room. The knot of uncertainty that once gripped her heart began to unravel as she absorbed the strength inherent in their collaborative efforts.

They spent the next few hours sketching ideas, drafting goals, and outlining messages for the upcoming gathering. It felt as if pieces of a larger puzzle were falling into place, weaving together narratives and experiences that would carry their fight forward.

Despite the challenges that lay ahead—and the lurking threats from Coral Reef Enterprises—Alison felt an undeniable sense of belonging with this newfound collective of advocates. They had each other's backs, their dreams melding into a collective purpose that transcended any fear.

That evening, as they dispersed, Alison lingered for a moment, witnessing the connections warmly exchanging numbers and plans while laughter and hope filled the air like a hymn. The scars of loss and betrayal dulled slightly by the strength of the new ties forged among them.

As she stepped outside, the cool breeze embraced her, and looking out at the horizon where land met ocean, something inside her clicked into place—a sense of certainty. The battle against Coral Reef was far from over, but together, they were more than allies; they were interwoven threads in a vibrant tapestry determined to reclaim the reef and protect its legacy.

Every heartbeat echoed as a reminder of the journey ahead and the promise of a united stand against the tide. They were no longer just individuals on a quest—they were a movement, and their collective resolve would carry them through the challenges awaiting just beyond the horizon.

~ Thirty Three ~

The days following the Coastal Community Gathering had been a whirlwind of activity and transformation. Energies heightened by a collective sense of purpose and renewed determination rippled through Cairns as the community fully recognized the weight of their fight against Coral Reef Enterprises. With the evidence in hand and the support of activists ignited at the gathering, Alison and her allies were ready to strike the blow that would expose the corruption undermining the reef.

The sun rose on a pivotal day—a day earmarked for the press conference that would unveil the evidence they had painstakingly compiled, showcasing the unlawful practices of Coral Reef Enterprises. The tension in the air was palpable as Alison, Samuel, Eva, Tommy, and Jeff gathered outside the local press room, their hearts racing.

"Is everyone ready?" Alison asked, her nervousness masked with determination as they stood in front of several journalists preparing to broadcast the unfolding story.

"Let's make our voices heard," Samuel replied, his confidence bolstered by the success of the rally and the growing support of various community organizations.

With the cameras rolling and eyes trained on them, Alison stepped up to the microphone, her heart pounding in her chest. "Thank you all for being here today. We are gathered not just to voice our concerns but to call out the unscrupulous actions of

Coral Reef Enterprises, a corporation that has put profit over the preservation of our vital marine ecosystems."

As she spoke, Alison felt a sense of the weight of history resting upon her shoulders—the echoes of her father's advocacy guiding her words. She detailed how the community had discovered numerous fraudulent practices: the falsified environmental assessments, the initiatives launched under the guise of conservation, and the backroom dealings that had put the reef's health at risk.

"This," she said, lifting the folder of evidence, "is proof of the blatant disregard for transparency and accountability. We owe it to future generations to ensure that our oceans are protected."

The crowd erupted in cheers and applause, solidifying the resolve that had begun to grow in the wake of their collective efforts. Eva, who had joined Alison at the podium, added, "We are not just here as a reactionary force but as the champions of restorative practices. We demand transparency, protection for the reef, and the end of exploitative projects that threaten our ecosystems."

The journalists scribbled furiously, capturing the essence of their determination, while cameras flashed. The message was clear: this was a battle they would not relent in.

As the press conference concluded and the crowd dispersed, a wave of exhilaration washed over Alison. It felt like a tipping point—the moment where the community's voice could no longer be ignored. But beneath that exhilaration was a deep-seated anxiety. Would Coral Reef Enterprises retaliate? Would they attempt to silence them?

Only days later, the news broke. Media outlets picked up the story; it went viral. The community rallied together, sharing the evidence on social media and organizing calls to action.

Under the weight of public scrutiny, Coral Reef Enterprises found itself cornered. Legal challenges mounted as environmental regulatory bodies-initiated investigations into the corporation's practices. News of a congressional inquiry into their dealings sparked outrage across the country, motivating more citizens to join the cause.

The chain of events set off a domino effect. Shocking reports surfaced about how Coral Reef had misled local communities, manipulating scientific research to push forward agendas that endangered marine ecosystems. Resignations followed swiftly as board members faced pressure and exposure of their unethical actions. The corporation's facade began to crack, revealing not only the greed that had driven their ambitions but also the profound disregard for the dire consequences of their actions.

In a breathtaking display of solidarity, local fishermen who had once faced intimidation joined Alison's group, advocating for the reef's restoration. Community workshops sparked action plans, revitalizing interest in sustainable practices that ensured a healthy ecosystem. Coral reefs around Cairns began to surface as symbolically intertwined with their shared identity—a testament to resilience and community.

Then came the announcement: a settlement hearing. Coral Reef Enterprises had relented, agreeing to halt all harmful projects and pay restitution toward restoration efforts in the reef. This outcome was not just a small victory; it marked a significant shift in how the corporation would operate moving forward.

As Alison stood on the shore one afternoon, gazing out at the beautiful, vibrant waters, she felt a mixture of emotions wash over her. The reef, her father's legacy, was still fighting. The tides of change had shifted, buoyed by the collective voices of the community. They had shown their resilience and ability to grapple with adversity head-on.

"Look at the waves," Jeff said, joining her at the water's edge. "They're stronger now, because the community stands together. And we can keep it that way."

Alison smiled, recalling the voices that had rallied, the stories that had intertwined, and the love they had shown toward the oceans they cherished. It was a profound reminder that even in the face of adversity, they could inspire change and protect what mattered most.

Together with Samuel, Eva, Tommy, and the community, she had woven a tapestry of hope—a plan that ensured their voices would carry on, mingled with the rhythms of the sea.

As the sun dipped below the horizon, casting a kaleidoscope of colors across the sky, Alison whispered a silent pledge to the waves. "We will always protect you."

Standing firm in their commitment, they knew the fight for the reef was far from over, but they were no longer alone on this journey. The bonds they had forged would carry them through whatever challenges lay ahead.

With the echoes of their past fueling their courage and the promise of a united future ahead, they remained vigilant protectors of the ocean—standing guard against the shadows and celebrating the light of hope that shone brighter than ever. Together, they would navigate the tides of change, ensuring that both the sea and their community would thrive, creating a legacy worth fighting for.

And with that vow, a new chapter began—not just for Alison, but for everyone bound within the tapestry of Cairns, woven together by love, commitment, and a relentless drive to protect the very lifeblood of their home.

I'm a dynamic storyteller born from the picturesque shores of Cairns, Queensland, I have always been enthralled by the power of words, transforming fleeting ideas into vivid narratives that captivate readers. With a love for crafting stories that inspire and entertain, Ashley is committed to exploring the depths of human experience through her writing.

Nestled amid the breathtaking landscapes of tropical Australia, I draw inspiration from the vibrant surroundings and rich cultural heritage. My unique perspective and creative flair shine through in my work, making each tale a journey into the heart of adventure and emotion.